Hello Handsome

by

CARRIE McGOVERN

Copyright © 2024 by Carrie McGovern

All rights reserved.

No part of this publication may be reproduced, distributed, or transmitted in any form or by any means, including photocopying, recording, or other electronic or mechanical methods, without the prior written permission of the publisher, except as permitted by copyright law.

For permission requests, contact info@carriemcgovern.com

The story, all names, characters, and incidents portrayed in this production are fictitious. No identification with actual persons (living or deceased), places, buildings, and products is intended or should be inferred.

Published by Embrace Publishing

Paperback cover art by Lauren Osbourne

Edited by Helen Bowman from In The Detail

ISBN – 978-1-7384973-2-4

Dedication

I dedicate this book to my husband, who inspired some of this book, especially the bit about building a patio.

Love you!

Chapter One

Hannah

It's just typical of my life really, the day goes by super slow and nothing much happens and then when you need to get yourself out and home, the world and his dog want your attention. We've been sitting in the café, twiddling our thumbs most of the day. Some of the regulars have popped in for a cuppa and a chat, but not much else. So, with the day almost at a close, things start happening.

Firstly, Cynthia got a phone call about one of her grandchildren getting something stuck up their nose and needed to go to accident and emergency. I can't say I was surprised, it isn't the first time. She was meant to be closing up at the café but with only half an hour to go until we shut, I sent her off to help out with wrangling the dozens of kids in the family.

I thought I'd get the place ready to close. I mean we've not had anyone in for at least the last hour, so I thought I'd start clearing and mopping up. That way, as soon as I flip the closed sign, I can grab my stuff and go. But my phone started ringing and I answered without checking caller ID. Big mistake! It was my mother, with the same conversation we have every time she rings. I can predict exactly what will be said.

"Hannah, you're wasting your life working in that café."

"Hannah, your stepdad can get you a job at his office."

"Hannah, photography isn't a REAL job!"

"Hannah, why can't you be more ambitious like your stepbrother."

"Hannah, why can't you dress more like a lady?"

"Hannah, when are you gonna get a boyfriend and settle down?"

"Hannah, you're not getting any younger, your biological clock is ticking."

Or words to that effect. But they all amount to the same thing. I don't fit into her neat little box of *normal* and she can't handle it. I'm 32 years old and still being lectured by my mother about my life choices. It could be worse in so many ways. I told her the same thing I always do. "Isn't it better to be happy than to be normal?" She hates it when I say that. What mother could get away with saying to their child they'd rather they were normal than happy, but I know she's thinking it.

Let me tell you about my mother. She's always had it in her head about living the perfect life. It's mainly because it didn't start out that way for us. At 18 she fell pregnant with me to a one-night drunken escapade with a friend of a friend. She was at university at the time and had to give it all up to become a mum. She returned to life in her small ex-mining home town of Winford in County Durham. You know the kind of place – big enough to not know everyone, but small enough for everyone to know your business. She gave up her ambitions to be the next big thing and that's when she started up her ambitions to be *normal*. I mean, what even is normal?

After a string of loser boyfriends, she met my stepdad, the hot shot business consultant widower, with a nice car and a young son.

He needed a mother figure for his child and she needed stability and normality, and so her obsession continued onto me.

She moved us into to his big house within weeks. I was a spotty fifteen-year-old with alternative tastes, strange clothes and a bad attitude. To be fair not much has changed. His son, Drew, was a spoilt brat of a kid. Even at nine years old, he was having tantrums to get his father's attention. Me and my mother coming into his life did not help one little bit, and he's been the biggest pain in my arse ever since.

My stepdad is very non-descript. You could easily lose him in a crowd. He has this perceived air of importance and to be fair he is important to some people. Mainly men the same age as him, and in the same line of work. This perceived importance makes him think that he has the right to tell people how they should live their lives. He's a very opinionated man with very little life experience of the things he has an opinions on.

The other thing about my stepdad that irritates me is the way he has moulded my mother. I'm not saying she wasn't complicit in it, but he's aged her beyond her years. She wears clothes of an 80-year-old and has a sour face to match. I often wonder if I was switched in the hospital when I was born. They've both become the poster child for those couples you see in the media, who complain about most things and are intolerant of pretty much everything different to them.

My stepbrother is your stereotypical misogynistic male, so the apple hasn't fallen far with this one. He compensates for his small dick with his flashy car and chucks round money like it's going out of fashion – his father's money, I may add. He has a string of blonde, skinny women on the go, god only knows why. My mother's vision of him being ambitious is very much deluded. With all that said, he still acts like the high school bully that never grew up.

At my age, she thinks I'm a disappointment, because I'm not married to a Hedge Fund Manager, living in the 'burbs with two point four kids. But on the other hand, if I got pregnant at 18 like her, I would have still come up short.

I manage to get her off the phone by agreeing to something or other, I'm not entirely sure what, to meet someone for something. Oh my god, I hope I haven't agreed to go on a date with someone who works with my stepfather. Best not to think about that. I just need to concentrate on getting out of the café on time and getting to the Hub to do a bit of work on my portfolio, maybe even process some film.

I grab a sandwich out of the fridge, it can tide me over until I decide what I might have for dinner. I head into the back to sort the rest of my things. Hearing the ding of the café door, my heart drops. Who in their right mind is going to want a coffee or a dried-up sandwich at this time of day?

I head out into the main part of the café to see who it is, hoping Cynthia is back to say false alarm, and that she's back to lock up. But no. Standing there, elbows on the counter with a smug grin on his stupid face, is Drew, my stepbrother, flanked by his equally gormless mates.

"Hannah Spanner Spencer!" He uses the name he knows will wind me up, but he never has the balls to say it in front of our parents.

"What do you want Drew? I'm about to close up."

"Well that's not very customer friendly now, is it?"

I roll my eyes, here we go again. "You're not really a customer, just a pain in the arse!"

"We'll have three cappuccinos to go," his face so smug, I want to slap it right off.

I have a feeling he chose those drinks because they are time consuming to make. But if I don't, it will just make things worse. So, I turn to face the coffee machine, make three perfectly passable cappuccinos and place them on the counter.

"That'll be -"

"Aren't you gonna ask us if we want chocolate?" He cuts me off.

"Do you want chocolate?" I say deadpan.

"I think I'll do it myself." His mates look to one another, so I know this is going down a sinister route. These guys would never make MI5 agents.

He takes the lids off the takeaway cups and picks up the chocolate shaker. Shaking chocolate all over the cups and my freshly wiped counter. "Sorry looks like I made a mess." A menacing grin etched on his face. "Oops!" and with one fluid motion of his arm, he sends the drinks speeding towards me, emptying their contents along the way.

Standing statue still my brain can't quite compute what is happening. Before I can do anything, I hear the ding of the door as they leave chuckling away to themselves, as I stand watching the coffee drip from the counter onto the floor and pool in a continuously increasing puddle. The coffee that caught me, starting to seep through my apron and onto my sweatshirt.

I'm not usually the kind of person that hates. If I don't like someone, I generally just ignore them and avoid situations where I have contact. But Drew I really fucking hate! And to top it off, I can't avoid him. He knows I won't tell our parents, because they won't believe me. They'll make some excuse or infer that I'm exaggerating the situation. But one day, the planets are gonna align and karma will come hunting for Drew. And when it does, I'm gonna be sitting on the side-lines watching with glee. I start the clean-up, there's nothing else I can do if I want to make it out of here anytime soon. What even is my life?

Barging through the door of the Creative Hub building in time to catch Tom, the caretaker, to tell him I'm in and I'll put the alarm on when I leave.

I head through the corridors and down the steps to the basement. The bowels of the building are where my darkroom is situated. It's a converted cleaners' room, still full of the smell of bleach and I really don't want to know what else. But this is my haven, my safe place.

This is the place I come to escape and to create. The place isn't perfect but it's mine. The room is pretty big considering it's just a cupboard. There's open wooden shelving against the wall to hold all the different types of chemicals I need. It has a massive sink, handy for rinsing, and a washing line strung from one side of the room to the other, then back again forming a V shape, it still has a few prints hanging up. There's a high bench where I can stand and develop film, and a low table where I can use my laptop to process my digital photos. Being in the depths of this old building, underground with no windows would turn most people off. But for a dark room it's perfect.

This place and my little terrace house are my absolute sanctuary.

Chapter Two

As if we're in some kind of groundhog type day, it's been another one of those days. I finished work late, again, this time without help from Drew, which meant that I had to rush over to the Hub. I needed to make sure the caretaker, was still on-site, this time I need to tell him about the flickering light in the corridor again, and to let him know I was working late.

As I walk in the main door, I see him chatting to another resident artist, but he finishes his conversation as soon as I approach and I'm able to tell him what I needed to. The last time I didn't tell him I was in the building, he locked up and put all the alarms on. To be fair, it is easy to forget that I'm downstairs. When I realised it was after 10pm, I rushed out of the building, setting off all the alarms. I stood there, frozen in a panic, alarms blaring, while a police car comes hurtling round the corner. Which in itself was impressive, since our town only has one police car. It's safe to say, that's not happening again. Now he knows I'm here, I can relax and concentrate on getting some work done.

I'm behind because I didn't get much done yesterday. With everything that kicked off, I was so wound up by Drew's antics, my head wasn't in the right place. I kept making mistakes, which set me back more. So I packed up and went home. I stop and take a few deep breaths, trying to calm my jumbled mind, today is gonna be different.

Continuing back down the corridor, I see a woman peering in through the glass of one of the art studio doors, swearing under her breath. She is dressed in corduroy dungarees with a rainbow puffer jacket covering her. Her hair is an explosion of curls, trying to escape a simple hairband she has holding them back.

"You okay?" I ask as I approach. She turns quickly with a quizzical look on her face, as if she didn't expect me to be there.

"Not really. I'm late for my class."

"Surely they'll let you in?"

"There's a no late entry policy, they won't let me in, even if I begged. I'll have no excuse now not to go back to work."

"What was your class?"

"Life drawing." She points at her portfolio. "I really needed the escape today as well." She ponders as if speaking to herself. She shakes her head as if to rid her mind from the thoughts running through them. "What are you here for?"

"Oh I'm going down to my dark room."

Her expression is puzzled. "Your what now?"

"Dark room, for my photography. I develop and print photos there."

Her face softens as if she understands and then pulls again to ask another question. "That's a bit old-school, I thought everyone worked in digital now."

It's nothing I haven't heard before. "Well I work in digital as well, but I like the look of black and white photos and I love the smell of the chemicals. My art shots look better that way."

She ponders the answer for a moment they shakes out of her thoughts. "Sorry, I'm Dionne." She gives me a big warm smile.

"Hannah. You wanna see it?"

"Huh?" Her eyes knit together.

"The dark room?"

"Hell, yes I do." She smiles back at me, I think I have given her that excuse she needed. I point in the direction of the stairs and we head into the depths of the hub.

As we reach the basement, I look back as Dionne slows, takes in her surroundings and falls behind. "Erm Hannah, this isn't a plot to murder me, is it?"

"What do you mean?"

Dionne points up at the strip light that flickers on and off. "If this isn't the start of a horror film, I don't know what is."

"Nah, it always goes a bit flickery. I keep asking our caretaker to fix it. Then a week later it starts again. It may be possessed." She gives me a little panicked look. "Anyway, I have to work first thing and I'd not have time to clean up and dispose of the body."

"Reassuring!" Dionne's eyes widen and I turn to unlock the door, pushing it open and gesturing for her to go in ahead of me.

She walks into the room. "Dionne, do you always go into creepy places with someone you've only just met?"

"You'd be surprised how many times I do."

"Remind me to never be on your emergency contact list."

"It's okay, I get feelings about people, I can usually read them really well and you've come up as okay on my dickhead detector."

"Good to know." I smile back at her.

"Do you always invite people you've just met down to your dungeon?" She smiles at me.

"You'd be surprised how many times I do." I laugh back. Dionne is definitely my kind of person, I think we'll get along well. I flick the light on and the room glows red.

She looks round at all my bits of equipment and turns suddenly when she hears me lock the door. "Don't worry, I always lock the door, it's like muscle memory. The door needs to be locked because if anyone walks in when I'm processing, and the light gets in, everything is ruined."

"Right." She still sounds a bit suspicious.

"Do you want to see some of my work?"

"Yes, that would be great." Her tone has lifted and we both stand over my pile of recently printed photographs. "So what images do you take the most? Is it people, things, nature?"

"Depends what mood I'm in really. What I'm focused on. I try to put collections together in the hope that one day I can show them in a gallery." She looks at each individual photograph, taking in all the aspects, like she's obviously someone who enjoys searching out the detail.

"Being in a gallery would be amazing. I don't think my drawings would ever be good enough to exhibit." She pulls a face. Pulling out a photo she directs it towards me. "I like this one, it's the shadows that make the rest of the subject pop out. Tell me more about why you take photos with an old camera."

"Analogue and digital are two completely different entities. Putting it in simple terms, digital is a shoot multiple shots and decide later which ones to use. Analogue you need to compose the piece more, take your time over it because you only have a small number of shots, depending on the film you have. It's a slower process. I like digital as well, that's great for action stuff, like when I take photos at events."

"I never really thought about it like that."

"Come on then, let's see yours." I point to her portfolio case.

"I don't know if I want to. They're not very good and I only do them to take my brain away from work."

"I bet they'll be great. What do you do as a day job?"

"I'm an accountant." She rolls her eyes.

"Numbers, nice!"

She looks at me quizzically, "You're not going to tell me that it's weird mixing art and numbers?"

"Why would it be? Just because you're academic doesn't mean you can't be artistic, they are not exclusive."

"See that's what I say. People just don't get it. Why do we need to be put in an either/or box? I love numbers but I also love images." She shrugs. "Do you have a day job?"

"Yes, I work in a café on the high street, *Grub's Up*. It pays the bills and it means I can focus a lot of time to my photography. I also sell some of my prints online. The café is a means to an end. My parents want me to get a *proper job*. They just don't get it. This IS my proper job, and some day I hope it will make me a living."

"Yes, my parents don't even know I draw."

"Let's have a look then." She stares at me for a moment as if weighing up whether or not she should, but then she picks up her folder and opens it out on the work table.

"Wow Dionne!" I say as I leaf through the sketches, all different shapes and sizes. Some of objects, some of people. Black smudges front and back, the intricacy of the pieces are amazing. Some very life-like, and others abstract. "These are amazing."

Dionne's face lights up. "You really think so?"

"I really do. Have you decided on a style? You have a lot of different ones here."

"No not yet, I'm just playing about, trying to find the ones I feel most comfortable with."

"Do you show them to anyone?"

"Not really. I've shown them to my friend Megan, but she's not seen my new stuff because she's travelling for the next few months."

"I wish I could go travelling. Well actually I just wish I could get away from here."

"You don't like living here?" Dionne questions.

"There's loads of stuff I do like about being here, this hub for example. But there are other sides, like the constant glare of my family... it's complicated." Dionne gives me a knowing look and then goes back to looking at the photos, while I take in her artwork. "I mean I feel comfortable here, I like my life, but I feel like there's more out there for me in some way."

"I get it."

We make general chit chat and it feels so comfortable, like we've known each other for a lifetime and we're just catching up on new events.

The ping of a phone has Dionne reaching into her pocket. Her expression changes to something I can't quite put my finger on.

"Is that the time? It feels like we've been here five minutes. I'm gonna have to head out, my lift is here. Are you staying?"

"Yeah. I've just got a few things to catch up on."

"I've really enjoyed this. Maybe we could exchange numbers and catch up again?"

"I'd really like that." She hands me her phone and I put in my number, she takes it back and I can feel the buzz in my pocket.

"You have mine now. I'll drop you a message."

"Great." Dionne gathers all her things together as I unlock the door and open it to let her out. She waves goodbye, shudders a little when she sees the flickering light again and rushes off out of view.

I've never really made friends easily. Well I made them, but never really kept them. I was always someone at school that was friendly with everyone but didn't really have many actual friends. And those sets of friends I did make, I was never really anyone's priority.

I'd be the last person someone would call. Or the person that would be dropped at the slightest sign of a better offer. Sometimes I'd find out the next day that a group of them had all met up and not thought to ask me. Eventually they'd move to something new and forget about me. Surprisingly it didn't really faze me, because through my life I've not known much different because my mother was the same, choosing other things than me as her priority. Men, friends, hobby's all came before me. Maybe this time things can be different.

I think I'll stay here looking through some recent negatives, then I'm going to head off home.

Chapter Three

Sean

I'm feeling totally out of sorts. I'm annoyed at the situation I currently find myself, which is unusual for me because I can normally just go with the flow. But I have lost my two best friends. Okay, I'm being a little over dramatic, but it's just how I feel right now.

Firstly, there's Ben, we've been friends since university, got up to all kinds of crazy shit. I helped setting up his business and have been working with him since forever. Ambrose Holdings, although Ben's brainchild, has been something we started together. We worked together, we played together, lived the high life in Edinburgh. That was until about two years ago, when he met the love of his life, Emma.

He decided the only way they could work was for him to move to England, which I thought was a bit drastic at the time, but I suppose it was what he needed. He set up a satellite office down in a small town in County Durham and we started accumulating more properties to renovate down there. There had been lots of potential and funding for regeneration there, so it was a good business decision. He would come back to up to Edinburgh and I went and stayed down there a few times a month. But now things are all change.

This is where my secondly comes in. My other best friend, Megan, kind of came with the deal. She's one of Emma's friends and we struck up a friendship. She's like the sister I never had. Trips down to Winford weren't so bad because I would be able to spend time with her. That is until she met her boyfriend and they decided to *get to know each other* for six months, galivanting around the world.

When Ben and Emma decided to relocate back up to Edinburgh, the best business decision, was for me to head down south, live in the North East. He'd be able to spend more time with his young daughter and I'd take care of the day to day running of the office and projects. Not much of a change, I suppose, except Megan isn't there to soften the blow.

In Edinburgh I had people, I had places I liked to visit, I had bars that had the right atmosphere. It was home. Now I say it out loud it does seem a bit pathetic. But I do have a set of friends here, even if I have only really acquired them through Megan, so I shouldn't feel so... I don't know, lost.

And then there's the living arrangements. When Megan needed somewhere to live, we kind of got a place together. It was mainly hers but I lived there when I came down for work or just to hang out. It's small. A lot smaller than my apartment back home, but it's more homely. It has cushions and throws on the sofa, there are scented candles all over the place. The only downside was the masses of long hair in the bath plughole.

But now she's not here and her friend has taken her place. Dionne moved in after her flat had a flood and had to be gutted. It's nice to have to company, but I don't really know her. She's not my person. It's not awkward because she's really chilled, but I don't think I have made enough of an effort with her to truly feel comfortable.

I think the overarching reason I'm feeling like this is because my friends are all pairing off and finding people they want to spend their forever with, which in equal measures makes me queasy and jealous. There is absolutely no way I want a relationship, not ever. But it would be nice to be someone's first and last thought.

My phone rings for a video call – it's Megan. It's like she has some kind of sixth sense.

"Alright lovely!" I answer as her face fills the screen. She's got a glow to her and her freckles have made an appearance.

"Hey misery."

"I'm not a misery, I am just deep in thought."

"Tell your face that!" She pulls a goofy face and all the melancholy ebbs away. She brings the sunshine back into everything.

"Where are you now?" Megan and Myles have been travelling all over the world, I really can't keep up with them.

"Do you know what? I'm not sure I even know what day it is. Malaysia, but which city, I couldn't tell you."

"What time is it there?" We have this conversation every time.

"It's 8pm here, we are just about to go out and have some food, but I felt the need to ring and check in. How's it going living with Dionne?"

"Fine."

"Just fine?"

"Well she's not you." I say curtly.

"Okay what's going on? Come on, spill. You know the rules."

"It's just... I honestly don't know. I feel out of sorts. Nothing should really have changed, but I feel like everything is totally up in the air. It's just dawning on me that I won't be going back home."

"This has been on the cards for a while now though. You could have employed someone else to run things in England and just stayed in Scotland."

"I know but I would have had to be here anyway for at least the first few months, so what was the point?"

"Well you can't have it both ways. You either relinquish the control or you go with the change."

"I know." And I do know. It was my choice, so why does it feel so disorientating.

"You've got plenty of people down there though. What about Jonathan? I'm sure he'd love to go out for a catch up."

"I know all this. Like I said, I just feel out of sorts."

"Do you want me to ask Dionne to go out and get your favourite biscuits?" She's teasing me now, but her big smile does lift my mood slightly.

"Yes, I do!" I laugh. "You know the one good thing about living with Dionne? At least she can use the coffee machine!"

"Rude!" There's movement and noise behind her. It's probably Myles trying to get her moving. "I've got to go." She leans into the screen. "But are you okay? I mean really?"

"Yes, I'll be fine. You go and enjoy your evening, I'm gonna have to find a decent sandwich shop so I don't get even more homesick." She waves and blows me a kiss before ending the call. I blow out a breath and log off my laptop.

It's lunch time and I need to head out of the office, find somewhere decent to get some food. It's a completely different kettle of fish being here compared to Edinburgh. Step out the door and there'd be at least five places in a 50 metre radius. The office down here is in a town on the outskirts of County Durham. It has a small-town atmosphere and only a handful of places to eat. I could drive out of town to one of the big shopping outlets and get something from a national franchise, but I am very aware that our company is trying to build these communities up and that means supporting the local businesses.

As I head out onto the street, I pull up a map on my phone. I still don't really know my way around and it will show me where the nearest place is. The high street has a few options, so I head to the nearest.

I push through the door of the coffee shop and it makes a dinging noise, drawing attention to me coming in. The place is a good size with a fridge of pre-made sandwiches and cakes. There's a professional coffee machine behind the counter, so we're off to a good start.

The woman behind the counter looks like she could be a former soviet shot putter in an apron. She looks up from her open magazine and gives me a toothy grin. "Hello Handsome, what can I get ya?" I'm just a little bit scared.

"Can I have a Macchiato and a look at the sandwich menu?"

Her face drops and she gives me a look through narrowed eyes, then without breaking eye contact she shouts. "Hannah!" she draws out the name for effect. "There's someone here wanting one of your poncey coffees." I'm considering whether to make a quick exit when someone emerges from behind the scenes and I can't believe my eyes. She's the most beautiful thing I have ever seen.

She doesn't notice me a first, which gives me the opportunity to take her in. She's petite with blonde hair, pulled off her face and up into a ponytail. The ends are coloured with a faded pale pink. Her face is oval and pixie-like with huge eyes and long lashes. She is wearing a baggy sweatshirt covered with the same apron.

Shot-putter nods over to me and the woman turns and lets out a small gasp, like she wasn't expecting me to be standing there. "Can you serve him? He wants one of those fancy coffees you make."

"Hi." She says in half a voice. She clears her throat and takes a deep breath. "What can I get you?"

"I was hoping for a Macchiato, but now I'm not sure." I watch as shotput woman heads out to the back.

"Don't mind Cynthia, her bark is worse than her bite. I can do a macchiato. Are you staying in or taking away?"

"Take away, and I was wanting a sandwich to eat at my desk too."

"We've got some in the fridge but if you don't fancy any of those, I could make you something up. Name?"

"Sorry what?" I start to fidget. For some reason I feel like I can't form words. I've never been nervous around a woman before.

"What's your name to put on your cup?" I look around the deserted shop, it's not as if my order is gonna get mixed up.

"Erm Sean."

She writes my name on a paper cup with a marker and turns away to use the coffee machine. I divert my attention to the fridge to stop myself from staring at her. I really wished I had said I would stay in, just so I could keep looking.

I think about asking her to make a fresh sandwich, just so I can stay longer, but my mind has gone a complete blank and I just pull a plain ham sandwich out of the fridge and set it on the counter.

She turns back round and places the paper cup next to the sandwich. "You spelt my name right." I don't even know what is coming out of my mouth right now. She has my head all messed up.

"That's because it's the correct way." She smiles back at me, then rings through the food through the till and I tap my card. Her face drops for a moment. "Is that your real name?"

"Yes. Why wouldn't it be?"

"Usually customers use false names, so the café weirdos don't shout after them in the street." She gives a little chuckle.

"You're wearing a name badge." I look at the badge on her apron. It reads *Gertrude*. She looks back at me with a cheeky grin and the realisation crosses my face.

"The only reason you know *my* real name is because of big mouth over there." She thumbs towards the shot-putter.

"Funny, you look like a Gertrude as well." Her face drops again and I think I may have just put my foot in my massive, stupid mouth. Say something to make it better, open your mouth and say words Sean, I'm begging myself. But nothing comes to mind, so I pick up my cup and sandwiches and head for the door, and mouth *thanks* as I scuttle off.

I get onto the street and head back to the office on auto-pilot. Never before have I been affected by anyone like this. Maybe it's just because my head is all over the place. But I know for sure I have found my favourite coffee shop now.

Chapter Four

It's been a week since I first saw her, and I've been to the coffee shop every day since. Well, excluding the weekend, because I didn't really have an excuse. But she's not been there. I wondered if I imagined her for a minute. I know I couldn't have because the shot-putter has been there every time, informing me, as soon as I step foot inside, that Hannah wasn't there to make my *fancy coffee*.

I just can't get her out of my head. I think about every bit of the conversation and kick myself for not saying something funny or asking for her number. But my brain totally seized up and I bet I looked like a total dickhead.

I need to put this woman out of my head because I'm driving myself completely insane. My phone rings and pulls me out of my daydream.

"I see we've got you for good then." Jonathan's dulcet tones hit me.

"You must have been good in a former life."

"Ha. I was just ringing to ask if you want to come out with me and some of the footy lads on Friday. We need some new recruits for both nights out and to play."

"Sounds good. When do you play? Be aware I've not played a full match for a year or so, so I'm gonna be a bit out of shape."

"Mate, half the guys on the team have never been IN shape. Well, not since police training."

"Ah... so it's a police team?"

"Mainly but we let in outsiders too, if they pass the *I'm not a knob* test. We play Sunday mornings. But you can find out more if you come on Friday."

"Message me the details and I'll be there."

"Will do." As he hangs up, I think maybe giving myself something to do is just the right thing. Firstly to forget this woman, because nothing can come of it. I have sworn off relationships for good, so at most it'll be a quick hook up. And also it might get me out of this mood and make me feel more like I belong here.

Pushing through the door to the pub, I spot the group straight away. Jonathan is laughing at something as the others nudge him or shake their heads. This isn't like the Dog and Swan, Megan's local. It's less friendly, more testosterone filled, walls adorned with football memorabilia and black and white photos from past times.

Jonathan spots me and waves me over.

I make my way over to the crowd of men. When I reach them, the crowd erupts with laughter.

"Sean. Meet the guys." I nod at them. "Guys this is Sean, he'll be joining us in..." He looks to me to fill in the blank.

"Defence."

"Well thank god, I thought we'd have someone else vying for a striker spot. This is Titch, he's in goal. Onions, Deano, Woody, Charlie." They all nod back as their name is announced.

"What was so funny?"

"Charlie is in the doghouse with his missus."

"How come?"

"Come on Charlie, let's get an opinion from a self-confessed permanent bachelor."

"Well, she kept going on about this new amazing mop she's seen on TikTok or something. So I bought it for her." Charlie explains.

"I don't see a problem with that."

"Charlie!" Jonathan pushes him for the rest of the story.

"Okay, well I bought it for her birthday."

I let out a gasp. "Even I know that you never buy a woman appliances for her birthday. Was this recent, can you pull it back by buying her something else and saying it was a joke present or something."

"It was two weeks ago."

"You're screwed," I reply, pulling a face.

"That's what I said!" Deano pitches in.

"And she's still mad?" I continue to try and get more information.

"Like, really passive aggressive and brings it up out of the blue."

"I think you deserved that one," says Deano. "I got told off last night by my missus for cooking her a pizza with different toppings from what she asked for. Went absolutely ballistic."

"Is she hormonal?" asks Charlie.

"Probably, but there's no way I can actually ask that without getting my head ripped off." Everyone sighs and nods in agreement.

"Can we stop talking about women. I come out with you lot so I don't have to deal with this shit," says Titch.

Jonathan leans in to me and explains under his breath, "Titch's wife is pregnant, and he has a toddler too. Life is a bit hectic." God this lot make me feel like my life is all roses.

We stay in the pub until just before closing time, chatting about all kinds of things, until one by one all the lads leave to head back to their families. Finally, it's just me and Jonathan. "How you finding being here permanently?"

"I dunno. It shouldn't feel different, but it does somehow."

"You'll get used to it. I don't think you'll be out on the town every night like in Edinburgh."

"It wasn't quite that exciting. But there's definitely a slower pace here."

"You can say that again. Right I best get going. If you need anything, just message." Jonathan gets up and pulls his coat on, pats me on the back and heads for the door.

"Will do," I say to his retreating back. I finish my pint and head out for the walk back to the house. Luckily, it's not too far.

Chapter Five

Hannah

Why do I do this to myself? Sunday mornings are for sitting on the sofa in pyjamas and fluffy slippers, watching reruns of sitcoms, drinking tea and eating rubbish. But no, I'm here, on the side of a cold, damp football pitch, watching 25 unfit men run around, covered in mud. I have at least seven layers of clothes on, plus fingerless gloves and a woolly hat. All because I told my Uncle Mitch, who isn't even a real blood relative, that I'd take some photos of the team he was sponsoring.

My rucksack is weighing me down and I'm not in the best of moods, my digital and analogue cameras are ready to shoot, but I can't bring myself to focus on what's happening. I do take action shots, but Sunday League football really isn't my scene.

I have a mental word with myself – once I get going and get a few shots, I can head home to the warm. I look up towards the action. He's here! I feel like my heart has stopped and I might just drop down dead. I watch as he shadows one of the opposition players. I realise I'm staring, so I pull up my camera and start shooting pictures. They are all of him, so I quickly scope the rest of the pitch to capture the other players.

"Hi" I hear a voice next to me and I jump out of my skin. All I have been focused on is gorgeous Macchiato Man. I remove my eye from the view finder and lower my camera to see a woman with the face of thunder. I take her in from her boots, right up her full-length puffer jacket, to her woolly hat with a fluffy pompom on the top. "Are you taking photos of my man?"

"Erm well..."

"I'm just joking." Her face cracks and there's a slight turn at the side of her mouth. I can tell this woman is no nonsense and would be a force to be reckoned with. She points out onto the field. "That's mine, number five, on the blue team. What are you taking photos for?" Her tone less accusatory.

"Mitch asked me to get some action shots because The Dog and Swan are sponsoring them."

"Ha! Action shots? You'll be lucky. They all look like they had a heavy session last night. I think we may need an ambulance on standby."

"Maybe. I don't usually do football, so I'm not sure what to expect."

She points to my camera. "Can I have a look?"

"Sure." I turn the screen so she can look while I flick through the photos I have taken.

"There he is," she says, when we get to a photo of her number five. I carry on flicking through until I realise that the only ones left are all of Sean, so I pause after the first four. "So you've got a good few of Sean then?" I think I would have gone red if my face hadn't already felt like it was going to fall off.

"Who?" I say, trying to hide the fact that I have blatantly been stalking this man. The woman points at the screen and gives me a knowing little look. I shrug "I was testing the light and he was the nearest to me." I wonder if she can hear the lie in my voice, I'm not even convincing myself.

"Hmm. I'm Lizzie by the way." She points to the pitch again. "That's Jonathan, my... well I don't know, father of my children I suppose."

"So he's not your man... or is he? If you're not together, why on earth would you be out here in the cold."

She shrugs, "Showing willing I suppose. It's a complicated situation." She looks at me and gives a kind of smile. "Plus he looks good in a pair of shorts. Scroll back and I'll tell you who they are." I scroll to the end, then start back through them.

"That's Deano, Woody, Onions."

"Do any of them have normal names?"

"No, not really. They are grown men, but most of them still have nicknames from when they were 14. A lot are based on their surnames, but others are just outright weird."

"Onions?"

"Because he has layers apparently." She rolls her eyes and we go back to the camera screen. "Charlie." She points at another player.

"Well Charlie is vaguely normal. Is he called Charles or something."

"No he's in the drugs squad!" I give an undignified snort at the idea. "Jonathan, but they call him Jono. And that's Sean or Hutch as he has been named."

"Don't tell me... because he has a rabbit?"

She laughs. "No, his name is Hutchinson. But I think yours is a better reason." She points to another player. "Titch, he's the big one in goal. It's ironic, and apparently it's because he's big elsewhere too." She gives me a wide eye and I laugh. The bloke is a man mountain.

"Well I don't think I can stand here much longer, my fingers are freezing and I'll soon not be able to press the buttons," I say.

"Do you think you could send me some of the pictures if I give you my number?"

"Yes, sure." I put my hands in my pocket, giving them some light relief from the frost bite, and pull out my phone. I hand it to her, unlocking it before she takes it completely. "I'm Hannah."

"I'll leave you to it," she says, handing the phone back to me. "The more I distract you, the more time you'll have to spend out here. I might actually go and sit in the car for the second half." She waves goodbye and heads down the touchline.

She's got the right idea. But I think I might just take some analogue shots, for art purposes obviously, and absolutely not because I'd have to stare at Sean for hours on end. As I take a few more shots some kind of situation develops at the other end of the pitch, so I head down the touchline to see what's going on. The referee moves people away from an opposition player on the floor. Lizzie is knelt next to him, tipping his chin skywards as she inspects the cut, oozing with blood, above his eye.

I pull my camera up to my eye and take some shots. This is exactly what I need for my new exhibition. I then pull myself behind the crowd and make my way out of the park and head home to try and get some feeling back in my limbs.

Chapter Six

It's been a few days since I saw Sean at the football, but I haven't stopped thinking about him. It's been longer since I saw him in the café. I thought he might come in again, even if it was just because I make a good coffee. Maybe I've scared him off? It wouldn't be the first time. I expect a man like him would get lots of attention, you can't help but notice his handsome, sculptured face and his buff, tall body. His Scottish accent was so smooth, but he seemed a bit nervous. Surely you don't need to be nervous when you look like him. I don't think he realises how seriously hot he is.

Seeing him at the football only confirmed what I suspected – he must work out, his shirt strained across his chest, like it was hiding the most perfectly chiselled specimen. I thought he'd be someone who would like a bit of flirting, but that first time we met, he had rushed out of the café with no backward glance.

For the first few days, every time I heard the ding of the bell, I would rush to see if it was him. But no, and the disappointment would rush through my body like an ice-cold drink. After a few days, and a few changes in shifts, I was no longer on high alert.

The ding of the bell sounds now and Cynthia puts her head round the door to the kitchen where I'm lurking, pretending to do something important.

"Your mate's just come in." Now when Cynthia says *mate*, she often means it ironically, like it's actually the person I would least like to see. But then sometimes really it is a friend of mine. So it's just pot luck and head out to investigate.

"Verity. Oh my god, I've not seen you in ages." This time it was my friend. "You look amazing." A big smile spreads across her face.

"You too!" She's lying because I look a mess, but it's a nice gesture.

"Do you have time for a chat?" I probably shouldn't ask because I'm meant to be working myself.

"Yes, sure. I'm on a break."

"I'll bring over your drink." Verity makes her way over to an empty table and sits down.

I can't get over how much better she looks. The last time I saw her she had sunken eyes, her skin was grey, she just looked like a ghost of her former self. I turn and make her coffee, then make my way over with it.

I know Verity through the hub. She was a regular and we became friends. Then one day, she just didn't turn up. We didn't think anything of it at first but after a few no shows we became worried. I messaged her and went around to find out where she was, but she was in a very traumatised state. It took a long time for me to get her to open up and tell me what happened.

"You look like a whole different you." She gives me a little smile. "No you really do, you look like you have so much life back in your face."

"I feel like I've got my life back. Did I tell you I have been taking some self-defence classes?"

"Wow! That's awesome. Tell me you have a really hot instructor."

"Well, not exactly. But there's another who bring the hotness." She gives me a sly little grin and I know there's a story there for another time. "It's just given me so much more confidence. I feel like I'm almost back to the old Verity."

"That's amazing to hear."

"I don't think I'll ever be the same as before though."

What Verity went through really bought things home to a lot of us. Because really, it could have happened to me or any of my friends. She was just walking home and got attacked. I want to say she was lucky in one aspect, but luck may be the wrong word. Someone disturbed the assault or it could have been a whole lot worse.

"Do you remember I took a photo of you not long after it happened?"

"I vaguely remember, it's all a bit of a haze."

"Do you think I could take some more to compare them, and maybe add them to a collection I'm putting together?"

"Yeah sure, I'm not sure who would want to look at me though."

"You are joking right?" This woman is beautiful, inside and out, even on her worst days. "Can we do it in the same place at yours, so the comparison is true."

"Yeah sure, just drop me a message when you have time available."

"Have you been able to get back to anything creative?"

"Well actually I started sketching again." She takes her phone out and finds some pictures. She turns her screen towards me.

"Geez who's this guy?" Verity's cheeks pink up and I know it's someone she likes. The sketches are brilliant, I wonder whether he looks this perfect in real life or is this just how she sees him.

"He's just someone... I like. I don't want to put a label on it just yet."

"But you like him?"

"Yes I do. He's kind and strong and funny."

"And hot?"

"Very!" There's a little glint in her eye and I know she's absolutely smitten with this guy. And good for her, I hope he's her prince charming. We chat for a bit longer until Verity has to leave and I have to go back to work.

The café is pretty empty and I'm thinking about Verity and her new man. I rest my elbows on the counter and drift off into my own thoughts. I'm really quite happy with the way my life is heading. I'm not like my mother, in need of validation from others to tell me I'm happy. My photography gives me a sanctuary and it surrounds me with people of a similar outlook. But is there more?

"You look deep in thought." I flinch at the voice, I didn't even notice Sally come in. She's here to take over from Cynthia. "What's up?"

"Just contemplating life."

"Well that's a bit deep."

"Verity has just been in and she's glowing. She's got a new man."

"AND?"

"And nothing. I was just saying."

"You always say you don't need a man to *complete you*." She does a circle motion with her hands to reiterate her point.

"I don't." She gives me a wide eye, knowing full well that I'm holding something back. "I'm not like you. I don't need to always be in a relationship. I'm happy on my own."

"I don't know what you mean. I was on my own before I met Owen."

"No you weren't. You cheated on Steve with Owen."

She looks sheepish. "You knew about that?"

"Everyone knew about it Sally. Well except Steve, obviously." I blow out a breath, because in all honesty I don't know what I want. The best of both worlds, I think. She comes around the back of the counter and starts putting her apron on. "I mean I don't need someone, and I totally love my independence, but maybe it would be nice to do things with someone else, you know?"

"Sometimes it's more trouble than it's worth. I'm at my wit's end with Owen. He's driving me mad saying he's doing one thing, then does another. He says 'Babe I'm gonna be five minutes' sorting something with that stupid car, then it's an hour and a half later and he's nowhere to be found, I'm waiting around for him like an idiot. I could have been doing something more valuable with my time."

She ties her hair up into a high pony tail, produces her phone and poses all pouty lips and peace signs. "What are you doing?" I ask.

"Posting on Instagram."

"You've just made out that your life is a shit show and you're posting all happy vibes?"

"Yes, well it's social media, none of it is real."

"Yeah, but none of it is real because people like you post unreal images. Then people think everyone else's life is so much more rosy." I don't know how many times I've had this conversation with Sally, and it's one of the reasons I don't put things about myself online, only my art. And then sometimes, even that's anxiety inducing when people say its rubbish and you should get a proper job. Come to think of it, is that my mum commenting on my posts?

The ding of the door goes again but it's not enough to pull me out of my head.

"Hello Handsome." Sally's words jolt me into reality and I quickly stand up straight and meet his startling blue eyes. God he is just as gorgeous as I remember. Even though it was Sally that greeted him, he hasn't acknowledged her, and still hasn't broken eye contact with me.

"Hi…" It's like the rest of the world has fallen away, it's just me and him standing there, like he's trying to talk to me without words. "Please can I get a Macchiato?" And I suddenly pull out of my trance.

"Sitting in or taking out?"

"In."

"I'll bring it over." He takes a few moments, taps his card for payment and walks over to the seat in the corner, as I turn to the coffee machine.

"Wow!" Sally is watching me, arms folded across her chest with a huge grin on her face. "So, now I understand the conversation we just had."

"I don't know what you mean."

"I think you do." She gives a little laugh as I go around the counter to deliver the hot guy a coffee.

Chapter Seven

Sean

It's been a funny week. Monday was tough, but mainly because I played football the day before, for the first time in a long while, and used some of those muscles haven't been used in a while. Plus, it was freezing. So much so that Lizzie spent the second half sitting in the car. Then there were the obligatory few pints in the pub to warm up afterwards. Which then led onto the pub Sunday roast dinner, and before I knew it the day had gone, and I was prepping for Monday morning mayhem.

There's been a lot of site visits this week too. A few teething problems at one of the new sites and a bit of vandalism on the other, not to mention having to temporarily shut down a site because of the rain. Not big issues at all, just things that needed handling in person.

So today is the first time I have had chance to go back down to the coffee shop. Mainly an attempt to see for myself if the girl did, in fact, exist and was as gorgeous as I first thought. I'm strictly sworn off relationships, so I'm not sure why I've been a bit obsessed with her. Nothing can come of it. If she's not how I remember, I can easily put the thoughts to rest.

I stop outside to gather my thoughts before going in, and I see her through the door. She looks like she's daydreaming with her elbows on the counter while her colleague chats away and takes weird selfies. And yes, she is as stunning as I first thought. Maybe even more so. Just keep it casual Sean, go in, get your coffee and leave.

I push through the door and am greeted by her colleague. The girl snaps out of her daydream and stands to attention. I meet her piercing green eyes and my mind goes blank.

"Hi...." I just stare at her, trying to get the words out of my mouth. "Please can I get a Macchiato?" I can't pull my eyes away.

"Sitting in or taking out?" she says, as if on autopilot.

"In." What are you saying? The plan was to leave quickly.

"I'll bring it over." I pull my stare away and tap the contactless tab, turn and make my way over to the furthest table. Maybe some distance will distract from the fact I'm acting like some kind of crazy man.

I pull out my phone, so it looks like I'm unaffected by her. But I watch her make her way to my table over the top of my phone. The apron ties hug around the curves that her big baggy jumper tries to hide. I know I'm not going to be able to look away from her arse in those skinny jeans once she heads back to the counter.

She puts my coffee on the table but doesn't turn to leave.

"Back again then?"

"Yeah, this place has the best coffee. Well seemingly only when you're in." Her eyebrows raise.

"Well thanks for the compliment."

If I say anything else it will just be noise and I'll make a dick of myself so this time I stay silent.

"So are you working around here? You don't sound local."

"I've just moved here with work."

"What do you do?"

"I run a Property Management company. What about you?" My face falls, of course she works in a coffee shop, I already know that.

She smiles and I'm waiting for her to call me out for being an idiot. "Apart from working here I'm a photographer." Interesting.

"Can't anyone take photos now with their phones?" What a dick thing to say, I need to pull this back before she hates me. "Sorry I didn't mean it the way it came out."

"Nothing I haven't heard before." She turns to head back to the counter.

"What kind of thing?" I'm desperate for her not to leave. She stops and turns back round.

"Huh?"

"What kind of photos do you take?"

"Really depends what kind of mood I'm in, or what project I'm doing. Sometimes people, sometimes things, nature, sometimes football." She gives me a cheeky little grin but I'm not sure why.

"Right." I can't form words when she's around.

"Well maybe I'll see you around? Seeing that I make the best coffee around here." She gives me a grin and heads back to the counter. My brain is whirling. I pick up my phone, so it looks like I'm concentrating on that, but in reality, I'm going over that conversation again.

When we go out in Edinburgh, I'm usually described as the flirty one, the one that makes the first move at chatting a woman up. It seems that has gone completely out of the window with this one. She completely shuts my brain off.

I can see them over at the counter talking in whispers. Her colleague is laughing and obviously teasing her as she gives a shoulder bump. She's probably telling her she's attracted some weird bloke who can't string a sentence together. I need to get out of here before I embarrass myself even more.

I finish my coffee and head to the door, hoping I don't trip over my feet as I leave. I nod a goodbye.

· ♥ · ♥ · ♥ · ♥ · ♥ ·

I don't know what's got into me. I rushed back to the office after seeing Hannah. I went over the conversation we had, beating myself up for the things I said, for the things I didn't say and then for the fact of how much this whole thing is affecting me, when I don't even want to be in a relationship.

I've spent the day looking like I'm working but achieving absolutely nothing. I packed up my things and went home, there was no point in staying. I'm currently making some pasta while searching for some kind of crime drama I can binge watch to distract myself.

Dinner is served and being eaten sitting on the sofa. I've not heard from Dionne so I have left plenty for her in the pan, and maybe some for a lunch. We make sure we eat together at least twice a week and have a catch up. Usually just how work is going and sometimes we have a joint video call with Megan.

I hear the key in the lock and the door opens. "Hi honey I'm home!"

"Hi Babes!" I laugh. It's our little joke because everyone questions if we are dating because we live together, and they can't really believe that we aren't. I turn and look towards the door and my heart stops. Behind Dionne stands a very sheepish looking Hannah. "Hannah?"

"Sean."

"You two know each other?" Dionne questions pointing between us.

"Kind of."

"I didn't know you lived with someone." Hannah looks to Dionne.

"Well yes, but not like that."

"It's just a joke, we're not dating!" I jump up from the chair and head over to the kitchen, while Hannah stands in the door way.

"I've saved you some pasta." I say to Dionne.

"Oh brilliant, I'm starving."

"You're welcome to have some Hannah, I've made plenty."

"No thanks, I'm not hungry." And just on cue her stomach rumbles and uncovers her lie. Her face flushes and, oh my god, it's the most amazing thing I've ever seen. I start to dish up two more bowls.

I don't know what to do with myself now. The evening of trying to forget about Hannah has gone and I'm pacing the kitchen not knowing where to put myself. Dionne comes over and grabs the two bowls and takes them over to Hannah, where they've settled on the sofa. "So how do you know each other?" she asks.

"From the coffee shop."

"Oh I've not been yet."

"Apparently I make the best coffee in town." Hannah smirks at me and it's my turn to go pink.

"And you two?" I ask, trying work out this weird triangle.

"Hannah's dark room is in the hub where I take my life drawing classes."

"What are you both doing here?" There I go again, sounding like an arsehole.

"I live here!" I give Dionne wide eyes until I get a proper answer. "Hannah lost her keys, so she's hanging out here until she can get hold of someone who has a set."

"Don't you have a spare?" What is the matter with me? I sound like her Dad.

"I have one of those safe boxes, with the code. But last time a forgot my key I used it and didn't put it back."

"You should have replaced it straight away." I'm not usually so abrupt or this much of an arsehole.

"No shit. Hindsight is a wonderful thing." She turns to Dionne. "Maybe I should go."

"No! Sorry, I didn't mean to sound rude."

"What's got into you?" Dionne looks at me like I have been possessed.

"Nothing. Why don't you choose something to watch." I start to tidy up in the kitchen, I wouldn't be able to focus on a film anyway and if I went upstairs, I'd look even more rude and I don't want to stop looking at her.

They settle on a film and I eventually admit defeat and sit on the end of our massive L shaped sofa and scroll through my phone aimlessly. The girls are chatting, and it washes over me until my ears prick up. "There's lots of sex in this film, I'm feeling a bit jealous right now. I mean do people really have that much sex? I haven't had it for so long I'm not sure I'd remember what to do." Hannah laughs.

"I know what you mean." Dionne replies.

"Pah!" It comes out of my mouth without thought and before I can rein it back in both of them are staring at me.

"Have you got something to say?" Dionne glares at me.

"Nothing no!"

"Spit it out!" she orders.

"How can you say that when you're sleeping with two guys?"

"Well..." She looks sheepish, and so she should.

"You what? Like two guys separately or two guys together?" Hannah's eyes are wide.

"Both." I answer for her, at least the heat is off me.

"Both?"

"Yes. I sleep with them separately and I have slept with them together." Dionne is giving me the death stare. "This was maybe a subject I would have liked to lead up to. Thanks Sean!"

"Well there must be something wrong with me then, cos I'm not even sleeping with one."

"There's nothing wrong with you." I snap. "Dionne is just being greedy."

"I need to know more about this." Hannah is laser focused on Dionne for more answers.

"It's complicated. Tell me why you don't have anyone. You're an intelligent, beautiful, strong, sexy woman." I couldn't agree more with Dionne on that.

"Aww thanks. I don't know. I seem to attract the wrong type of men. The last two men I dated were polar opposites of each other. The first was a bit controlling and wanted to fix my life, a life that doesn't need fixing, might I add. And the second couldn't make a decision to save his life. You know the kind. *Where do you want to go out to eat? Wherever you want, I'll have what you're having, It's up to you,* kind of person. Drove me nuts."

"You can't have it both ways." I reply.

"I don't want it both ways, I just want something a bit in the middle. It's not like I'm asking for the world. And I'd rather not have anything than compromise too much and lose myself. I'm actually quite happy with how my life is going." She says curtly putting me in my place.

Well I managed to kill the conversation, again, and we all sit in silence as they watch the film. I continue to look at my phone but am just thinking through the fact that Hannah isn't with anyone at the minute. I don't want a relationship, but maybe we could help each other out with the sexual frustration part.

My mind is wandering off down all kinds of different avenues with this one and I'm vaguely aware of Dionne saying she's going to the bathroom. I try and focus on my phone and not look at Hannah. My attention is drawn to the TV when I notice the credits running. Dionne hasn't come back downstairs and on closer inspection Hannah is fast asleep.

I run through what I should do and most of the scenarios have me looking like a creep. I head upstairs to check on Dionne, and hopefully ask her what to do, but when I get to her room, she is also flat out on her bed.

I could leave Hannah on the sofa, but what if something happens? What if someone breaks in? She'll be in the line of fire. It also means that she can leave without me knowing and I quite like her being here.

Decision made, I go back downstairs, put her phone in my back pocket, and scoop her up in my arms to carry her up the stairs. I kick open the door to my bedroom and gently place her on my bed. I untie her boots, slip them off her feet and place them next to the bed. I cover her up, plug her phone in to charge and leave it on the bedside table.

She hasn't stirred once. She must have been exhausted so I take a few moments to fully look at her. She looks so peaceful, her frown lines gone, her face looks younger and innocent. She isn't pulling that face that says *Sean you're acting like a prick*. I pull myself away because if she wakes and sees me standing over her, I'm gonna be in big trouble. I quietly close the door and head downstairs to the sofa, find something to watch and pull a throw over me.

· ♥ · ♥ · ♥ · ♥ · ♥ ·

I'm woken by the sound of footsteps on the stairs and the creak of the third step up. I'm glad I didn't get that fixed now. I open my eyes and Hannah is creeping through the living room. "Morning." I say and she visibly jumps, then stands statue still.

"Morning. What happened last night?"

"You fell asleep. You seemed like you needed it so I put you in my bed."

"I could have just stayed on the sofa." I shrug to brush off the explanation.

"Coffee?"

"I should get back."

"At…" I look at my watch, "7am on a Saturday morning?" I raise my eyebrows at her.

"Fair point." I get up and head to the kitchen, flick the switch on the coffee machine and it starts making noises.

"What a coincidence." She looks up from her phone and gives me a quizzical look. "That we just met and you know Dionne."

"Maybe the universe wanted us to meet."

"You don't believe in all that do you?"

"Yeah, why not? I believe people come in and out of your life for a reason at a certain time."

"So why has the universe brought us together then?" I flinch as I say the words, because we are very much not together and never will be.

"I don't know yet. It hasn't made its plans known. I take it you're not thrilled we met."

"Why would you think that?"

"I wonder." She crosses her arm in front of her chest.

"I think we got off on the wrong foot. Things seem to be coming out of my mouth that I don't mean and I apologise. I am a nice guy, honestly."

"You know only creeps say *I'm a nice guy, honest*."

"Well you like Dionne and Dionne likes me, so I can't be all that bad."

"You didn't really say how you came to be living together."

"Well, it's a bit of a long story."

"Do you need to be somewhere at 7am on a Saturday morning?" She throws back at me.

"Fair point." I gesture over to the sofa so we can get comfortable. "I kind of part-time lived with Megan."

"Dionne's friend?"

"Yes. I lived in Edinburgh but had to come down on business every so often. Megan couldn't afford all the bills on her own and I needed somewhere to stay, so it seemed like a good idea. Fast forward to a few months ago when Megan decided to go travelling the world, Dionne's flat gets flooded and I have to move down here on a more permanent basis."

"And you still don't believe in the universe bringing people together at the right time?" I shrug because I have never really thought of it in that way. "You were there for Megan at the right time, Megan was there for Dionne, I was there for Dionne and here we all are."

"Isn't that just friendship?"

"Well yes. But how did you meet Megan? Have you been friends your entire life or was it a chance meeting."

"Okay, I see where you are going with this, but I'm not totally convinced."

We both sit cradling our cups and contemplating. We're pulled out of our thoughts by Hannah's phone ringing and she pulls it out of her pocket. She looks at the screen and rolls her eyes. "It's my mum." She answers the phone and I listen to her side of the conversation.

"Hi... Yeah, I know, I didn't mean to...I've been staying at my friend Dionne's... Well can you wait until I can get over there?...I'll set off now... There isn't one in the box... I wouldn't call it irresponsible, I just misplaced them. Right... Bye... Well if you let me go, I'd get there quicker." She hangs up and swears under her breath.

"Everything okay?"

"Just my mother catastrophising again. But I do need to go. Thanks for the coffee."

"Do you need a lift anywhere?"

"No I'll be fine, as long as I set off now."

"If you're sure."

"Yes, and thanks for letting my stay in your bed. It was very comfortable." She gives me a cheeky smile and I feel my heart rate pick up. Before I can say anything else, she's closing the door behind her, and I feel the loss immediately.

Chapter Eight

Hannah

After getting yet another lecture about how my life is going down the pan and how irresponsible I am for losing my keys, plus how it wouldn't have happened if I had a man looking after me, I got into my house. I need to do everything I can not to have to ask my parents for the key again. Not losing it would be a plan, but I know myself too well, so needed something else.

I got more keys cut and have put one in the safe box, I found my original key at work in my apron, but I also gave Dionne a key to keep at hers, just in case. Is it because I trust Dionne? Yes. Is it also because it gives me an excuse to go over and see Sean? Also yes. But we'll not tell anyone else about that.

I can't believe he carried me upstairs and put me in his bed. I mean, how did he manage that? I woke all snuggled and warm, surrounded by his smell. His aftershave was on the pillow and his sheets smelt like a freshly showered Adonis. Well that's what I was picturing when I smelt it. Not that I go around smelling people's sheets. Gross.

Sean has got my head in a bit of a mess. I just can't work him out. I can see him watching me and I think he may be into me. But then what he says makes it seem like I'm just a silly girl to him. He did apologise the next morning and said I'd got him all wrong. But I don't know and I didn't really hang about to find out.

He didn't come back into the café this week either and I've only briefly seen Dionne at the hub. But to be honest, I've had my head stuck in my photography. I did a photoshoot with Verity and developed them yesterday. The comparison in pictures is unreal and I am putting these as the centre of my new collection. The working title, I think, will be Healing or Recovery... or something like that. I'm not quite sure what yet.

I had someone contact me on Instagram too, asking about my collections. The messages didn't seem like the usual spam so I'm hopeful that something might come of it.

It's the last hour of my shift at the café, so I'm just going through some cleaning and restocking. I decided to give my brain a rest tonight and just chill out at home. I'll find a series to binge watch and eat a whole load of junk food. Sounds like the most perfect night – fluffy pyjamas and an array of throw cushions and blankets littering the sofa.

My phone gets my attention and I see the caller ID and answer straight away. The caller speaks before I get the chance to say hello.

"Hey! How's my favourite girl?"

"Now I know you want something." My lips turn up into a smile, because although I know he's after something, he's one of my favourite people.

"But you are my favourite niece."

"Mitch, I'm not even your niece though am I? So you're not starting out very well there if you are going to be asking me for a favour." Like I said, Mitch isn't actually my uncle, but he is as close to one that anyone can be.

I've known him all my life and he has been my one stable male influence and protector. I think he was a friend of my Dad. But Mitch stuck around when my father didn't even want to know. Plus he doesn't fall for any of the rubbish that my mother dishes out.

"True. But can you do a shift for me tonight? I know it's short notice, but I don't really trust anyone else." Mitch runs one of the local pubs, The Dog and Swan. It's not what you would call *high end*, but it's definitely not the roughest around. The great thing about The Dog is its sense of community. People look out for each other. And Mitch is like some kind of, I don't know, godfather for want of a better name. He seems to know everything that goes on. If you mention anything in the Dog, Mitch knows about it.

"I was planning a pyjama party with myself."

"I'll make it worth your while."

"What, you'll actually pay me?"

"Well no. But think about the good karma."

"If it was anyone else, Mitch, it would be a hard no. What time do you want me?"

"Well it won't start getting busy until about eight, so any time before that would be great."

"No problem, but you owe me!"

"You will get your reward in Heaven. Thanks." He hangs up, leaving my night of relaxation in tatters.

I decided not to bother getting changed, so I'm still in my denim pinafore dress with jumper over the top. The pub is definitely not the place to go without my armour. With my friends it's kind of a joke that I'm always wearing a baggy sweatshirt, even in a heatwave. But my body shape is so top heavy that without it I get a lot of unwanted attention. I have paired the ensemble with my favourite stripy knee length socks and some black lace up boots. The shin length of the dress hides the tops of the socks, so they actually look like funky tights.

I push through the doors of the pub and am greeted with the familiar smell of beer and bodies. The place is not full by any means, but there is enough of a crowd to have to squeeze past people to get to the bar. I make my way through the open hatch, behind the pumps and through to the store cupboard/staff room to find Mitch.

"Hannah! Thanks so much for helping me out, you're a lifesaver. Me and Ollie probably could have managed but I heard one of the football teams is out on a bender tonight and it's bound to get messy."

"No problem." I look at him up and down. "Do you ever wear anything other than that t-shirt?" It's now an off black colour because it's been worn so much. It's adorned with the words *The Best and Most Talented Barman in the World* in white writing.

"It's my favourite."

"Whatever! Right where do you want me?"

"Can you collect a few glasses and get them in the dishwasher, then serve when it gets busier."

"Sure can." I pick up an apron from the rusty old hook sticking out of the wall, pull it over my head and make my way through the tables picking up glasses.

The night is progressing well without too much drama. The football team came in, were very loud, downed a pint and a shot, sang some strange nonsensical song and left. They didn't need escorting out and there were no fights or spillages, which has got to be a first. Mitch says it must have been my influence because I served them. And to be fair, I did warn them in a very jokey way and they all just grinned at me. I'm not sure what that was all about.

I come out from behind the bar in search of more glasses again and spot a group of women on the sofas in the corner. When I look closer I spot not one, but two familiar faces. Dionne is sitting and laughing with the other women, one of whom is the one from the football match I photographed. I head over to say hello.

Dionne looks up at me and her face lights up. It's nice to have that effect on people. "Hannah! What are you doing here?"

"I'm just helping Mitch out." She jumps up and gives me a hug.

"Let me introduce you. Everyone, this is my friend from the hub, Hannah." They all give a little wave and Dionne points out who they are. "This is Beth, Kateryna and Lizzie."

"We've actually met before," Lizzie says. "And I keep forgetting to drop you a message about the photos."

"Where do you know each other from?"

"A very, very cold football pitch. Hannah was taking a fair few shots of our Hutch." Oh god, the cat's out of the bag now.

"Hutch?" Beth pulls a face.

"Sean."

"Were you now? You didn't mention the other day that you were at the football," Dionne says with raised eyebrows.

"Well he didn't see me and I didn't want it to seem weirder than it already did."

"Why weirder?" Beth asks.

"Because we've bumped into each other on a few other occasions and I didn't want it to look like I was stalking him."

"Do you want to join us?" Lizzie points to an empty space.

"I need to get back to the bar." As I turn around, Mitch is behind me. "I'm on my way back," I say to him defensively.

"I was just coming over to tell you to stay and relax with your friends." He takes the glasses I have picked up from the table and heads back to the bar.

"Are you sure?" He just waves his reply.

"Great. It's my round, what would you like to drink?" Lizzie stands and I perch on the extra seat. "We're all on fruity cider."

"Oh I don't drink, just a lemonade would be great."

"You don't drink? Okay we'll be revisiting this once I get back from the bar."

Lizzie is back from the bar in record time and doesn't beat about the bush asking me questions. "So tell me why you don't drink. I'm not being a dick about it, I'm just curious." Lizzie has

a *takes no shit* tone, but it must just be her voic
the same at the football.

"A number of reasons really. I'm not keen on the taste of
of it. Beer and cider, I mean it tastes vile. But also in the past I have done dumb things while I have been under the influence and I just don't like the feeling of being out of control."

"Good reasons if ever there were any."

"Plus no hangovers are great and I'm the one that not only always has the camera but remembers everything."

"You're not invited out with us," Beth states, straight faced before breaking out into a giggle.

"She's only saying that because, after a few, Beth is the one dancing on the tables."

"But I don't get hangovers. Which is great when you have to deal with two mental kids the next morning."

"You no get hangover if you drink the good stuff."

"By good stuff, Kat means the 100 percent proof Ukrainian Vodka she drinks. It's her answer to everything."

"Because true," she answers in her thick accent.

"Anyway, we were talking about Beth's son Johan." Dionne fills me in.

"Yes, he's one of these kids who is enthusiastic about one thing for about six months, then drops it completely for something else with just as much enthusiasm." Beth explains. "At the minute, it's kick boxing, and he's mainly trying it out on poor Steve. I'm hoping he gets bored of this one very quickly before we have to find him some kind of fight club. This kid, though."

"I'm hoping he comes to my school when he gets to year 7."

"You really don't Lizzie. He'll be a nightmare."

"They're the kids I love to deal with."

"Lizzie works in a secondary school," explains Dionne.

"Rather you than me." I say, taking a welcome sip of my lemonade.

"I like the kids. Senior Leadership, not too keen on." She pulls a face and I think there's a story there.

"I didn't get on with secondary school when I was a kid."

"You'd be surprised how many don't. The whole system is completely flawed. But I'll save that rant for another day."

The conversation flows in and out of different subjects – Dionne and Kateryna's work, Beth's family life and my photography – until it's time to leave. We've talked for hours but it seems like a few minutes. I say my goodbyes to Ollie and get a big bear hug from Mitch, before heading to the door.

We walk up Dionne's street arm in arm, chatting about different things. She's a little bit merry and I wanted to make sure she got home safely, although I didn't need to worry because apparently there's a kind of rota where the men take it in turns to make sure they all get home safely. This time it was Beth's husband Steve, but as we didn't have far to walk, he drove round and parked at the bottom of the street until we got inside.

"Hi honey, I'm home." Dionne giggled as she pushed through the door.

"Hiya babes." Comes the voice from the living room. "I'm just about to order Pizza if you want some?"

"Yes! Me and Hannah are starving." I follow her into the house and Sean sits bolt upright, indicating he didn't anticipate me joining the party.

"Are you two drunk?" I'm not sure whether it's and accusation or he's a bit amused.

"She's maybe a bit happy, but I don't drink so I'm definitely not."

"You don't drink?" His eyebrows raise as if he doesn't quite believe me.

"Nope."

"Well I'm gonna file that away for now, but I do need to know what pizza you want."

"Can I have Hawaiian?" Dionne asks.

"Pineapple on pizza? Remind me again why we are friends?" He answers back.

"We're not friends, you just have me on loan. You just got stuck with me."

"Now, you know that's not true. You definitely have had too much to drink, you always do the *I'm not worthy* thing when you've drank too much."

"On that note, I really need to pee." Dionne bolts upstairs to the bathroom, leaving me standing, not sure what to do with myself.

"Hannah?" I give him a questioning look. "Pizza?"

"I like it hot and meaty."

"Okay noted, but what kind of pizza would you like?" He smirks.

"Something spicy with extra jalapenos."

"Are you hungry enough for fries and onion rings."

"Hell yeah."

Sean taps on his phone before putting it down. He turns back to me. "No alcohol, eh? I bet you get questioned about it a lot.

The reason is absolutely your business and I'm not going to pry but the one question I do have is, do you drink alcohol free stuff that imitates it, or do you stick to juices?"

"I get that people drink zero alcohol beers and gins, but that's not for me. I don't like the taste for a start. I do like virgin cocktails though, because they are usually just fruit juices."

"Okay, next time I do a shop, I'll make sure we have some options for you."

"You don't need to do that."

"Why wouldn't I? You've got to drink something while you're here and coffee isn't great at this time of the day."

"Are you expecting me to be coming round more?"

"I'm hoping." He looks away as if he realises he said it out loud. Well that's interesting, because the way he has spoken before, gave me the impression that he wasn't all that bothered. "Are you just gonna stand there?" He nods to the sofa for me to take a seat, so I take off my coat and make my way over to get comfortable.

"What's the film?"

"Some weird MMA film. Jonathan said films two and three are the best, but you need to get through the first one to appreciate the others."

"Any good?"

"Well I'm now on the third film and none of them have been any good. I've wasted five hours of my life that I'll never get back."

"Not been out with friends?"

"Didn't fancy it. I only really have a few friends down here – people from work and the football team. Some of them were going on a bender, I just couldn't be arsed."

"What would you be doing if you were back in Edinburgh?"

"Probably out with my friends." He shrugs.

"Tell me about them and what you'd get up to."

"There's Ben, Joel and Piers. It's Ben's business I work in but I helped him start it up and Joel is our accountant. Piers did some work with us, he's a banker, and we decided to keep him. We'd probably grab something to eat and then hit a few bars and clubs."

"I bet it would be a bit more sophisticated than The Dog and Swan."

"Don't knock the Dog! I think when the city is what you're used to, you take places like that for granted. They're homely and community-spirited, which are hard to come by in the big city centres."

"I'll tell Uncle Mitch you said that. He'll be buzzing."

"Uncle?"

"Yeah. Not really but the closest thing I have to an uncle. I was actually doing a shift for him tonight to help out, when I came across the girls."

"Oh so you've met them then? And what's your verdict? A bunch of crazies or the best people ever?"

"Definitely both. I love a bit of crazy."

Dionne makes her way downstairs to join us and we chat a little bit more. She fills Sean in on the pub conversations, and it seems like he knows all the girls well too. The doorbell sounds and Sean checks his phone, it seems they have a camera doorbell.

The Pizza has arrived and Sean brings them in and places them all on the coffee table before grabbing some plates from the kitchen.

We munch through the pizza like we haven't eaten in weeks and laugh and joke with each other, especially when Sean tries my pizza and tears stream down his face as he rushes to the kitchen for a glass of water.

Dionne's phone beeps several times in quick succession and she rolls her eyes as if, without checking, she knows exactly who is messaging. Then it rings and she has to pull it out from her pocket. She answers abruptly and stands to move away so we can't hear much of what's being said.

Sean raises his eyebrows at me as we have a silent conversation with our facial expressions.

"Oh for fuck's sake Sebastian!" Dionne's raised tone gets our attention.

"He's getting the full name treatment, it must be serious," Sean says, as he tried to hide a smile.

"That can't be the reason you are calling me on a Friday night." She shouts down the phone, then goes back down to a whisper. She ends with a *Whatever* and comes back over to the sofa.

"Are you going to enlighten us?"

"Nope."

"Are you going to see him?"

"Looks like it."

"So it was a booty call?"

"I expect so, but he frames it like it's a work emergency. I wish he'd just be upfront."

"But if he was upfront would you accept it?"

"Says you, Mr Sean *I don't do relationships* Hutchinson." Her phone beeps again and she gets up. "Am I just at everyone's beck and call?" It rings again and she puts it to her ear and shouts. "I am!" and storms out of the door leaving me and Sean sitting on the sofa.

"Well that was weird," I say.

"It's getting to be less weird. I'd think something was up if she didn't get a call like that now."

We eat some more pizza and watch some generic late-night TV until Sean breaks the quiet. "You know what you said about not having enough sex?"

"Yes." I immediate wonder where this is heading.

"Well, maybe I could help out."

"How's that?" I can feel my face flush at even the thought of what he might say.

"Nah, forget it, bad idea." He backtracks, but I really want to know where this is heading.

"No, you started. I'm intrigued now."

He thinks for a moment before start again. "Well you said you had too much going on for anything else, so what about just the sex?"

"With you?" My eyes shoot up. Not because it's an unpleasant though, but because I didn't expect he'd find me that appealing.

"Why not with me?" He seems offended.

I ponder the question for a moment. "I don't know. It just seems a bit too close to home for a one-night stand."

"I'm not suggesting a one-time thing." He looks serious.

"Well what are you suggesting then?" This has just got very interesting.

"A friends-with-benefits kind of situation."

"And who says I find you attractive?" I bat back to him, wondering if he can tell it's all bravado.

"Tell me you don't find me attractive and we can just put this to bed, so to speak, right now."

I'm not going to admit that I do, so I deflect. "I don't know, what would we tell people?"

"It's no one else's business what we do."

"What if we aren't, I don't know, compatible?" He smirks as if that wouldn't even be a possibility.

"Well why don't we see? A try-before-you-buy type situation."

"I'm not sure how that would work." I say as if I have never fantasied about him.

"What about I give you an orgasm, without you having to do anything, other than relax." I can't quite believe what he's just said. The heat rises up my face at the thought of what he's suggesting.

"Seems very one sided." It's the only thing I can think to say.

"Just this once, but I'm okay with that. If you don't enjoy it, we don't have to do it again." Don't enjoy it? More likely he'll ruin me for anyone else.

"I don't know." My eyebrows knit together.

"It's fine, just forget I said anything." He waves it off.

I feel like I need to explain, and I'm not totally adverse to the idea. "It's just that I need to feel comfortable with someone before I can do anything."

"Well get comfortable with me then." I look at him for a moment. "We'll need to get closer." Are we really gonna do this. I mean who goes from chatting and eating pizza to full blown orgasm in the space of minutes?

But I mean, it's just a one-time thing, can't do any harm, can it? I mean he's hot, and I have been thinking about him, a lot. So I nod at him and he moves from his end of the sofa to my place in the corner of the L. He lifts my feet off the floor and places them on his lap and starts to untie my boots and slips them off one by one.

He places the boots on the floor and starts to squeeze my feet. I flinch a little.

"Ticklish?"

"A bit, just on the bottom." He massages my feet one by one and then moves up my calves. I go ridged. I'm not used to being touched. He notices and turns the TV up as a distraction.

He waits until I've settled a bit more and my shoulders have relaxed. "How far do these go up?" He runs his hand up my socks.

"Only half way," I whisper.

"Can I see?" I nod as I'm now incapable of words. He pushes my dress up to mid-thigh, bunching it up as it goes and his eyes never leave mine. My heartrate picks up with every inch higher his hand goes, still massaging his way up. The further up he gets, the more he has to stretch to reach, so he shuffles a little closer.

He has a hand at the top of each one of my legs and the anticipation is immense. He squeezes and I jump a little and he frowns. "You need to relax."

"Easy for you to say." I manage, and it doesn't even feel like it was me speaking. He squeezes a few more times then moves further up. He gently brushes his thumbs over the outside of my knickers, he must be able to feel the moistness seeping through and I feel myself flush as a little moan escapes. I don't know why I feel embarrassed with him, but I do. I fling my arm across my face and hide it in the crook of my elbow.

"Eyes on me, Hannah."

"I can't!"

"Okay well I'll need you closer anyway." He tries to pull me towards him but I don't move. He leans over, takes my hand from my face, moves it to his mouth and dusts my finger tips on his lips. As if he just realised, his attention moves to the baggy sweatshirt covering my dress. The one I try to hide my body underneath. "Why these baggy jumpers?"

"Keeps the attention off me."

"What do you mean?"

"People can't seem to keep their eyes on my face otherwise."

"Okay. Well you didn't want me to see your face anyway, so you might as well take it off." He smirks. I lift the hem, pull it over my head and discard it on the floor. His eyes widen but he tries to reign in his expression.

"You get my point now?" He can't take his eyes off the strained fabric over my more-than-average cleavage.

"Amazing. I don't know why you want to hide them away." I roll my eyes and he gestures to me to come closer. I swing my legs back over the edge of the sofa and stand. He grabs my waist as I come near and pulls me to sit on his lap. His sweatpants don't hide the fact that he's liking what he sees. He moves my legs so they are on each side of his knees, his legs stay closed. He pulls me back so I'm laying on his chest, my head touching his cheek. The position feels intimate but comfortable. I try to relax but his breath on my skin makes the goose bump rise.

We stay still for a moment, getting comfortable with the proximity before he starts to unbuckle the straps of my dress. I feel a pang of disappointment that he's acting like every guy I've had this kind of contact with. I don't know why men are so obsessed with breasts, but I let him carry on. His hand slips under my dress and finds the bottom of my t-shirt, but he only lifts it a few inches and spreads his finger across my middle holding me in place, gentle caressing my skin.

He moves his head down so his lips are on my cheek but he doesn't try to kiss me and I can feel his breath skate across my skin.

With one hand firmly holding me in place, the other caresses the inside of my thigh and eventually, every so often, grazes the cotton of my knickers. I wish I'd worn something a little more sexy than my home-brand underwear.

"Okay?" He speaks so softly I can feel it more than I can hear it. His warmth is radiating through me. I have a jumble of feelings going on in my head, one part of me wants to rip my clothes off, then his, and the other wants to run away and forget we ever started this. I give a slight nod and he takes that as the green light.

His fingers travel up, skimming over the soft fabric again and again but don't give the friction that my body is now desperately waiting for. Hovering over the elastic he pauses for a few seconds, but it feels like an eternity. At last he dips inside my knickers and his fingers hit the spot. I let out a moan. I have no control over my body now and I am panting with desire. My body heats and a wave of pleasure flows through and pools at the base of my spine.

I can't believe how quickly he has got me to this stage and I can't control any of it. He opens his legs which parts me, giving him more access, as his fingers slide down and briefly dip inside me. I pant as my body relishes his touch. He moves his fingers back up through my folds and circles and I can feel his breath again on the side of my face. I feel a moan pull through me again as he moves down and inside me again. All of my muscles tense without warning and with the motion of him pushing inside and retreating, over and over, my brain misfires, my body explodes, and the wave of ecstasy hits me as my body begins to shake.

I've never felt anything quite like it, my head is foggy and it takes a few minutes to get my senses back. But when it becomes clear again, a wave of panic hits and I freak out. I pull his hand away, move my legs so I can jump up out of his lap and start gathering my things. "I've got to go. This was a mistake."

"Wait Hannah, no! Don't rush off, what happened?" I pull myself together at lightning speed and head for the door. "Wait." Something in his tone makes me stop still. "I'm not going to make you stay, but I can't let you go out on your own in the middle of the night."

"You let Dionne leave without another thought."

"I didn't, I heard Seb's car outside, or I wouldn't have let her go either. I'll drop you home." I don't answer but I also don't move. "You don't have to speak to me if that makes you feel better."

"Fine." He gets up and picks up his hoodie from the arm of the chair, grabs his keys from the kitchen bench and we head for the door.

He unlocks the car with a beep and I head for the passenger side as he locks the house door. He gets in, pulls his seatbelt on and stares through the windscreen ahead. He presses the button and the engine comes to life. "If you put your postcode into the satnav, I'll take you home."

I type in the code and the journey is calculated at taking only a few minutes. He sets off and taking it slowly, giving us more time sitting in silence. My face is pressed against the glass trying to cool the flush from both the experience and the embarrassment. I just want to get back home, I feel a jumble of different things but the one that's coming out on top is the mortification of it all.

We come to a stop and before I can get out, he speaks. "Can we talk about what happened?"

I blow out a long breath. "I freaked out a bit."

"No shit." He obviously finds my answer almost comical. "But why?"

"I don't know. I was just overwhelmed."

"Did I hurt you?"

"No."

"Well we can't have you freaking out every time I make you come." The corner of his mouth raises in amusement.

"Who says it's gonna happen again?" Why would he want to do it again with a girl who turns into some kind of crazy. I just feel so out of my comfort zone.

"Are you gonna tell me you didn't like it?"

"I never said that." I turn back to look out of the window, feeling a wave of embarrassment again.

"Well what exactly is it then? Do you feel embarrassed?"

"A bit. I don't really want to talk about it."

"I think we should." I reach for the door handle and crack open the door. "Would you feel more comfortable if we weren't face to face?"

"Maybe." I open the door and step out.

"Then I'll give you my number and we can call or message instead, if it makes you feel more comfortable." He leans over the handbrake to get a better view of me.

I hesitate but then agree and hand over my phone. He types in his number and looks at me. "Can I have yours?" I nod and he presses the call button. I hear the ring tone from the car's handsfree breaking the silence.

I take my phone back, kill the call, slam the door a little harder than I intended and fumble for my keys before letting myself inside. I close the door and sag against it. The car doesn't leave at first and I hold my breath wondering whether he might get out and knock on the door.

It takes only a minute more for my phone to start vibrating. I look at the caller ID. It reads *Your hot friend* and I give a little smile.

Chapter Nine

Sean

Well I have no idea what has just gone on. Maybe it was a bad idea to suggest a no strings, *friends with benefits* kind of relationship. The fact that we got so close and she just bolted makes me think either there's something wrong with me, or there's something wrong with her, or we're both messed up.

I've just dropped her at her door and drove off, but I didn't want her over analysing and thinking what we did was a bad thing. I redial straight away. It rings until I think it's gonna click onto the answer machine, but the line goes live. She's not speaking. "Hannah?" I say softly. "Talk to me."

The pause makes me think she's hung up, but eventually she whispers, "I don't know what to say."

"Tell me what happened."

"I feel stupid."

"Why?"

"Because I freaked out."

"It's okay to freak out. Just tell me why, so I can fix it." Another long pause while she's gathering her thoughts, and I've come to a stop outside my house. "You didn't enjoy it?"

She blows out a breath. "It's not that I didn't, you could tell I did, it's just I don't usually do that kind of thing. Well not without a connection first. I don't even know you, Sean."

"I know, it was maybe a bit soon."

"I'm not sure I'm cut out for *Friends with benefits*, especially since we're not really friends."

"Okay I get it, so can we try to be friends? I don't want things to be weird."

"Are we friends though? Do you actually like me?"

"Are you kidding? Of course I like you, or I wouldn't be practically begging you to talk to me. I don't have many friends here, and I'd really like it if we could hang out, get coffee, whatever friends do."

"Do I have to make you the coffee?" She laughs, and I finally feel like it's a breakthrough.

"Probably, although I do know this place that makes the best coffee round here."

"I suppose." She whispers.

"So we can be friends!" I sigh with relief.

"I guess so."

"Shall we set a date for something?" I want to get her to commit to something straight away so she can't back out later.

There's a long pause and I'm surprised by her answer. "Well, if you want to come out with me next week? I'm going out for a walk to take some nature shots."

"That would be nice." The relief that she's willing to try this is unreal. What is this woman doing to me?

"Okay, I'll message you with the details."

"Right. I'm already looking forward to it!" and it's the truth.

"Whatever!" She laughs and hangs up.

Thank fuck for that. I don't know what it is about Hannah, but I have a real urge to please her, get to know her more, which is really unusual for me. I would never have even contemplated calling a woman for even a few days after we'd been together, let alone 90 seconds after she's left. I'm not sure what's come over me.

I head back into the warmth of the house and throw myself back on the sofa. It feels like she's all around me, I can smell her light perfume and I'm suddenly hit with flashbacks. The feel of her weight sitting on me, the soft feel of her skin under my fingers, the gasping sounds she makes.

I can't be doing this. I jump off the sofa as if it's on fire and take the stairs two at a time as if I can outrun the memories. Sleeping it off might to be the only solution, but I have a feeling she's going to be haunting my dreams too. As my head hits the pillow, I curse myself for not changing the sheets since the last time she was in it. I had put it off, giving myself all kinds of excuses, but really, I felt good knowing she'd been here and being surrounded by her scent.

In a fit of rage, I jump up and start pulling at the covers, ripping them off the bed, bundling them up and throwing them over the banister, down the stairs so they would be as far away from me as possible. And then I throw myself back on my bed. This was a really bad idea. I don't want to be in a relationship and Hannah seems to be a relationship kind of girl. It never ends well, I'm not risking having my heart broken again.

· ♥ · ♥ · ♥ · ♥ · ♥ ·

Keeping myself busy was the only way I could get that woman out of my head. I've been laser focused at work. So much so I've had several calls from Ben asking if I'm okay. I've joined a local gym to get my frustration out and an hour run on the treadmill wears me out enough to stop me thinking about her when I drop off to sleep.

I have this rage when I think about her, like I'm mad at her for the fact that I am having feelings that I don't want. There's been times where I've nearly messaged her and said 'no thanks, I don't want to be friends, after all'.

I played football again on Sunday and had to be told to calm the fuck down because I was making the rest of them look out of shape. But to be fair, that's not too hard. My phone beeps and I pull it out of my pocket.

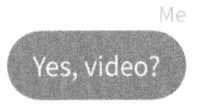

Megan

> You free?

Me

> Yes, video?

The phone rings in my hand immediately and I answer. Megan's face appears on the screen.

"Hey freckles," I say.

"Hello. Nice to see your face. You look different."

"I've been working out."

"Nice. Any particular reason? You haven't been a regular at the gym for a long time. I didn't like to mention it but you were letting yourself go a bit." Cheeky, but I know she's just messing.

"It's this friend of Dionne's."

"What about her?"

"She's got me all…. I don't know."

"You like her?"

"She gives me the rage."

"Why?"

"I don't know. I'm just so angry thinking about her."

"What's she done to wind you up?"

"It's not what she's done, I'm angry because I can't stop thinking about her."

"I don't get it." She wrinkles her nose.

"I don't do relationships." She rolls her eyes at me and I know she still doesn't get it, maybe because the only person who knows the full story is Ben.

"Look! I understand you've been hurt before, but that's doesn't mean you shut yourself down to everyone else."

"It actually does."

"I didn't let what I went through stop me from being open to finding someone who actually deserved me."

"Myles doesn't deserve you, he's a muppet!"

"Stop it, he'll hear you, it's a small apartment."

"So?"

"You're being a bit of a dick, you like Myles." She chastises me.

"Yes sorry." And I am, she's my best friend and I'm happy for her.

"There's more to this story. Come on, spill."

"I kind of propositioned her."

"For what exactly?" She looks perplexed.

"*Friends with benefits*. And we kind of did stuff and she freaked out. She says she can't do it with no connection."

"So you step away." She folds her arms across her chest, I know she's about to get annoyed with me.

"I've tried."

"Try harder. Okay, turn this round. If I told you that someone had asked me for a no-strings hook up, what would your advice have been?"

"To tell him to get lost, that you're worth more."

"So maybe she feels she's worth more."

"She is worth more, I just can't give that to her."

"I still don't see why."

"You wouldn't. Sorry Megs, I've got a call coming through for work, I need to go." I hate lying to her but I can't carry on with this conversation.

"Okay, just think about what I said."

"You know I won't, bye." I hang up the call and I'm back to square one. Maybe finding something to hate about her will stop the thoughts. But trying to focus on the bad is hard, because there isn't anything that comes to mind. And when I search it means I'm then thinking about her AGAIN.

My phone vibrates and I think it's gonna be Megan nagging me via message.

Hannah (don't call her)

> Hey, are you still up for meeting?

Me

> Yes, sure

What the fuck am I doing? And why am I smiling? The anger evaporated the moment I saw her name. I really need to change her contact name too.

Hannah (don't call her)

> I have a day off on Thursday, but you'll probably be working.

Me

> I'm sure I can take some time, I'm pretty much the boss.

Hannah (don't call her)

> I was thinking about 10am at Western Park, I need to get my duck pics. Do you know it?

Me

> Duck pictures? Was that auto correct? No I don't, can I pick you up and you can show me the way?

Hannah (don't call her)

> Not auto-correct *eye rolls*

> Okay, see you then.

And here I am feeling all happy and fluffy just because she texted me, and I get to see her again. I absolutely hate myself.

Chapter Ten

Hannah

I can't stop thinking about Sean and it's really beginning to piss me off. I feel like a love-sick teenager and I hate it. I stand at work and look out into nowhere, thinking about what happened the other night.

It's fair to say I have never come that quickly in my life. The way he touched me, he knew exactly what he was doing. The closeness and the heat and his smell had me gooey before we'd even started. This man is amazing and unbelievably gorgeous. Which again makes me wonder, *why me*?

I'm not sure if I freaked out because I'd let a practical stranger touch me so intimately. It's just not me. Or whether it is the fact that I've never had someone like him interested in me, which immediately makes me pull my defences up. When he called me as soon as I got through the door, it stopped me over-thinking about what I'd done and what he thought of me. He seemed genuinely concerned about how I was feeling and that he wanted to see me again. Which is nice, but is that just because he wants to get in my knickers without putting any effort in?

He hasn't been in the café all week and I was hoping he'd pop in so that things weren't awkward. And also so that I didn't have to initiate contact with him. I pulled his contact details up on my phone about 50 times before having the nerve to actually message him. He replied straight away and I'm looking forward to spending time with him, even if I have all this nervous energy about it.

I see his car pull up outside and I grab my camera bag from the hall and pick up my keys. I've tried to keep it casual and make it look like I've made as little effort as possible. I'm wearing my tight jeans, a stripy chunky knit jumper, finished off with a big, thick wool coat. I pulled my hair up because it's a bit windy, so it won't get in the way while shooting.

As I leave the house and turn towards him, I realise I didn't really acknowledge his car last time. It's a sleek, black Range Rover with leather interior and it seems to fit him very well. He obviously hasn't got a run of the mill job, and he's definitely not a labourer, even though he mentioned site visits. But the thing that stands out the most is the lingering smell of him. It's not just his cologne, it's something that I can't quite put my finger on.

"Hey."

"Hey." I'm not sure how to act towards him, and I still can't quite make eye contact. This feels weird but also really normal too.

"Got everything?" he asks.

"Yes."

"Put the postcode in the sat nav and we'll get going." I put in the address and it calculates it's just over 20 minutes away. I wonder if that means 20 minutes of awkward silence and one-word answers.

"So tell me about this place and why we are going."

"Okay so, it's a country park that I used to go to as a kid. It's got long walks and a lake. I'm wanting to get some duck photos, which I know sounds weird, but they do really well."

"Do you sell them?"

"Yes, online. Animals sell really well. That and landmarks. I save the weird stuff for my collections. But really, because of the diversity of the place you can get all kinds of shots. It has a coffee place too. There's a big hill with a pathway winding all the way round and at the top you can see for miles. It's really beautiful."

"Okay. You can point out all the local attractions that I'm missing out on," He's concentrating on the road, and I can't help but stare at his face, taking in all the details. He gives me a quick glance, catching me watching him. I feel like I've been caught perving. "So, you've always lived round here then?"

"Yes, mostly. We moved a bit further out when my mum married my stepdad, but once I'd left home, I moved back in again. It's familiar, you know?"

"Yes. I'm kind of missing the familiar right now."

"Tell me what you like doing back home."

"Well we're very social. We go out a lot, into town. I sometimes go and watch Ben play rugby, mainly because we sponsor the team. I sometimes play football, but I couldn't really commit to being in a team full time, so generally just if I had time and they needed someone."

"So it's a bit of a culture shock living in a pit village in the middle of nowhere?"

"A bit. I don't hate it, I'm just not settled yet."

We pull through the metal archway entrance, into the car park and find a space straight away. It's quite empty today. Most people will be at work or school, so it's ideal for me to get some clear shots. I jump out of the car and pull my camera ruck sack on my back, only to have it immediately taken away from me.

"I can carry my own bag."

"I know, but at least I have a purpose."

"Be careful, I'm very precious about my kit." I narrow my eyes at him, but he shrugs and gestures me to show him the way. We walk down the long path towards the lake. The weather is crisp and every now and again a swirl of wind whips up the natural debris from the path.

We sit down on a bench on the bank of the lake and I pull my camera out, fit the lens and check all the settings. There are a lot of ducks on the water today and I've brought bread, just in case I had to entice them over. There are always people here, so the wildlife just gets on with it and doesn't shy away.

I point the camera at the water. "See that one there? The one getting mouthy?" I point to a pair of ducks, one of which has not stopped squawking and flapping his wings. They look like a couple having an argument, the bloke going on and the woman just rolling her eyes. "He's called Freddy."

"You know their names?" He looks so serious.

"No." I laugh at his expression. "He just kinda looks like a Freddy. All mouthy. Who do you see?"

He looks round the lake and I go back to looking through the camera and take a few test shots. He taps me on the arm and points to the other side of the lake. "That one there, with his beak up in the air. He is Bartholomew."

"You mean bill."

"No, Bartholomew."

"I mean it's a bill not a beak. But yes, he does look very grand."

"Alright smarty pants." He laughs. "You knew what I meant."

"That one over there…" I point to a duck swimming round all chilled, bobbing his head every now and again. "He's Marv. Just a bit too cool for the rest of them."

"Yes, definitely a Marv." Sean smiles back at me.

We take a few moments and sit quietly. Sean is taking in his surroundings and I'm taking some scenic shots. "I can see why you liked this place so much as a kid. It's so vibrant yet peaceful."

"Yes. And with the different seasons, everything changes and it's like a totally different place, but still familiar."

As he looks out onto the lake again, lost in thought, I take another sneaky photograph of him. I think he's becoming my obsession, my muse. I take a deep breath. The sun has come out and I lift my face so it bathes in the warmth. We sit there in silence, but its not awkward. It's easy, natural. Being here with him feels like we have know each other our whole lives.

I look over to him again, his features tell me he's deep in thought. But he must sense me watching and turns. Our eyes meet and he gives me a smile, then looks back to the water.

"See that one over there?" He points across to the centre of the lake. "The one being all sassy, that's you."

"Well you see that one over there? The one who's swimming up to the others and bossing them about. That's you!" He laughs. "Do you want to go up the hill, it's a great vantage point?"

"Sure, let's go."

I pack my bag up and put the cameras round my neck. Sean automatically takes the bag from me.

I've always been so independent. I can do things on my own, but it feels nice to have someone doing things to help with no expectations. We set off up the hill. I've not been up here for years and I'd forgotten how massively unfit I am. "Oh my god, I think I might die. I don't remember it being this steep."

"Not far now." Sean grabs my hand and pulls me along with him. "You can do it." He laughs.

"Don't make me laugh! I can't breathe and laugh and the same time."

We make it to the top and I try to catch my breath. I feel so comfortable with him.

"Well this was worth the hike," he says, scanning the horizon.

"I'd kinda forgotten how beautiful it is." I look across the greenery of the hills that span for miles. "See over there, that tower?" I point into the distance. "That's some old furnace. And over there you can kind of make out the change in the landscape. That's where the mine was." I find something else. "That hill over there has some kind of folk legend attached to it, something about if you climb it, you'll come into fortune.

Or have an untimely death. Or something. I don't know, I can never remember."

"Two very different things to get mixed up. I'm not sure I wanna risk it." We continue to look over the scenery in silence. I take a few shots, mainly just to remember this moment.

"Do you do anything like this back home?"

"Not anymore. Me and Ben used to go up Arthur's Seat every couple of months. Same as here, you can see for miles. I don't think I really appreciated it though. It makes you think."

"Do you miss Edinburgh?"

"I do, but not in the way I thought I would. This place is totally different, it's been hard getting used to it."

"Not as exciting?"

"Just different. Back home it's faster paced than here, but I'm not sure whether that's a good or a bad thing. I suppose being here has made me stop and think about, I dunno... life."

"That's very deep."

"Yes. A little too deep. Shall we go back down before I have some sort of epiphany."

"Probably best. If we go this way," I point to the path leading away from the direction we came, "we can see the swans, head to get a coffee and it will bring us full circle."

"Literally or metaphorically?"

"Both." He smiles and takes my hand, although I don't need the help because the rest of the walk is downhill.

We sit back near the lake with our drinks and make general conversation about work and friends. After a while we decide we've had enough sightseeing, it's time to head back home. The day has been nice, unexpected. I feel so much more comfortable with him. He seems like he's more relaxed with me, nothing like the snappy Sean I first met.

Chapter Eleven

Sean

I hate to admit what a good time I had going out on a shoot with Hannah. If I was trying to find ways in which I could dislike her, I failed miserably. She's funny and doesn't take herself too seriously, but I'm struggling to see how we can just be friends. She's really sexy, mainly because she doesn't see it herself. The women I usually hook up with are all preened and polished, to the point where I'd probably not recognise them without their make up or a filter.

She's different and I have no idea why she doesn't have a boyfriend. How amazing would it be waking up to her every morning? I need to push this shit out of my head. I had such a nice time on our walk and it scared the shit out of me. As a result I've effectively ghosted her ever since and I feel really bad about it.

I'm sitting on the sofa, aimlessly scrolling through Netflix for something to watch, when Dionne walks through the front door. "Hi, Honey, I'm home!"

"Never gets old, that!" I say, sarcastically.

"I know, right. What are you up to?"

"Not much, trying to find something to watch. You're home late, everything okay?"

"Same shit, different day."

"By shit, do you mean Seb?"

"Who else?

"Is he gonna call in two hours to get you back in."

"I'm turning my phone off!"

"Must be bad." Dionne never turns her phone off.

"What's for tea?"

"I'm not your wife, you know." I bite back.

"Could have fooled me. You'd make a lovely little wife one day Sean."

"Never gonna happen." I pull the face of a child that doesn't want to partake.

"Talking about potential wife material, have you heard from Hannah?"

"She's just a friend." Dionne pulls a face. "And no, not since we went out to the park."

"Funny, she's not replied to any of my messages. That's just not like her." I sit up straight and my mind goes spinning with all the possibilities.

"I'll drop her a message." I pick up my phone and send her a quick hello.

"Great, let me know. But back to the important stuff, what are you cooking for dinner?"

"You really should learn some kitchen skills, I won't be here forever."

"Then I'll just need to find someone else to look after me."

"Like Seb?" She sticks her tongue out at me like a five-year-old. "I can't be arsed to cook, I'm sure it's your turn to get take out."

"It probably is, what do you fancy?" she says, looking at her phone to pull up the app.

"I can't think, just order something like tapas with loads to pick at."

"Get you! You're not in the city now, Mr Hutchinson."

"Whatever!" I look down at my phone and the message has been delivered to Hannah, but she's not read it. She might be in the darkroom or something. She might even be on a date. Oh god, I do not like that idea one little bit.

I send her another few messages.

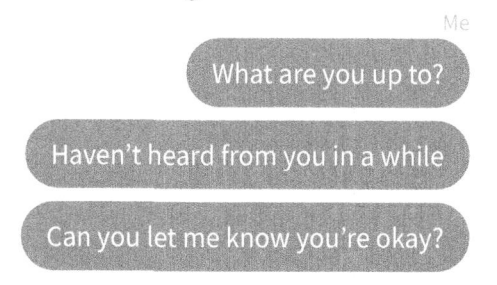

> Me
>
> What are you up to?
>
> Haven't heard from you in a while
>
> Can you let me know you're okay?

I put my phone down, trying not to look too eager. There's a knock at the door and I check the camera to see the delivery guy. Dionne has disappeared. Was I really in my own head for that long? I pull myself up and answer the door. God knows what shit Dionne has ordered. She makes her way downstairs and we plate up some non-descript food and continue flicking through the film choices. I press play on one. I have no idea what it is but I'm losing my mind trying to calm my thoughts.

After half an hour, the food is gone and I haven't been able to engage with the TV. I check my phone again.

"Di, have you had anything back from Hannah?"

She looks up from her phone. "Erm no, it's still not read."

"I'm gonna call her." It rings and rings then eventually cuts off onto voicemail. So I ring again, and the same happens. Then my phone beeps as a message comes through.

> **Hannah**
>
> Sick

> **Me**
>
> Do u need help?
>
> I'm worried
>
> I'm coming over

I jump up and grab my keys.

"I'm going over. Where's her spare key?"

"What's happened? Her key is by the door, do you want me to come?"

"She's sick, so I'm gonna check she's okay."

"You might want to take over some supplies."

"Like what?"

"Paracetamol, flat cola, bread for toast. When you're ill what do you have?"

"Point taken." I search through the cupboards for supplies and Dionne hands me a bag to put them in. I head for the door picking up her key and leave, slamming the door behind me.

As I pull up my phone beeps.

Hannah

No

Me

Tough shit, I'm here. I have your key so I'll let myself in.

Hannah

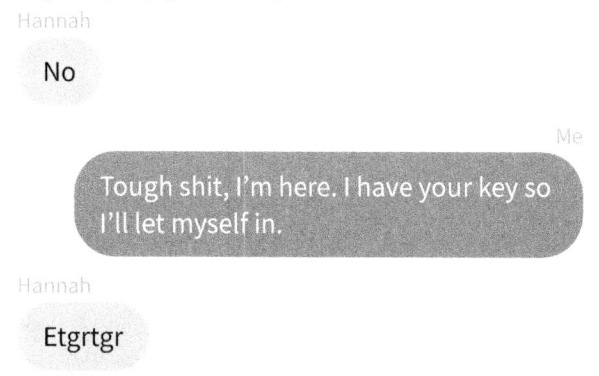

Etgrtgr

I park in the only space available, a few houses down. I close the gap to the door in long strides, unlock it and rush in. I've never been inside her house before and it's pitch black. I flick on the hall light and lock the door behind me.

"Hannah?" There's no response so I step into the first door to find it also in darkness and empty. I step back. If she's sick, she'll be upstairs in bed. I head up.

"Hannah?" I hear a moan coming from the front of the house, so I follow it, putting the torch on my phone to find my way. "Where are you?" And where are the light switches in this house?

"No light… bad head."

"Okay, I'm gonna have to turn something on or I won't see you."

"Good."

I step into the room next to where she is and flick the switch. It lights up a spare room and the hall. I open the door to the front bedroom and can see a double bed, with a Hannah shaped lump in the middle. Oh god what am I even doing here? Even the thought of her in bed in front of me has my pulse racing and I'm rock hard. I need to adjust my dick before I set foot in that room.

"Hey." I hesitate, then make my way over and sit on the bed.

"Eurgh."

"That pleased to see me?" I whisper.

"Can't lift my head." I instinctively put my hand on her forehead.

"Hannah you're burning up, have you taken anything?"

"Can't move."

"Good job I brought supplies." I find one of the bottles of water I brought and pop out some of the painkillers. "Can you sit up to take these?"

"No!"

"Well you're gonna have to if you want to feel better. I'll help." I gently lift her to sitting up and prop her against me while I open the bottle and hand her tablets. She puts them in her mouth and takes the bottle.

"Thanks" she whispers.

"How long have you been unwell?"

"Few days. Can't get rid of this headache. If I lift my head I vomit."

"Keep sipping that water. When was the last time you ate?" She shrugs then winces, so I lower her back onto her pillow.

"Why are you here?"

"Cos you're sick. I was worried."

"I look awful."

"You're very hot."

"Thanks."

"I mean you are radiating lots of heat." She shivers.

"Thanks for bringing supplies, but you can go now."

"As if! Dionne said flat cola was good for putting minerals back into your body, so I have that, and some bread, and maybe having a bath and getting some fresh air into here will help."

"Eurgh."

"We'll let those pain killers kick in first." She closes her eyes and I automatically stroke her head.

"Nice."

"You like that?"

"Mmm."

"Is that headache easing off yet?"

"Yes, more stroking."

"Okay bossy." I continue stroking her head. The time passes by in silence but it's natural, like it's totally normal that I should be here with her. "Hannah? I'm gonna run you a bath, okay?" As I stand up, she moans when she realises I'm no longer stroking her. Those little moans give me some unwanted flash backs.

I find the bathroom and turn on the taps, rummage through the baskets on the floor in search of bubble bath, and pour it in. I leave it to fill up and go back to collect her. Tapping her gently she slowly comes back to consciousness. "What are you doing here?"

"I came to look after you, remember?"

"Oh."

"I'm gonna get you up and take you for a bath." Without questioning she makes a move to get up but the way her eyes float about, I know she's not capable of doing anything herself. This is going to be a lesson in restraint if ever there was one.

I pull her to standing, wrap my arm around her waist for stability, as she puts one foot in front of the other. As we get to the bathroom, she winces at the light, but needs must. "You need to take your clothes off."

"With you here?"

"You can't stand by yourself, what other option is there?"

"I need to pee."

"Well you pee, I'll go and find a towel. Shout when you're finished, and I'll help you into the bath." She pulls her sleep shorts down and sits on the toilet. Her baggy t-shirt is so long I didn't even know she was wearing them.

"Cupboard in the hall." I take it she means the towels, so I leave her to it and go in search.

I find what I'm looking for and pause to take for a few breathes. I'm not sure what has come over me, I've never reacted to a woman like this before. I know I have the urge to protect every one of my friends, but this is so much more. I shake the thoughts out of my head, grab a towel and head back to the bathroom.

She's still on the toilet, head down as if she fallen back to sleep. As I stand over her and place my hands on her shoulders, she turns her head up to me but doesn't open her eyes. "We need to get you in the bath."

"Mmm."

"You have to stand up and take off your t-shirt." She stands and her legs are wobbly as she places her forehead on my chest for stability. "T-shirt Hannah." But all she does is lift her arms in the air and I compose myself as I prepare for this woman to be naked in front of me. Grabbing the hem, I lift the material up, over her head and drop it to the floor.

She's your friend, she's your friend, she's your friend. I focus on the mantra, but I need to get a grip and get her in the bath. "Let's go. Step in." I hold her as she steps in the bath and lowers herself down. Even sick she looks like an absolute goddess. Her curves make ripples in the water, bubbles cover her plump, firm breasts, her hair fans out in the water as she sinks in. This was a bad idea.

"I'm gonna leave you here to soak for a bit while I change your sheets, where are the fresh ones?"

"Under the bed."

I take one last look at her, all peaceful, before I stride back out and into her bedroom. I flick on the light switch and I can finally see her room. The first thing that strikes me is the number of photographs covering the walls. Literally covering every available bit of wall. There are some big, framed photos and others just stuck onto the wall like a whole-room collage.

I make my way over to the window, stepping over the pile of scatter cushions that no doubt would usually be on the bed. I open the blinds and the window to get some fresh air into the place. There is a vintage-looking wardrobe, filled to bursting, and next to it a chair that looks like it may collapse with the weight of clothes thrown across it. The bed looks like someone has thrown all the pillows up in the air searching for something. I pull the duvet off the bed, undo the poppers and get to work. The drawer under the bed holds an array of different bedding sets and I try to match them up. Women can be funny about that kind of thing, but I know a fresh bed will make her feel so much better.

The bedside table has a number of empty glasses and empty blister packs. She obviously set out well, then ran out. I take the glasses and head downstairs, into the kitchen. I check in on the bathroom to make sure she's okay on the way.

Opening what seems like every cupboard door, I finally find some glasses. I grab two and take them upstairs. I fill one with the cola and I leave the other one empty. "You okay in there?"

"Hmm."

I walk back into the bathroom and the sight of her takes my breath away. I pull my thoughts back out from the gutter and prepare myself for dealing with her like a friend. "Can you sit up and drink some of this for me." It's a gentle command rather than a question.

"What is it?" She pulls herself up, the water cascading down her body. She's going to think I'm a complete creep looking at her like this when she vulnerable.

"It's flat cola. I think you must be a bit dehydrated."

She takes the glass but I keep my hand on it as her hand shakes a little.

"Thanks." She takes a slow, shaky sip followed quick by another.

"How's the headache?"

"Not as bad. Like, it's still there but not making me feel as sick. It's more of an all over pain than a piercing one."

"That's good news. I'll make you some toast in a bit, it will help with energy levels."

"You don't need to."

"Will you be able to do it yourself?" She opens one eye and closes it again. "Didn't think so."

"Thanks. It just feels weird having you here looking after me."

"What are friends for?"

"Usually not this."

"Sit forward and I'll wash your hair." She does as I've asked, and I start to massage the shampoo into her scalp. I'm not used to washing longer hair, so I have no clue what I'm doing, but I'm secretly enjoying it. It hits home how intimate this really is. I rinse out the shampoo and do the same with the conditioner. All the while Hannah makes little noises of pleasure, which are doing nothing to tame my dick.

Once I've finished, I stand up and grab the towels. "Time to get out."

"Hmph. Do I have to?"

"You do if you don't want to catch a chill." Her face contorts into a frown and she makes a move. I grab her arm as she wobbles and steadies herself. Then with two hands on her, she steps out. I wrap a huge bath towel round her and a small one on her hair as, again, her forehead rests on my chest.

Can she hear my heartrate going through the roof? I guide her back to her room and sit her on the fresh bed. Her head rests on my stomach and I hold my breath, willing my body not to react. I'm well aware that her position is one that I have thought about before, but really not in this context. I take the towel off her head and she looks up at me with her big green eyes.

Grabbing the brush from the bedside table I slowly drag it through her hair. "Ouch."

"Sorry."

"Don't give up your day job to become a hairdresser."

"Noted." I laugh. There she is, back from the brink, giving me attitude. I help her into a fresh t-shirt and shorts and her head lands back on my stomach. I wrap my arms around her. "Time to get back into bed."

"Don't let go."

"I have to let go to get you into bed."

"No. Get in." Oh god this really will be a test.

"Well you get in and I'll get in the other side." She seems okay with that and swings her legs up into bed. I make my way round the other side. On my way I close the window and blinds and take off my sweatpants. It's not the best idea but I know, because of the heat coming off her, I'll die of heat stroke if I don't.

I get in and pull her close. She wraps herself around me and lays her head on my chest. I kiss her forehead and she sighs. I'm in big trouble here. But my eyes begin to get heavy and before I know it, I'm out like a light, exhaustion pulling me into sleep.

Chapter Twelve

Hannah

I'm pulled out of my dream by the sound of my name, but I can't tell whose voice it is, or even where I am. The bed dips and I come further back to the land of the living.

"Hannah, babe." I prise my eyes open to see a blurry vision in front of me. "It's time for some more painkillers, but you need to eat something first." Sean comes into full focus.

"You're here?"

"Of course I am. Who would want to miss seeing you wake up with dribble all over your face?" A wave of panic sets in as I wipe my face. He's lying, at least I hope he is. "Now sit up and eat your toast."

"What time is it?" It's dark outside, but even if it wasn't I'd still have no clue. I seem to have been sleeping on and off for weeks but is maybe just two days. I vaguely remember him being here and getting into a clean bed.

"7am. I didn't want you waking up later in pain and you haven't eaten in days."

"I had some really weird dreams."

"Like what?"

"Well I dreamt that you were here, and we had a bath together."

"True. Well, you had a bath and I watched."

"You're kidding right?"

"Nope. What else?"

"That I bought a new comfy bed and you cuddled me in it."

"Also true."

"That's not true." I feel my face flush.

"Well, I changed your bed sheets and you insisted that I cuddle you to sleep."

"I did not! God, I'm so embarrassed."

"Eat your toast. You were a bit out of it to be fair. No-one could get hold of you, then when I rang, you messaged me saying 'sick'. So I came over, used your spare key. Good job I did though. You couldn't get up to get a drink or take painkillers." I hunt round for my phone and find it plugged in. When I pick it up I see a number of messages and missed calls. "I knew your parents had a spare key, but the way your face grimaced when your mum called last time, I thought me coming round might be mildly better."

"There's a distinct lack of concern from them anyway. God, I need to tell work."

"Oh yes, Cynthia from work rang so I answered. Is that the one who doesn't like the coffee machine? I said you wouldn't be in."

"Ah yes. Hang on, you watched me in the bath?"

"Well I had to get you undressed and also make sure you didn't drown. You were really quite out of it. I changed your sheets because who wants to get back into a manky bed?"

"So you've seen me naked?"

"Yes. And in the spirit of transparency, you also tried to touch me up in the night."

"Wwwhhhaattt!!!!" I have never felt so embarrassed in my life, I cover my face with my hands so he can't see how mortified I am. "So to save you from watching me die of embarrassment, are you going into work?" I can't even look at him.

"No. I took the day off, just so I could watch the humiliation set in." He gives a little smirk, but I'm actually dying inside. "I'm kidding. It's been a pretty rough night and I didn't want to leave you. They can manage without me. I made you a latte. Well, it's just a coffee with loads of milk, but you get the sentiment."

"Thanks."

"There's no reason to get up, so once you've eaten, get your head back on that pillow."

"What will you do?"

"I'll probably go downstairs and watch something. Save me being molested. Not that I didn't like it." He raises his eyebrows. I take a few more bites of my toast before I feel full. The coffee is nice, but I just can't manage anything else. Maybe this will help me lose those few pounds I seem to keep hold of.

I put my head back on the pillow and he leans in to stroke my head. Did I really touch him up in the night? My eye lids flutter as I try to keep them open and I feel him get off the bed and leave the room.

The sound of voices pulls me from my dreams and I search my mind trying to place them. As the voices become clearer, I recognise them as Sean and another man, on speaker phone, I think. It's not particularly loud but the house is very quiet. I pull my legs out of bed and stand, finding my balance before setting off downstairs.

"I'm just being a friend," I hear Sean say.

"This goes above and beyond friends, you didn't even take a day off for your Nan's funeral."

"Then I am at least owed some time."

"I'm not begrudging you the time, mate. I'm saying you're kidding yourself if you think this isn't more than a friendship."

"Ah just don't Ben. You know I can't even entertain the thought of a relationship."

"It's been a decade."

"You're only saying that because of Emma."

"Yeah, I probably am. But what if she's your Emma?"

"She's not!"

"How can you be so sure?"

"Because I'll never have my own Emma."

"For fuck's sake Sean, you're an idiot." The last step creaks under my foot and Sean look towards me from the living room before quickly hanging up the phone. His face softens and he gives me a little smile.

"Hey, you're alive."

"Yes, barely. Who were you talking to?"

"It was just work. You must be hungry by now, what do you fancy?"

"I don't know, but I can guarantee I don't have it in the house." I glance around the room and into the kitchen. "Am I in the right house?"

"Oh I did a clean-up, hope you don't mind."

"Mind? Can you move in?" He laughs.

"So, food?"

"I dunno, a cheeseburger maybe. But I don't know if my stomach could actually handle it."

"Why don't you get dressed and we'll go to the drive-through, park up and people-watch while we have something. At least you'll get a bit of fresh air and change of scenery."

"Sounds like a plan. I'll go get ready." I make my way upstairs to get washed and pull on some sweatpants and a hoodie. I pull my hair up off my face. I can't believe he's been here looking after me.

Forty minutes later, we're sitting in Sean's car, in the middle of nowhere, watching the wind blow through the trees, slowly picking away at my greasy burger. I look over at him for a moment, taking in his handsome features as he looks out over the fields. "Thanks for this."

"It's only a burger."

"I don't mean the burger. I mean coming and looking after me. You didn't have to do that, but I really appreciate it."

He shrugs it off, "that's what friends are for."

"Well I have never had a friend that would have taken care of me before."

Our eyes lock and something, I don't quite know passes between us. "You do now." I do indeed, but is this really what friends do for each other?

Chapter Thirteen

I'm back to work after the best part of a week in bed, and it's as if I was never off. The café did not implode, although I have had a few people thanking me that I'm back. They are mainly the coffee drinkers. Cynthia still doesn't want to learn how to use the machine. I'm unsure whether it's because she thinks it's a bit of a faff or so that she doesn't have to clean it out at the end of the day.

Not only did I miss out on being at work, but also my time in the dark room. And coming back to work today has left me too exhausted to go afterwards. One of the staff at the hub sent me a link to an advert for a gallery in London, an exhibition for new artists and photographers. I'm not sure it's 100 per cent legit, as it's kind of an intern job, but it's worth a shot. I have to submit my application, which includes pieces from a recent collection, by the end of the month.

The bell tinkles on the café door and I look up to find those two big blue eyes staring back at me.

"Hey stranger." I say as he walks through the door, a big smile on his face.

"You're looking better."

"I'm feeling better."

"Good." He looks at me for a long time before he shakes his head, as if to release a thought.

"Coffee?"

"I've heard they're the best around." He smirks.

The bell chimes again, but I don't move my eyes from Sean's face. His expression suddenly drops, and I see who it is. A younger man, dressed in smart clothes, comes in and is beaming, looking between Sean and me. "Ah, now I know why you keep this place a secret."

"Huh?" I have no idea who this bloke is or what he's talking about, but Sean rolls his eyes. The man comes to stand in front of me.

"I'm Liam, and you are?" He holds his hand out to shake and I instinctively take it.

"Hannah."

"I work with Sean and he'll never tell us where he gets his amazing coffee. But now we know, and I'm sure I, for one, will be a regular." This bloke is pretty full of himself. I don't know why, he's not as tall or good looking as Sean, as well as the lack of sultry Edinburgh accent.

"Is this to go?" I ask Sean.

"It'll have to be now. So is yours." He points to Liam. "We've got a site visit to prep for." I turn to the machine to make Sean's and put it in a to-go cup.

As I put it on the counter, I meet his eyes. "That's on me as a thank you."

"No need." I shrug and he picks it up.

"Liam, what's your poison?" I turn to the other man.

"Cappuccino."

"Thought as much. You can tell a lot about people by the coffee they drink."

"Do tell me more." Liam leans on the counter to get a bit closer and I can see Sean's jaw clench as I turn back to the machine.

While the steam whistles I can hear them talking in muted tones, but I can't make out the words. I turn and put Liam's coffee on the counter.

"So what does my coffee say about me?" His attention is back on me now.

"It says you're full of hot air and I'm smooth. Now let's go!" Sean virtually man-handles Liam out of the door, as Liam tries to wave goodbye.

"Bye then!" I shout out and Sean looks back, giving me the glimpse of a smile through the window. That was a bit odd.

"God, what a sandwich that would be." I nearly drop the milk jug I'm holding. I don't know how long Sally has been standing there. "I'd love to be that filling."

"Eh?"

"Them two. Ones all tall and brooding, the other cute and chatty. I was gonna ask who you'd pick, but why should we have to choose?"

"Get your mind out of the gutter."

Before she can go any further by phone beeps in my pocket. "Is that them?"

I look at my phone. "No, it's Dionne."

Hannah is added to the chat

Dionne
> Are we going out to the Dog tonight? I neeeed some girl talk

Beth
> Oh god yes

Emma
> I can't believe how much FOMO I have right now

Beth
> We really should boot her out of this chat for leaving us

Kateryna
> If I find babysitter

Beth
> Bring Tomasz round to ours

Lizzie
> I'm in

Dionne
> Hannah?

> **Me:** Dunno. Still tired from this flu

> **Dionne:** That's something we need to talk about too

> **Me:** What? Me being ill?

> **Dionne:** No, your Florence Nightingale

> **Me:** *eyeroll*

> **Beth:** Erm what are we missing? Never mind, leave it for tonight

> **Dionne:** Hannah????

> **Me:** Fine

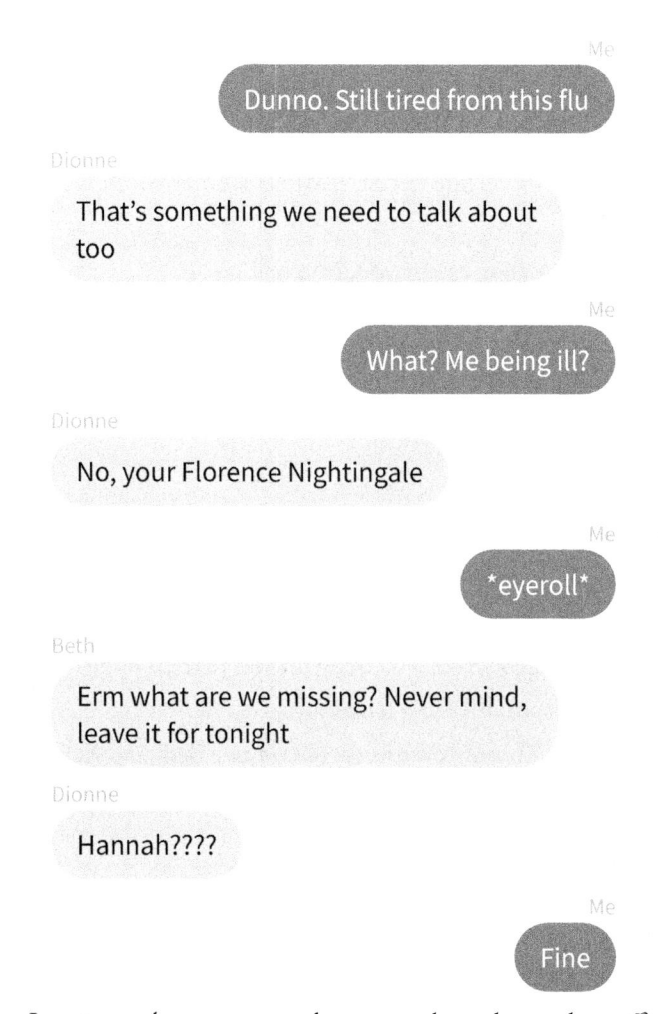

I put my phone away and start to clean down the coffee machine. I have a feeling I'm going to be in for a grilling tonight. Maybe they could give me a bit of insight because they know him better than me.

• ♥ • ♥ • ♥ • ♥ • ♥ •

I push through the door to the Dog and Swan and the familiarity fills my senses. There are only a few people in tonight, but it's only early. I walk straight to the bar.

"Hiya Han, feeling better?" Mitch saunters over, cleaning cloth in hand.

"Does anything escape you, Mitch?"

"Nothing worth the mention. So, better?"

"Yes, still shattered but a lot better."

"Did your mum come over?"

"No, why would she?"

"Cos you were ill."

"Are we talking about the same person?" He pulls a face, knowing that my mother is not particularly maternal at the best of times.

"Oh actually. I have something for you to try. The girls are in their usual spot, I'll bring it over."

"Thanks." I turn towards the sofa where Beth and Kateryna are chatting and Dionne is looking at her phone and rolling her eyes.

She looks up from her phone and sees me and a broad smile crosses her face. Dionne is just one of those people who radiate loveliness. She's the kind of person that when she smiles it's just infectious. The girls get out of their seats one by one and give me a hug. I've never really thought of myself as a hugger. Mainly because my mother didn't really hug a lot, well not me anyway, so I've never really been one to do it. But these girls are huggers and it feels really nice. "I've missed your beautiful face." Dionne says.

"Well you'll be glad because it wasn't that beautiful at the start of the week."

"Ah, bless you. Lizzie is running late, but I got the drinks in, lemonade for you because I wasn't sure what you'd fancy."

"Lemonade is great. Mitch says he's got something for me to try, and I'm a little bit scared." Right on cue, Mitch arrives at the table with a bulbous cocktail glass containing a reddish concoction, straw and umbrella. "Oh god Mitch, what even is this?"

"It's a non-alcoholic Sex On The Beach."

Lizzie walks in, as cool as anything. "What's the occasion?"

"I wanted Hannah to try out my non-alcoholic cocktail."

"What is it?"

"Sex on the Beach."

"Oh the irony of a Virgin Sex on the Beach." Lizzie smirks.

Mitch's face drops. "I didn't think of that."

"Get some more straws and we'll give you our verdict." Mitch passes me the glass and I have a sip. It's actually really nice. Quite sweet.

He rushes back and hands out the straws.

"You know what this needs?" Kateryna says.

"Don't tell me, good Ukrainian vodka?" Beth says rolling her eyes.

"How did you know I say that?"

"That's your answer to everything." Everyone tastes the drink and nods in approval. I think it's a hit and Mitch goes back to the bar, happy.

"What made you late Lizzie, it's not like you?"

"Well Jacob was having an online argument with someone over a racing game on the Xbox, had himself a bit of meltdown. So I had to calm it all down before I left."

"How old is Jacob?" I ask.

"He's nearly 15. He thinks he's mature and tough but he's not really."

"Have you left them on their own tonight?" Beth asks.

"No, Jon's with them."

"Couldn't he handle it?"

"God no. He'd go all Police Interceptors on them. It was just a normal squabble. Jon would probably ring one of his mates to go and pay the parents a visit."

"Really?" I ask.

"Well probably not, but he'd definitely threaten it."

"Oh god, I can't wait for Jonah to be that age," Beth says sarcastically.

"Does he get in trouble a lot?" I ask Beth, trying to get a feeling for all the girls' families.

"You could say that. He's just too clever for his own good. He's always getting told off for answering back. And it's not that he's generally cheeky, he just likes to point out when his teachers are wrong." She lets out a big sigh. "You'll never guess what the teacher suggested to use when they were building a castle? That expandy foam!"

"What's that?" I ask.

"You know that yellow foam that builders use to fill voids in walls. It's in an aerosol, comes out in a thick spray, expands into a foam, then goes hard. But it keeps on expanding, if you spray too much it's effectively filled your house and is oozing out of every hole. Can you imagine Jonah with that? I had to ring the school to tell them under absolutely no circumstances was he allowed to use it, or even be given the idea."

"Oh god, I can imagine that going wrong."

"I just know that Jonah is going to take over the world eventually, Lex Luther style, but I'd rather it wasn't on my watch." Beth sighs.

"They're just so fearless at that age. Tomasz same. I hate to think what the two of them are getting up to now. Poor Steve." Kateryna laughs. "They're so head strong."

"Wonder where he gets that from?"

"What you mean? It not me, just people strange. Work yesterday I had Sophie cry when I asked to do job. And then there's Sam, keep watching me, waiting for my mistakes."

"That's not why he's watching you Kat," Dionne points out.

She pulls a questioning face. "Then why?"

"Because he's a bit scared of you but also totally in love with you."

"No. He just a boy."

"He's 29."

"Yes boy! How he in love with me?"

"I popped down the other day and he'd bought your favourite doughnuts. Wouldn't let anyone touch the one you liked."

"No he bought for the team."

"Nope! He literally slapped my hand when I went for one." Dionne explains.

"Don't understand men."

"You and me both." Dionne's face drops.

"Seb?"

"Bloody Seb!"

"Has Di told you about her fling with Seb?" Lizzie asks me.

"I've had a brief outline, but he seems very demanding. Is that as a boss or as a boyfriend?"

"He's not my boyfriend. And there is absolutely no way I could tolerate him full-time. I don't know whether it's the job or him, but I don't think I can handle this CFO job."

"CFO?"

"Chief Finance Officer," Dionne explains, and I still have no idea what she's talking about, but she reads my facial expression and starts to expand. "So a few months ago, we caught our CFO trying to frame me for, well let's just say fraudulent activities. It all got a bit nasty and I ended up kicking him in the balls. Nothing he didn't deserve, I might add. He got fired and they needed an interim CFO, so I got the job. It's not a hard job, it's just longer hours and a bit stressful. All that would have been fine if Myles had carried on being my boss, but Seb stepped in. And let's say he's a bloody nightmare to work with."

"How come?"

"Bloody late-night calls to look at things and come into the office."

"Is that him pulling you into work, or is that him wanting a booty call?"

"Now I come to think about it..." She pulls a face as if she's thinking through the last few times of meeting. "Bloody men!"

"You feeling better now Hannah?" Kateryna asks me, concerned.

"Yes, I'm still really tired, but pretty good."

"Did you hear about who went over to look after her?" Dionne says and my eyes go wide and I can feel the heat rise up to my cheeks. I was hoping not to have to divulge that information.

"Come on then, spill." Lizzie's eyes seem to penetrate my soul.

"Oh god, it's so embarrassing. Sean came round and looked after me."

"I didn't even know you two were friends. The last time we spoke, you kept bumping into each other."

"Well, yes, we've become friends. We cleared the air a bit and we got to know each other a bit better." The girls give each other a look. "I was totally knocked out and couldn't lift my head off the pillow and he kept ringing. So I just messaged I was sick and before I knew what had happened, he's sitting on my bed."

"How did he get in?" Beth asks.

"We have Hannah's spare key because she's notoriously bad at keeping them safe." Dionne explains.

"Okay, so what happened. And what's the embarrassing part?"

"Do you mean other than the fact he's seen me at my very worst? He also stripped me and put me in the bath."

"Wow, he saw you naked?"

"Yes. The only saving grace is that I don't really remember it because I was pretty out of it. He fed me, gave me painkillers and he even tidied my house."

"Wow! Where do I get one of those?"

"So he wants to be boyfriend?" Kat questions.

"No, he definitely doesn't. He's asked to be *friends with Benefits*, but I said I can't handle that kind of thing."

"Was that before or after he saw you naked?"

"Before. But he does loads of boyfriend type things."

"Oh that's just Sean. It's the way he's wired. I don't even think he knows that it's a bit above and beyond friendship." Dionne says.

"Yeah, we thought that there was something going on with Sean and Megan, but it's just the way he is. He wants to, I don't know, be the one who people rely on." Lizzie says.

"Were Megan and Sean ever romantic?"

"No, it was more like a brother and sister thing."

"So he could genuinely not want to be in a relationship and do all those things?" I'm hoping the disappointment doesn't show on my face. I shouldn't have even contemplated that I may be something special to him.

"Well I think it's a bit different from what he has with Megan. He never asked for *Benefits* from her." Lizzie points out.

"This is definitely different. Sean is so together and suave usually, but he seems to lose his head when you are around." Dionne points out.

"I don't know what you mean, he seems normal talking to me."

"When you came around the first time, he was a bit rude. That's not like him at all, like you'd thrown him off balance. I thought you might punch him."

"I very nearly did. But then I couldn't be mad with him because he carried me upstairs and put me in his bed, then slept on the sofa. So all these cute things he does, it's just him?"

"Pretty much."

"He was acting weird the other day when he was in the café. Well he wasn't until someone he works with came in. He acted like he didn't want him to know we were friends."

"Weird. Who even knows what goes through the small minds of men anyway?" Beth exclaims with a sigh.

"How is it going with Jonathan then Liz? Are you back together?"

"In a fashion and only when it suits. Because we aren't officially together, there's nothing to make us stay and work things out when we have a disagreement. He just goes back to his flat and festers for a bit. I mean we have been making the effort. I go and stand in the freezing cold to watch him play football like a doting wifey."

"What does he do?"

"Dunno, picks me up from places, buys me things he thinks I might like, the little things. But I think we're in this limbo, not together, but not apart. We need to either completely split or, I dunno, get married."

Beth spits her drink out and nearly chokes. "What? I can't see you being married Liz."

"Me either. So we might have to totally split. But to be honest I've not fully formed any thoughts yet. Change the subject before we all want to cry." Lizzie looks sad, I'm pretty sure that means she doesn't want to split.

"Do we know what Megan is doing when she gets back?"

"Gets back?"

"Yeah. She's on a six-month *finding yourself* trip with her boyfriend. I think they're leaving all the decisions for the very last moment."

The girls continue to chat about different things that are going on, television programmes they've watched and so on and I try to get Lizzie's attention away from the group. "You know the match I saw you at? With the lad that had his head cut open? Do you know who that was? I need to get another photo of him."

"Oh yeah, that's Carl. He's a bit yummy. Anyway, usually they wouldn't play each other for a while, but that was a cup match and they play them again in the league this Sunday, you'll probably catch him there. He was quite taken with you."

"Really?"

"Yes, he kept asking who you were. Called you that *little Pixie*. But he did also have a mild concussion. It would be good for you to come down, at least I'll have some company."

"I'll try. I'm really behind with my developing and printing after being sick. So I'll see how it goes."

We both turn back to the group and the conversation flows again. It feels so natural with these girls. This is only my second night out with them and I feel so comfortable, like we've known each other for years. I feel like I could spill all my secrets and they'll be there to support me, no matter what.

Chapter Fourteen

Sean

The people I work with are absolute massive dicks and I hate them! Ever since Liam saw me in the coffee shop talking to Hannah, it has been non-stop. I told them we were just friends but they wouldn't give up. That was fine, I had it a lot with Megan. People don't get how a man and a woman can just be friends. But then it changed, and they started going on about how nice she looked and that if I was just a friend then they had a chance at dating her. As you can imagine I saw red, made them swear never to go in to see her and never touch her, which then fuelled more of the same talk about me being attracted to her.

Of course I'm attracted to her – she's amazing, beautiful and funny. But I can't date her. There's just too much hurt involved. I learnt my lesson years ago and I'm not going back there again. Plus, if it didn't work out and I ended up hurting her, I don't think I could forgive myself. She deserves so much better.

So my days have been filled with thoughts of Hannah in one way or another. Either thinking about her naked or thinking about how someone else will eventually be her boyfriend, her fiancé, husband and there will be little versions of Hannah running around but without my features too.

I've honestly never felt like this about anybody before, not even *she who must not be named*. I need to quickly get a grip or I'm going to give myself an ulcer, or worse. At that moment Liam walks in my office with a take away coffee cup and places it on my desk. He doesn't say anything, just winks, and I feel the heat rise up through my body. Before I can explode, he makes a quick exit. Twat!

Maybe I need a distraction, maybe I should go back home and have a night out with the boys?

Me

> Oh dickhead, what you doing tonight?

Ben

> Not really got a plan, was gonna be pizza and a film, why? You up?

Joel

> I had a date but she ghosted me

Piers

> I'm up for anything

Me

> I'm gonna leave work early and drive up

HELLO HANDSOME

Ben: You're nearest to town, shall we come over to you before heading out?

Me: Yep about 8, c u then

Ami: Can I come?

Me: Who added her?

Ami: Is that a no?

Me: Boys only

Ami: Charming

There's someone else I think I might message. It'll help get Hannah out of my system.

Me: On for a hook up tonight?

CP: Hello stranger, you back?

> **Me:** One night only
>
> **CP:** Then maybe, msg later

Well that's that sorted, I'll be able to get rid of this built-up sexual tension with no worry of anyone catching feelings.

· ♥ · ♥ · ♥ · ♥ · ♥ ·

I sunk the first three drinks in quick succession and I'm ready for my fourth, I better slow down or I'll be no good later, when it's most needed.

"So why the sudden urge to have a night out with us?"

"It wasn't an urge. I have been thinking about it for a while. I've just been too busy to actually sort it out."

"This isn't anything to do with a certain blonde, is it?" Ben raises an eyebrow at me.

"I don't know what you're talking about."

"You know, the one that you drop everything to go and look after. The one that, every time she's mentioned in the office you look like you're about to burst a blood vessel."

I roll my eyes. "Can we sack Liam?"

"No, why? He's good at his job."

"He's a dick."

"So are you."

"He's brought lots of revenue in though." Joel pipes up.

"Always about the money with you Joel. Tell me about this woman that ghosted you."

"Not much to tell. I thought she liked me but then she just stopped replying."

"What was the last thing you said?"

"Dunno something about meeting up and promising I wasn't a serial killer."

"That's why then." We all shake our heads, he has absolutely no clue.

"I'm not though." Joel looks at us for answers, confused as to what he's done. Bless him.

"Yeah, but you don't say that out loud." Ben rolls his eyes, Joel is so naïve about women and always goes for the ones that will chew him up and spit him out.

Piers arrives back from the bar with the drinks. "What have I missed?"

"Well Joel has been ghosted and Sean is trying to avoid talking about Hannah."

"Joel always gets ghosted. So Hannah, what's she like?"

"She's a friend, and the whole point about coming out tonight was to get away from questions like this."

"Sean is pissed that he likes Hannah, but won't admit it, but also refuses to have a relationship with ANYONE, and is annoyed that the other lads want to ask her out on a date, would rather sack them all and see our business go down the toilet than admit it all." Sometimes I hate my best friend.

"Fuck off!"

"True though."

"I've never really understood that about you mate. Why won't you be in a relationship? Don't get me wrong, women are a bloody nightmare, but still..." Piers takes a gulp of his drink.

"I don't want to talk about it."

"But you've had loads of women." Joel states.

"Just hook ups. Sean doesn't do feelings," Ben explains and roll my eyes for what seems like the hundredth time.

"How's your love life Piers?"

"Non-existent."

"Is that because you are secretly in love with Emma's friend Sammy?" Ah I forgot about Sammy. She's the reason we met the girls I suppose. They came up to spend time with Sammy, who also lives in Edinburgh. I totally forgot about Piers colluding with the girls and having video calls with them.

"You've got a thing for Sammy?" I ask.

"No I haven't. We're just friends."

"Yeah, she's way out of your league." Joel smirks.

"Fuck off."

"Harsh but fair mate," I say.

"Why are you here again? I preferred it when you were back in England." Piers narrows his eyes at me.

My phone vibrates in my pocket and when I check it I can feel my heart speed up, some kind of rush of adrenaline I'm hoping no one else can see.

Hannah

Hey, you okay?

> **Me**
> Yeah up in Edinburgh

> **Hannah**
> Okay I'll not disturb you

> **Me**
> You can disturb me whenever you want. I'm heading back tomorrow, maybe I'll see you.

> **Hannah**
> Have a good time

I look up from my phone to all the lads looking at me, eyebrows raised. "Who's that then?"

"Someone I'm planning on hooking up with later." A lie.

"So not Hannah?"

"No, why would you say that?"

"Because your face lit up."

"Just because I know I'm getting a shag tonight."

"Whatever." Ben huffs.

My phone beeps again, as if by some divine intervention.

> **CP**
> Home in 20 minutes

I turn my phone to the boys to show the message on the screen and they all shake their heads.

> **Me**
> Great, see you soon

"My round, one last drink before I head off," I say, draining the last of my drink.

"When are you heading back down south?"

"Sometime tomorrow. I have football on Sunday." I head off to the bar.

Forty minutes later my cab pulls up outside Cheryl's flat, and for the first time ever I hesitate, wondering whether this is a good idea or not. I shake the thought out of my head, get out and head for the front door. I press the buzzer.

The door clicks and I pull the door and head upstairs. Her front door is still shut and I knock gently. She pulls the door wide and stands there like a model posing for a magazine shoot. "Hello Handsome."

Her long blonde hair is wavy and hangs down past her chest. She's wearing a silk and lace vest and matching shorts that show off her long slender legs. Her make-up is perfect as she stands at the door and pouts. I look at her for a few moments. Usually by this time I've grabbed her and shut the door with my foot. But I can't move.

Her face falls. "Are you coming in or not?"

"In..." is the only thing that I can utter. I'm wondering if that last drink was one too many as she turns and makes her way inside.

I've never really taken much notice of Cheryl's flat before because I've always been pre-occupied. But it looks more like a hotel room than a lived-in flat. There're no photos, no mementos, no random odd cushions. It looks like something out of a magazine, unlived in. And then it strikes me – so is my flat.

It's all sleek and modern with no personality. Not a thing out of place. Not like the house in Winford. Why is that? Megan furnished the house when she lived there. Back then I thought it was too girly and fluffy, but actually it feels cosy and homely. Nothing like where I am standing now, or in my flat. Does that reflect my personality? Or lack of?

I think about Hannah's house with its eclectic furniture and throws everywhere. It totally reflects her. So does this flat reflect Cheryl? Fake and empty?

"Drink?" Cheryl's voice pulls me out of my head.

"No thanks. How long have you lived here?"

"About eight years, you've been here before."

"I know I've never really noticed before."

"Because you've usually got me pushed up against the wall by now."

"Mmm."

"Is everything okay?"

"Yeah. Why wouldn't it be?" I think about Hannah and what she would think it she knew I was here. Would she hate me? Would she look at me differently? Would that completely close the door for us? Let's face facts, the only person who has closed the door has been me.

"Because you look like you either want to run out of the door or vomit. Are we doing this Sean or do I need to call someone else?"

"I've just had too much to drink."

"It's never been a problem before."

"No." And she's right, it never has been a problem before. But my dick feels like it'll never get hard again. Cheryl is one of a long line of woman I found attractive, who I'd hook up with for meaningless sex every weekend. But now it just seems, I don't know, wrong I suppose. "Look maybe you should call someone else."

"Are you losing your touch Sean Hutchinson?"

"Looks like it." I turn swiftly and practically run for the door, slamming it behind me. I run down the stairs so fast that I think I may go head first down them, and bolt through the main door.

I come to a stop, bent over, hands on knees trying to catch my breath. I may vomit after all. What the hell just happened? I pull out my phone, but instead of calling a cab, I look at the photos I took of Hannah at the park when she wasn't looking. I need to shut this shit down. I can't be acting like this over a woman I'm never gonna be in a relationship with.

I start walking, to clear my head. But rather than clearing it, the same questions keep going round and round, until I realise I'm at the front door to my flat. I've walked five miles on autopilot.

I let myself in, fling myself on the sofa and pull out my phone.

Me

> What the fuck is wrong with me?

Ben

> Well I don't know what you're talking about, but I'll hazard a guess that you couldn't go through with shagging your fuck buddy and now you're questioning your existence. Like I said, she's your Emma!

> Me
> Fuck off. Wish I never asked

I think back to the time when Emma had dumped Ben and he was in a state. I just dismissed him, couldn't take any of his pity party. But is that how I'm feeling now? Or have I just had too much to drink and am feeling a bit lost, being in my home town?

· ♥ · ♥ · ♥ · ♥ · ♥ ·

I ended up staying in the flat all of Saturday. I didn't want to speak to anyone. I looked like shit and I couldn't form a coherent sentence. I put it down to lack of sleep. I ordered take away and sat on the sofa for hours. Then decided to give up and had an early night, ready to set off early to get home in time for football. At least that will keep my mind occupied and I can run off some excess tension while I'm at it.

Jon messaged to say that Lizzie would drive us to the match. I know it's so that she can hide in the car for the second half if it gets too cold or boring. I hear a beep outside and grab my bag. I got home an hour ago and put my kit on and then some layers on top.

I head out of the door and lock it. I don't know whether Dionne is home because she doesn't usually surface until lunch time on a Sunday. I open the car door and throw my bag on the back seat and get in.

"Morning!" They say in unison.

"Hmm"

"Like that is it? Heavy weekend?"

"No, not really." Lizzie and Jon give each other a look.

"I think Hannah is coming down to watch and take some photos." Lizzie says as she looks in her rear-view mirror to gauge my reaction. I don't give her the satisfaction as she pulls out into the street and makes her way to the park. Why is everyone obsessed with Hannah? I know they went out the other week, did she say something?

We pull into a parking space at the side of the park. The away team have already got here and are chatting on the touchline. I look round, but I can't see her. I was hoping that football would be a distraction.

Greeted by slaps on the back by the rest of the team, I strip off to my kit and start to do some stretches. Jon comes up behind me. "You okay?"

"Fine."

"Okay then." He walks off, my tone giving him the message.

The whistle goes for the start of the match and I try to concentrate. I get into the swing of things and the first half goes quite quickly. By half time there is still no sign of Hannah and I think Lizzie may have been saying it to get a reaction. The match is not particularly eventful in the second half either until the other team's centre half loses possession and Woody takes a run down the left and crosses it to Charlie, who powers it past the goal keeper and into the top right-hand corner of the net. The team celebrates with hugs and the momentum is lifted. Everyone has a spark of energy again.

As play resumes, I see her. She's standing with Lizzie. I may not have recognised her because I can only see her nose peeking out of her scarf, her eyes are shrouded by her hair. The giveaway is the two cameras around her neck. She lifts one up to show Lizzie a shot and they both laugh. Something in my chest warms and I feel like all the tension from the last few days just ebbs away.

I'm pulled right back to reality when I'm barged by an opposition player as the ball flies overhead. Luckily Titch catches it. But before the ball can make it to the other end, the referee blows for the end of the match.

Jon runs to catch up to me as I head off the pitch. "So Hannah is here again, is this gonna be a regular thing?"

"Again?"

"Yes, she came the other week, took some photos, but left before the end. Lizzie said she spoke to her before she knew she was Dionne's friend."

"Right."

We reach lizzie who hands us both our hoodies and I look down the touch line for Hannah. She is stood talking to one of the opposition players, who is unnaturally close to her. She smiles up at him and the rage in the pit of my stomach starts to grow. I stop still, watching their exchange and it is obvious that he is into her. The way she is chatting, I think she may be too and I suddenly feel sad.

She pulls her camera up to her eye as he steps back and she instructs him on what to do. He poses, she takes a few shots and they continue to chat and laugh. She gives him her phone and he types something in and hands it back with a smirk. I feel the bile rise up into my mouth and try to swallow it down, past the lump in my throat. I start to walk, head down, trying to get past them as quickly as possible.

"Sean." She's spotted me and I can't help but turn towards her. She says something to him and walks to catch up to me.

"Hi." I answer curtly.

"Didn't you see me?"

I want to say something sarcastic but I don't. "No."

"Did you have a good game?" I wish I could ignore her, but I don't have that kind of willpower.

"It was okay." She gives me a look, she knows I'm shutting down the conversation.

"Lizzie said I can get a lift home with you guys." She sounds unsure. "Is that okay?"

"Yes, sure."

We arrive at the car and Jon opens the boot for us to dump our bags in. He sits on the edge, taking his muddy boots off. I toe mine off in an effort to be away as quickly as possible. I pull my trainers out of my bag, throw my boots in and pull the trainers on before rushing to the back seat of the car.

The journey is made in near silence. Lizzie asks Hannah the odd question, but I don't really pay any attention. We pull up in front of my house and I get out of the car, say a curt 'bye' and grab my bag out of the boot. I close it with a slam and head to the front door without looking back. I'm being a complete dick, but I just can't help it.

Chapter Fifteen

Hannah

Come on Hannah, get your shit together. I am on a deadline and, as per usual when I need to get stuff done, something goes wrong. My time management has been pretty appalling because my head is elsewhere. There's a chance for me to exhibit at a small gallery in London, that internship that someone told me about, but I need to submit the details of my proposal and a lengthy application form by midnight today.

I've spent all my free time in the dark room trying to get the prints ready and form some kind of order. But I just keep getting pulled into other things. My mother called yesterday. I wasn't really listening to her and when I said I had to get my prints finished, she started going on again about living in fantasy world and needing to get my life together. Thanks for the support mum.

Then there's Sean acting like he didn't even know me at the football. I'm not sure what I did to upset him, but it's clearly something. And he hasn't messaged me since.

I'm just finishing the last bits off in the café before I head to the dark room. I've got just about everything sorted ready to go, but last night my laptop decided to do an update or something and when I came to turn it back on I got a blue screen. So I shut it down – and left it overnight to calm down. I'll get everything finished off tonight. I take everything to the dark room because at least, even though I have nothing left to print, I can lock the door and not be disturbed.

Cynthia goes out the back while I wipe down the coffee machine and the bell from the door sounds again. Typical – with only five minutes to go, someone wants something. "We're just shutting up." I say without turning round.

"Well it's not closing time yet." Drew's dulcet tones have the hairs on the back of my neck standing to attention.

"What do you want Drew?"

"Oh, you know, just to mess your day up."

"Well you've succeeded. Now jog on."

"No coffee?"

"No. The machine is off."

"I'll just grab a drink from the fridge then." He heads over to the fridge, picks out two bottles of fresh juice and brings them back to the counter. He opens one and takes a drink, his eyes never leaving mine, waiting for me to challenge him, but I stay silent. There's no point, he'll do whatever he's come to do and then leave. If I try to stop him it'll just take longer and I really want to get out of here.

He puts the half empty bottle back on the counter without replacing the lid, picks up the next bottle and does the same. With them both sitting on the counter, this time he doesn't even pretend to spill them. Instead, he picks them up at the same time and pours them out all over the counter and the floor. Once emptied he flings them over towards me.

"That'll be three pounds fifty." I say in a monotone voice, my face not reacting to his attempts to rile me.

"Don't fancy it anymore," he says as he makes his way out of the door, the bell chiming after him.

"What the hell happened here? I was gone two minutes." Cynthia walks back behind the counter and takes in the scene. I can't even put any words together to answer her. "Was it Drew?" I startle at her words.

"Yes! How did you know?"

She shrugs. "I'll sort this, you need to get going and sort that thing out for London."

"I didn't think you'd remember. Are you sure?" Who knew Cynthia would be my hero. I always knew she was a softy really.

"Of course. But this can't keep happening."

"What am I supposed to do? My parents have never believed me over golden child."

"Leave this one to me." She takes her phone out of her apron.

The battered old model phone has stickers all over the back, no doubt from her grandchildren. She puts the phone to her ear.

"Oh hello Mr Carmichael." She is using a voice I have never heard before and I see her in a whole new light. "This is Cynthia from Grubs Up. I was just wondering who I should make the bill for the damages out to?" There's a pause as she listens. "No not Hannah, she has left for the day. I believe Drew is your son... He came in and took some beverages and poured them all over the floor and counter... No not an accident... I thought you'd rather I came directly to you rather than take the footage to the police... I would usually let this go, but to be honest Mr Carmichael, it's not the first time this has happened, and we take customers threatening staff very seriously.... I absolutely agree, yes two hundred should cover it... Of course. I do hope you enjoy the rest of your day."

"Oh my god, what actually just happened? Do we have camera footage?"

"Nope, but he doesn't know that. And we just made two hundred quid."

"I'll still get the blame."

"Yes, but the money will soften the blow. Now go, you have photos to do whatever you do with them."

"Thank you." I rush at Cynthia and give her a big squeeze. I think she's a little taken aback. I grab my bag, rush out the door and head to the Hub.

· ♥ · ♥ · ♥ · ♥ · ♥ ·

Twenty minutes! Twenty minutes of time that I do not have, I have been trying to sort this laptop out. It still won't do anything and I'm starting to freak out. I feel like throwing it against the wall, but then I definitely won't get this application submitted in time.

I pull my sweatshirt over my head and dump it on the floor. The stress must be heating up my little room. I have been so distracted that I didn't layer up my clothes like usual, so I'm here in a tight vest top which does nothing to hide my blue laced bra peeking out. My corduroy skirt with big over-the-top buttons up the front, just looks unbalanced now. At least I'm hidden away here. My phone beeps in my bag and I search through the endless amounts of junk to where I dumped it.

Sean

Hi.

Me

Talking to me then?

Sean

Sorry

Me

I can't deal with your tantrums today. My laptop is being shit and I need to submit this application.

The phone rings in my hand and his name flashes up.

"What's wrong with it?"

"It did an update and now it's just a blue screen saying something hasn't loaded."

"Hannah... Han... you keep breaking up. Where are you?"

"Dark room in the basement of the Hub, the phone signal is patchy."

"Basement?"

"Yes, at the Hub." And then the signal completely goes and the line is dead. This is all I need, I can't even ring anyone for help now. I can't use another computer to submit it because all the photos are stored on this laptop. This is the time I really wish I drank or smoked. I throw myself onto the desk, resting my head on my arms, and try to arrange my thoughts on what to do next.

I nearly jump out of my seat as there's a thumping on the door. "Hannah, it's me."

"Have you got over yourself yet?" I turn the key and pull the door open to find him resting on the door frame.

"No not really, but you needed some help so here I am."

"Ever the knight in shining armour." I can't help the edge of bitterness that comes across.

"Do you want help or not?"

"Fine." I gesture for him to come in. I don't know how it's got to the point where we are being horrible to each other. He heads straight for the laptop and I turn the lock on the door.

"Did you restart it?"

"Yes." I roll my eyes.

"There's probably a corrupted file and when it updated, it didn't like it."

"Can you fix it?"

"Of course I can fix it, or I wouldn't be here."

"Your tone is really pissing me off. You said sorry and yet you come in here all not sorry at all."

"Let me sort this out then we'll talk."

"Fine!"

"Fine."

A few minutes later the laptop reboots and is working properly. But I can't risk it going wrong again so I pull it towards me and open my email. I attach the files I'd previously created and hit send. I blow out a breath of relief.

"What was so urgent?" he asks.

"An application to exhibit in a gallery in London. Closing is tonight and I needed it to go through. Once I get a received message I'll be happy." The email app pings with an automated response saying they've received my application. Now all I have to do is wait. And hope.

"Done?"

"Yes, thank you." I look up to him and search his face for what he might be thinking but I come up blank. "Are you gonna tell me what's up?"

He shuffles his feet about as he looks at the floor. "I got a bit... I don't know, annoyed at you flirting with that other player. I know I have no right to, before you say it, but I did. And then the thought of you taking his photo and staring at his stupid face all day, pushed me over the edge."

I laugh out loud and his face drops. "You were jealous?"

"I didn't say jealous."

"Whatever. Have you looked around this room since you came in?" He gives me a quizzical look and begins to survey the room.

The washing line zigzags across the room and has prints pegged up drying from the past few days. I've been so busy I haven't had chance to take them down. He focuses on the photo I didn't want him to, the one I took of Carl over the weekend, and his face darkens. "The rest of them now." He looks back to me and then looks at each photo one by one.

"I..." I don't know whether he's gonna be happy or freak out right now, it could go either way. He just stares at the photos, but I can't bear the wait anymore. I walk round him and, one by one, pull the photos off their pegs, gather them up into a pile and place them on the worktop. I close my laptop and generally start to tidy away.

"Hannah!" I turn on the spot. He's up close as he stares down into my face. He places his hands on the worktop, caging me with his arms. "When did you take these?"

"Well... If you saw me with my camera, then I have taken a photo of you."

"Why were you with Carl?"

"Not that I should explain myself, but I took a photo of him a few weeks ago, when he cut his head open, and I was taking a follow-up photo."

"You gave him your number?"

"Yes, because he wanted copies. I was asking if I could put him in my exhibition." He leans forward, so close that our lips are almost touching, but pauses. His hand wraps round my throat to hold me in place and he lightly kisses my lips. I feel like all the air has been sucked out of my lungs, I'm frozen to the spot.

He pulls back, stares into my eyes and then, as if deciding it was the only thing to do, he bends and pushes my skirt up my legs, moves his hands under my thighs and lifts me up to sit on the worktop.

He pushes himself closer so he is nestled in the gap between my legs. "This okay?" I can't form words so just nod in agreement. He doesn't need any other sign as his hand goes back on my throat, angling my head so he gets the best position. His tongue brushes over my bottom lip and I immediately open up for him and he kisses me deeper.

He's never kissed me before and I wasn't expecting it to be like this. The kiss is hot and frantic, like the built-up sexual tension between us is just pouring out. He uses his tongue like he's trying to charm my mouth into submission. Heat radiates through my body and pleasure pools at my spine. He pushes himself further forward but is met with the resistance of my skirt. He pulls away. Looking down he lets go and starts to undo the big button of my skirt until it reveals my underwear. He moves further into the space and I can feel him, rock hard, through his trousers rubbing in between my legs. He continues with the frantic kiss.

It feels like this is happening to someone else. I have never felt like this from just a kiss before. It's taken over all my senses. My whole body is throbbing and I just need more. Pulling out his shirt from the waistbands of his trousers I push my fingers up and over his hard body, passing over all the contours until I reach his chest. He pulls away and releases my mouth, my lips still tingling as he rests his head on my shoulder.

The movement of my chest makes me realise I'm panting, but so is he. "I need more," I say, not knowing where it came from.

"But it's not what you wanted." He takes in a few more breaths. "I can't give you a relationship. Will this be enough?"

"It's enough." I don't know if I'm trying to convince him or myself at this point. The only thing I know is that I need this man, right now.

"Once we do this, there's no going back. I don't want you to run again."

"I won't." He looks into my eyes, searching for the truth, but I don't know the truth myself. I just want the here and now. He nods and pulls at the elastic of my knickers. I wriggle to get out of them. He pulls them down my legs, over my feet and puts them in his pocket.

He hesitates for a moment as he takes in the sight of me. "Lean back." It's a command and my brain is frozen but my body knows what to do. I lean back and rest on my elbows. Both his hands are on the top of my thigh, gentle squeezes sending shock waves through my body. Slowly he makes his way up and uses his thumbs to gently brush over my core. The only sound is the thumping of my heart and my panting, getting more pronounced the closer he gets.

Until now his focus has been on his own movements, and mine has been on him. But his eyes rise to meet me and there's a twinkle of something there, lust maybe. " Hannah you're perfect." And without breaking eye contact he pulls my legs wider and dips his head, taking a long slow lick up my flesh. The vibration of his moan reaching my toes. He does the same again and my head tips back, noises coming from me that seem somewhat unfamiliar.

He takes a breath, and I focus back on him, my body still pulsating from the contact, then moves his hands to under my bum cheeks and tilts my pelvis to get better access and continues with the onslaught. This time using a shorter, quicker motion, as he shuts his eyes devouring me like he's eating a juicy peach. I can't take anymore and my legs begin to shake.

He can feel my climax building because he ups the pace. But just as the pleasure tries to explode through my body he pulls away. I'm both disappointed and relieved. I'm not sure I could survive something that big.

"I need to be inside you." I pull myself back to a sitting position and start to fumble with his trouser buttons, the fabric straining under the pressure from his erection.

His lips land on mine and I'm lost in him again. He releases me to rip open a condom packet as I push his trousers down his legs. "You sure?" His voice calmed for the moments but I can see the want in his eyes. I nod and he pulls me to the edge of the worktop. He pushes inside me, closing his eyes as the feeling sweeps over him while I hold my breath.

"Han, you need to relax, let me in." Easy for him to say. He sees the look I give him and he smirks, moving his mouth to kiss just below my ear and trails more down my neck. I know what he's doing as he pushes in deeper. "You feel so good." I whimper, and his hips move and he's further inside me. I feel so full of him, surrounded, overtaken.

He starts his movement and I move my arms around his body, just in case he lets me go. The rhythm of his strokes, has me making noises I never knew I could produce. I've never been vocal during sex, but this man just knows the spots to hit. I bite my lip to quieten myself, but the pleasure builds and builds until I feel like I'll explode. He must feel it too because his eyes roll to the back of his head and he lets out a groan.

As he carries on the train of kisses down my body, I just can't take any more. I grip him firmly as my body stiffens and the wave of ecstasy passes from my head, right down through my body. But he doesn't stop. He just gets more frantic and moves faster, harder. "Hannah you're squeezing this out of me."

And with that his body lets go with a jerk and a growl. He slows and his body sags on mine. "Fucking hell Hannah, you are amazing." He kisses me on the forehead and then on the mouth. And its at that point that I realise he's ruined me for any other man. Sean Hutchinson is a very high benchmark.

He pulls away and sorts himself out, but I don't pay much attention, my head is still mush.

We stay there in silence, trying to catch our breath, until he moves back to give me some room. "Can you jump down?"

"I can't really feel my legs yet. And I need my underwear." He frowns but gives me a smile and pulls them from his pocket. He hooks them over my feet and pulls them up my legs, pulling me slowly down from the workbench and onto the ground.

"That was...unreal. What now?" I'm not sure whether he means here in the dark room or in life in general.

"I don't know." Because I still can't think straight.

"Have you got more to do, or shall I drop you home?" And there it is. The barriers have come up. We've had sex and he needs to distance himself now so I don't become clingy.

"No, I'm done." In more ways than one it seems.

He picks up the pile of photos and flicks through. "I can't believe you took all these photos and I didn't know. Except this one." He shows me the one from the park with him smiling at the camera. "I actually have a bit of a confession."

"Go on!" This has piqued my interest but I continue to straighten my clothes out and button up my skirt.

"I took some of you too." He gets his phone out from his pocket and searches for what he needs. He turns the phone to show me. There's one on the park bench of me looking at the photos I'd taken on the camera, then one of me crouched down taking a shot. Then another of me laughing from the side.

"Oh god, they're not great."

"Well I'm not exactly a photographer like you."

"I meant the subject. I look horrific."

He narrows his eyes, looking at his phone as if in a trance. "You look perfect." He pulls himself out of his thoughts. After a few seconds he continues as if he'd just said something mundane like, *it's a bit foggy*. "Ready to go?"

"Nearly." I grab my sweatshirt and pull it over my head, then gather my laptop and the rest of my things and head for the door.

What just happened? We make our way out of the building and towards his car. So many things to think about but I just can't focus at all. What is this gonna mean for our friendship? I wish I could read his mind right now.

Chapter Sixteen

Sean

The car flashes as I unlock it to let us both in. I'm not sure how she's gonna react to what just happened, and I'm slightly concerned. Last time she ran, and I really don't want that to happen again. But I know she needs to process it when I'm not there to question her face to face. The radio blasts out as I start the engine and I quickly adjust the volume. "Tell me what's going through your head."

"Do I have to?"

"I mean it would be better to have open communication, rather than both of us guessing what the other is thinking. Or we can just forget it ever happened and wonder for the rest of our lives."

"Bit dramatic don't you think?"

"Could happen."

"Hmm... well I haven't really formed full thoughts yet."

"Well let's start with tasters of thoughts. Do you regret what happened?"

"No."

"Did you enjoy it?"

"Yes."

"Would you want to do it again?"

"Maybe."

"Why maybe?"

"I dunno. I don't usually… I don't know." She sighs and turns to me. "It's not usually that easy to get into my knickers." She says matter of factly.

"I feel like it's been coming for a while, so to speak."

"You said we were trying to be friends."

"You surprised me."

"Surprised you. How?"

"The photos."

"I mean who wouldn't want to take your photo. Have you seen yourself?" I can see from the corner of my eye that she's taking in my features, weighing up whether she'll ask me another question. "Which brings me to my other thoughts. Why me? I mean you could probably have anyone you want. Are you bored or something?"

I pull up outside her house, turn off the car and turn look at her. I can't quite believe she's asking me this. My eyes narrow, "Is that a joke?"

"Do you want to come in?"

"Best not. I think we both need to process what just happened, especially what you just said. And for the record I was not bored or something." I'm really quite pissed off at the thought that she could have that opinion of herself, of me!

"Do you regret it?" she asks in return.

"No, of course not."

"Then what is it we need to process?"

"Your feelings, away from me. I want you to think about what happens next. I don't want there to be any pressure on you. If you don't feel like you could do a *friends with benefits* arrangement, then I understand."

"Do YOU want to?"

"I'll be happy with whatever you decide to do." I've told another lie there. I would be devastated if she said no, especially after finding out how she feels being so close to her and those little noises she makes.

"That's not an answer."

"That's all you're gonna get. Just drop me a text with yes or no when you've thought about it."

"Maybe we should set some ground rules or something."

"Seems fair. What were you thinking?"

"Maybe we should keep this all to ourselves. I think people will be judgy."

"If that's what you want." She's got a point, it would be best to keep the outside world thinking we're just friends.

"And no kissing," she states.

"What? I like kissing. Are you telling me I'm not a good kisser?"

"No that's not it. It's just too *more than friends*. Along with touching and hand holding."

"Well what about only kissing with sex?"

"Sounds fine to me, I just don't want to stray into boyfriend/girlfriend territory."

"I can do that."

"The other thing that has been niggling me is wondering how many other *Friends with benefits* you have. I can't be one of many, if you have others then you'll not need me."

"I don't have others. Not anymore. I think we should be exclusive until one of us meets someone they might want more with, then we break it off."

"Right. I think that will be more you than me though."

"I can guarantee that won't be the case." She looks at me for a long time, trying to work out whether it's a good idea or not, then she gets out of the car, unlocks her front door, steps in and closes it without a glance back. My phone beeps almost immediately.

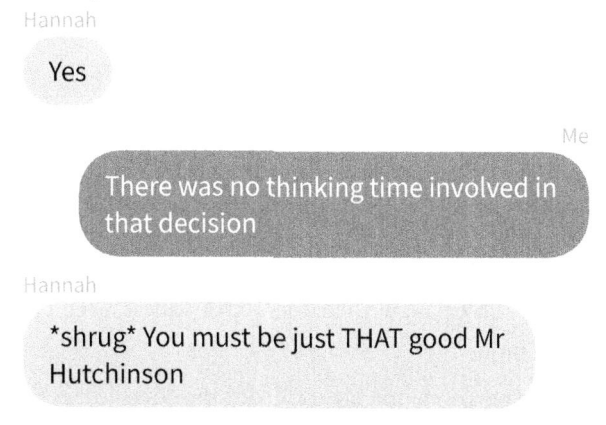

Hannah

> Yes

Me

> There was no thinking time involved in that decision

Hannah

> *shrug* You must be just THAT good Mr Hutchinson

I do a fist pump, something I haven't done since I was a teenager, but I'm elated that she said yes. I can't get the smile off my face. I throw my phone onto the passenger seat, pull the car out of the parking spot and head home. The drive home is quick and uneventful, so much so I think I've been on autopilot. I'm not sure what I have started is the best idea, but I couldn't do nothing. It was also very selfish of me to put in an exclusivity clause, but I can't bear the thought of her being with someone else. In the long run, I know that's exactly what will happen, but at least I can live in ignorant bliss, for now.

· ♥ · ♥ · ♥ · ♥ · ♥ ·

A few days have passed since she said yes to my proposition. We've had a few conversations via text, but nothing major. We've tried several opportunities to be alone but have been interrupted on each occasion. To say its frustrating is an understatement.

The doorbell app on my phone chimes and I check who it is, and her beautiful face fills the screen, and I rush downstairs to answer. "Well hello." I say opening the door.

"Dionne said she was running a bit late and to wait for her here, is that okay?" She gives me a little smile.

"More than Okay, in fact, while there is no-one else here, I have something for you to look at upstairs." I give her a cheeky smile and gesture to head through.

"Oh yeah?" She laughs then does a little squeal when I smack her on the bum.

We get to my room quickly and I kick the door shut as she sits on the bed. I stand over her, looking down into her big green eyes, eyelashes fluttering. I lean down and press a firm kiss onto her lips. My heart races as I remember all the things I want to do to this woman. Her breath hitches as takes hold of my belt. The same ideas obviously running through her mind.

I kiss her again. She made the rules of only kissing with sex, so I think I've made my intentions quite clear. But my ears are drawn to the sound of the door and my heart stops. I can hear Dionne shout for Hannah.

"For fucks sake." I whisper, clearly annoyed. "You'll need to say you're in the bathroom and sneak out." Hannah nods and tiptoes to the door and opens it and makes her way to the bathroom.

"Hannah, are you here?"

"Yeah, just needed the bathroom" She shouts back as the toilet flushes. She opens and closes the bathroom door in an exaggerated way. Looks up to where I'm standing, with my arms crossed and face not amused, gives me a quick smile and heads down the stairs to meet Dionne. They both shout their goodbyes and leave. Another chance interrupted, I'm beginning to think there is someone plotting against me.

After a few hours of sulking, and once I know she'll be home from the hub, I decide to try another tact.

I get my phone out and start to message.

Me

> When will you know about the exhibition?

Hannah

> Dunno, but I'm winding myself up about it already

Me

> Do you want something to take your mind off it?

> **Hannah**
> Sounds interesting

> **Me**
> Stop your dirty mind

> **Hannah**
> *sad face*

I pick up my phone and dial her number, this conversation will go better in real time. "Hannah Spencer, you are naughty!" She laughs. "Anyway, I need to go home for a meeting on Friday."

"When you say home, I'm taking it you mean Edinburgh."

"Yes. I was thinking you might like to come with me. It's a beautiful city and you could get loads of great shots, keep your mind off everything."

"I'll have to check with work, but I would love to. How long will you be away?"

"Well as long as you want. We could make a weekend of it."

"Where will we stay?"

"My flat. I was thinking of heading up on Friday morning, the meeting is at lunch time." I don't want to go the night before, I don't trust myself to make it to the meeting after a night away with Hannah. Plus, she might be fed up of me, realise what a fuck up I am, before I even get to the meeting.

"I'll try get my shifts covered and let you know, but it sounds like a great idea."

"Great. Speak soon."

Fingers crossed, this time I can get a chance at uninterrupted time with Hannah. Plus, this way, she definitely can't run, and the excitement flushes through me.

Chapter Seventeen

Hannah

The journey up to Scotland was pretty uneventful. I managed to get Cynthia to cover my shift on Friday and I wasn't on the rota to work the Saturday this week. We've generally chatted about things and I brought drinks and sweets for the journey.

We pull into a private underground garage in a modern-looking complex and get out of the car. Sean grabs both of our overnight bags, I carry my camera bag and head for the door. Sean puts in a code and the door buzzes open and heads up the stairs and through into a steel and glass lobby area. Sean nods at the security guard and we make our way up in a lift to the fourth floor.

As we walk down the corridor, only passing a few other doors, it's the only real difference from the look of a hotel corridor. He stops at one of them and unlocks it, pushing it wide and gesturing me inside. There's a little corridor to the right and a door to the left that opens up into a huge living space.

"This is not what I expected. It's a million miles away from the house you share with Dionne."

"Maybe it's the female influence, or lack of it."

It's so stark, minimalistic, straight lines and brushed steel with not a cushion in sight. It's like it belongs to a completely different person.

"Is it so bare because you don't live here?"

"Erm no. This is it normally, living here or not."

"You keep paying rent for this place while you're living in our little back water?"

"No, I own it."

"Very fancy. So is England just a temporary thing then?"

"I really don't know. That was kind of the thought initially. But even if it is a permanent move, I don't want to sell this place. I'll need somewhere to stay when I'm up here, and property like this doesn't come up for sale often. The housing prices here are on a permanent up. So looking for something similar in a few years' time, I'd be well out of pocket."

"Do you pay rent on Dionne's house?" He gives me a look. "Sorry, lots of questions, I'm just curious."

"No. the company owns the house. Megan, then Dionne, pay a below market value rent. But it just goes into a holding account for when they need a deposit on their own place.

"They don't know that so keep that to yourself. I know Megan won't accept it, but also Myles won't need it. He comes from money."

"Myles is her boyfriend?"

"Yes, but he's more than that. I wouldn't be surprised if they came back from this trip married. Let me show you around."

He gestures round the room. "This is the living room, with the kitchen." He walks over to the kitchen and pull open a door to reveal a large but sparse fridge with only the jars and sauces that everyone has in them. He places a shopping bag that I hadn't even noticed onto the work top and empties milk, juice and spread into the fridge and closes the door. "Coffee?" He points to the machine.

"So you really are a coffee addict. That's the same machine as at home. Yes, I'll have one."

"Yeah, it was the first and probably only useful thing I bought for the place down there. Megan furnished it all. Well, I did go with her, but I was just there to carry everything and pay."

"So, did you and Megan have anything romantic together?"

"God no. She's like an annoying little sister. Okay that's not a fair description. She's my best friend and I love her, just not like that. We just get each other, it's a bit weird, I know. People say men and women can't be friends and not be attracted to each other and I can see that in a lot of cases, but not Megan."

"Do you miss her?"

"Yeah." He looks sad.

I look around the rest of the room. There's an island in the middle of the kitchen area that looks like the place he eats. It has four stools along one side and a bottle rack at one end. Over the far corner of the room there are two large windows, with a massive TV in the space in-between. In front of that is a glass and metal coffee table and a very hard, square-looking sofa. The room has no *stuff* in it. No pictures on the wall, no old cards above the fireplace. In fact there is no fireplace. It just seems devoid of personality, colour or warmth. Which is surprising because I wouldn't say Sean is in any way shallow.

"Right, the rest of the flat." He gestures to the door and we head down the hallway. The first room is a small L shaped bedroom, with a window at the end. It's plainly decorated with not much furniture. "The spare room."

"You don't get many visitors then?"

"No, not really. There's an office on the other side, with a door onto the living room, but I only use it if I can't get into the office. I much prefer to work with other people around." He comes out and makes his way further down the corridor. The next door is a spotless bathroom. There is a large, deep bath, with one of those Victorian-looking shower heads resting above the taps. He continues to the end where there's a door that opens up onto a huge bedroom.

"This is my bedroom."

"Wow. My whole house could fit in here." There's a massive bed on one wall and huge windows on the other. There are two doors which I go to inspect. One is a narrow closet, housing clothes only on one side. The next is an ensuite bathroom, which is maybe bigger than the other one. There's a walk-in double shower that takes up the whole of one wall, with mirrored cabinets above the sink.

At least this room has some colour. The walls are a dark navy blue colour and the bed covers match. The floor seems to be the only carpeted place in the flat, its long pile must feel amazing between your toes. "I bet this place has seen a lot of action." I smile towards him, but his face drops.

"No actually. You're the first woman to be in this room, other than my cleaner."

"Is that so? I'm not sure I believe you."

"Believe what you want. I don't bring women back here, just in case..."

"In case what? They stay too long?"

"In case they get too comfortable maybe?"

"Hmm." Sounds about right.

"Anyway, that was the tour. Here's a key. Treat this place like your own."

"But don't get too comfortable." I laugh, he doesn't seem to find it funny for some reason.

"My meeting starts in less than an hour, it'll be a couple of hours."

"I'm gonna head out too, take some shots and generally wander around."

"Do you know where you'll go first?"

"No, I'm just gonna wander, and I have Google maps, so I'll be fine."

"If you need anything, just message, I'll be able to pick them up in the meeting." He looks down at me and I think he's gonna kiss me, but he seems to think better of it. He pulls me in for a hug and walks out the door. I grab my bag and follow him. Let's get this adventure started.

· ♥ · ♥ · ♥ · ♥ · ♥ ·

I knew Edinburgh was beautiful, but I didn't realise just how beautiful until today. I made my way to Princes Street and the hustle and bustle of people going about their normal day, mixed in with tourists, stopping to take photos of all the monuments, and through the beautiful gardens along the route. I have taken loads of pictures, especially from underneath the castle. I've made my way up through the old town and over the cobbled streets.

Sean has messaged me every half hour to make sure I'm not lost or have been kidnapped. It's kind of sweet but I am having the best time just being able to observe and take everything in. The old against the new is a wonder to see. I love the old-style shops selling tourist trinkets and flags. That reminds me, I must pick something up for Cynthia, she's a sucker for a fridge magnet.

My stomach starts to rumble and I realise I've been so involved I forgot to eat. I pull my bag off my back and rummage through the pockets. I always keep some kind of energy bar or snack in here for when I'm out on a shoot.

My phone beeps again.

Sean

How's it going? Taken many photos?

Me

Loads

photo sent

I send him a selfie of me with a bagpipe player. I sent the same photo for Sally because she loves a man in a kilt.

Sean

> Found a friend?

Me

> Yes, but I couldn't understand anything he said.

Sean

> We're just finishing up, the boys suggested going out for a late lunch/early dinner

Me

> Nice, enjoy yourselves

My phone immediately starts ringing.

Chapter Eighteen

Sean

This meeting has gone on a bit and I haven't been paying that much attention, just dipping in when I hear words that I know will involve me. I've messaged Hannah a few times to make sure she's okay. I'm a bit nervous about her being out there all alone in a place she doesn't know. But I needn't be worried – she seems like she's having a ball.

The meeting is to go through our end of quarter finances and our strategies for the next quarter. Seems everything is going along smoothly. Joel, our friend and accountant, has mainly taken us through a million slides about profit and growth. He explains it with such passion, but numbers have never been my thing. I leave that up to Joel here, and Dionne in England. Ben and our other senior project manager, Gareth, have taken us through the plans for the next quarter and beyond.

Something comes back into my mind, something Hannah said about Winford being temporary. I'd always presumed it was, mainly by the nature of how it happened. I didn't know whether Ben and Emma would decide to go back to England and I'd return back here. It's also the reason I didn't really look for somewhere else to live. I have never lived with someone full time before so it's been a bit of an adjustment sharing with Dionne. I think I needed it though because at least I had someone to keep me company while I got to know people better.

Being here with Hannah has made me think a bit more about the future. But I'm only skating by the ideas forming in my head, because they scare the shit out of me.

"Sean... Sean!"

"What?" Ben drags me out of my daydream.

"Are you actually with us today?"

"Of course."

"Joel just suggested we grab something to eat and a few drinks."

"I'm gonna have to rain check I'm afraid," Gareth says.

"We'll let you off, you have a good excuse."

"How long does she have left to go?" I ask. Not being up here permanently I'd kind of forgotten about the everyday lives of the guys in the office. Gareth's wife is pregnant and is a bit of a handful. His words not mine.

"It's her due date today. I got a lot of grief for being here already. But there are no signs of the baby. My sister says there would have been at least a few twinges. Safe to say, she's not too happy about it."

Me

How's it going? Taken many photos?

Hannah

> Loads

> *photo sent*

She's sent me a selfie of her with massive bloke playing the bag pipes, which makes me laugh because it makes her look so small.

Me

> Found a friend?

Hannah

> Yes, but I couldn't understand anything he said.

Me

> We're just finishing up, the boys suggested going out for a late lunch/early dinner

Hannah

> Nice, enjoy yourselves

I look up from my phone and Ben is watching me, eyebrows raised. I look down at my phone, perplexed, so I call her.

"Hey."

"Well hello there." Just the sound of her voice gives me a warm feeling.

"What do you mean enjoy yourselves?"

"Well you're going out with your friends." Ah I understand now, lost in translation, she had me a bit panicked for a minute there.

"No WE are going out with my friends."

"Oh. You want me to come?"

"Obviously."

"Okay then. When and where?"

"I'll drop you a pin of where we are going. We're heading off, but there's no rush if you are in the middle of something."

"Not really."

"Where are you now?"

"Royal Mile."

"The restaurant is back over this way. Do you want me to meet you somewhere or are you okay getting here?"

"I'll be fine. I'll just see you when I get there."

"See you soon." She hangs up and I breathe a sigh of relief. Although I'm not sure I want her round my friends, I do want her with me. I message her the location and put my phone back in my pocket to pay attention to the room again. They are all staring at me. "What?"

"Just friends then?" Ben asks.

"Yes."

"So your face lights up like that whenever I call you?" He smirks at me.

"Fuck off."

"You saw it too, right Joel?" He turns to Joel.

"No comment."

"Which in Joel language is yes, but I don't want Sean to batter me."

"Again, fuck off. We're just friends. Has anyone messaged Piers."

"Not yet. He'll be at work."

I open the group chat and send a message.

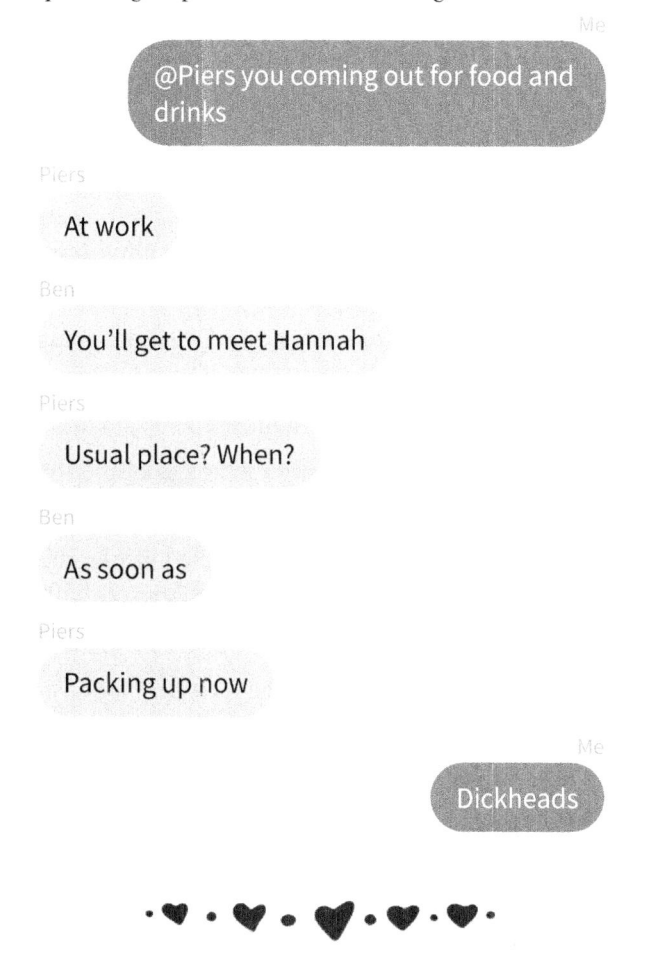

> **Me**
> @Piers you coming out for food and drinks

> **Piers**
> At work

> **Ben**
> You'll get to meet Hannah

> **Piers**
> Usual place? When?

> **Ben**
> As soon as

> **Piers**
> Packing up now

> **Me**
> Dickheads

· ♥ · ♥ · ♥ · ♥ · ♥ ·

We're all sitting round the table chatting away. They have all been briefed to be on their best behaviour, but that means nothing to this lot.

"What do you think Hannah will be drinking?" Ben asks as he's talking to the server.

"Something non-alcoholic. Maybe a virgin cocktail. She's quite liking them at the minute."

"She doesn't drink?"

"Nope."

"How does she cope with you then?" Piers says.

"Fuck off, I'm an absolute delight."

I keep looking over at the door and down at my phone waiting for her. I feel like there's a lot of nervous energy buzzing around me. I can't wait to see her, but I'm also a bit apprehensive of her meeting my friends. The door opens and I see her walk through. I stand up without thinking and head over to meet her. I'm totally not playing anything cool and I've just given my friends more ammunition to use against me.

She's wearing her oversized jumper – she must be roasting walking round in that. The spring sunshine has been out all day. Her camera bag is over her shoulder and all over a sudden I feel awkward. Should I hug her? How do I greet her?

"Hey, sorry it took me so long. I kept getting distracted."

"It's fine. Come over and meet the boys." We walk over to the table and she stands hovering, waiting for introductions. "This is Ben." He stands and shakes her hand. "Joel and Piers." I gesture for her to sit in between me and Joel, probably the safest place to avoid interrogation.

"I've got you a seat here Hannah," Piers says, and she moves to sit next to him.

"Okay I may not remember your names, I'm terrible at that kind of thing. So Ben, you are Megan, no, Emma's boyfriend?"

"That's right, but firstly I was Sean's best friend."

"The girls have told me a lot about you all."

"Wait what, the girls? You're friends with the girls?" Piers lights up.

"Well yes, some of them," I explain.

"Tell us how you know everyone, and how you two met." He points between me and Hannah.

"Well I met a few of them independently of each other, which was kind of weird. Sean came into my café for a coffee. I met Dionne in the Hub. She missed her art class, so I showed her around my dark room. She thought I was gonna murder her or something." Hannah laughs, a sound I just love. "I met Lizzie at the football, that Sean was playing in, but I didn't know he was playing. I was taking some photos for my uncle Mitch. Kateryna and Beth I met at the Dog and Swan when I worked a quick shift."

"Wow! Lizzie put me in my place when I first met her. Brutal." Piers laughs.

"It was hilarious. Wait, Mitch is your uncle? He is a legend," Ben says.

"Kind of. I call him Uncle Mitch but he's just a friend of my parents. And yes, he is a legend. Apart from wearing that bloody t-shirt."

"Megan bought him that for helping out with the ex." Sean explains.

"That was Megan? I never knew. I mean it's a nice t-shirt but he wears it constantly. I think it's actually now a second skin."

"So Hannah, what do you do?" Piers asks.

"In what respect?" She narrows her eyes at him.

"Your job."

"Well my job doesn't define what I do and who I am." That's my girl.

"I didn't mean…"

"I'm just messing with ya Piers." The relief on his face is immense and I laugh. "I work in a café by day, and by night I'm a modern visual artist."

"Eh?"

"A photographer."

"Ah right. Have you been taking some today?"

"Yeah. You wanna see?"

"Hell yeah!"

"Piers, you can't get away with a *hell yeah*, you sound too posh," Ben points out.

Hannah goes into her bag, pulls out the camera and turns the screen towards Piers. They move closer and put their heads together to look at them and a pang of jealousy trickles through my veins. I catch Ben's eye as he's looking for my reaction. How does that guy know me so well? She moves to her other side to show Joel and they both laugh at the photos as they flick through.

She leans over and hands me the camera. "Be careful!" she warns me.

"I'm always careful." I take the camera and Ben moves closer to see. The photos are amazing and she's captured the scenery with such professionalism.

"I'll need to get some of you guys, or the girls will go mad."

"They miss us, I know." Piers beams.

"I think it's just proof of life to be honest." I laugh as his face falls.

"You not been keeping up with your weekly facetiming Piers?"

"I mainly see Sammy and she tells me what's going on."

"You never told me you were meeting with Sammy." My eyebrows raise in a question.

"You never asked."

I hand Hannah back her camera. She leaves it on the table and we all order food. I'm pleased with how the night is going. Hannah isn't falling for the guys' charms and she's giving as good as she gets.

"Well I've told you what I do, I don't know what the rest of you do," Hannah notes while we wait for our food.

"Well my job doesn't define what I do and who I am." Piers laughs. "I'm a banker."

"Figures," Hannah quips.

"No, that's me!" says Joel.

"What?"

"Figures! I'm the accountant."

"Ah you'd get on with Dionne then, do you know her?"

"We haven't met."

"Dionne's got her hands full at the minute," I state.

"With what?"

"Megan's brother-in-law. She's kind of seeing him and he's her boss too. He seems quite demanding. He has her all worked up. But that's a story for another time. Can we order some more drinks?"

Everyone murmurs agreement.

Chapter Nineteen

Hannah

We've eaten and laughed about anything and everything. The food was delicious. I've tried things I never thought I would, and the company has been excellent. It's felt easy and comfortable and I don't often feel that way in groups of people, especially groups who know each other but don't know me.

I've heard tales of when Ben and Sean were at university and about how they all met each other. It's been really nice. I've taken a selfie of us all, just with my phone, and I'm about the send it to the girls. They all made out that Ben was the good looking one of the group, but it's definitely Sean in my eyes. Piers seems like on the surface he's full of himself, but underneath it's all just a show, he's very sensitive and unsure of himself. But I really like him.

Joel is obsessed by numbers, he would get on really well with Kateryna, but I think she'd eat him alive. He seems really shy and doesn't put himself in the forefront of anything.

I open the girls group chat.

> **Me**
> Look at the hotties I met up with
>
> *photo*

Emma
Oh I wish I could have met up with you while you were up, but I've got a work thing.

Beth
What a bunch of fitties

Dionne
Hot stuff

Lizzie
Punch Piers for me

Kat
Nice

> **Me**
> Kat – Joel says he's up for some number crunching if you are

Dionne
What about me?

> **Me**
> You've got your hands full

Dionne

sad face

I put my phone away with a little chuckle. "The girls say hi."

"I bet they didn't," Piers says.

"Actually, Lizzie told me to punch you."

"That's more like it," he says with a smile.

"Right, let's make tracks." Sean starts to get up from the table.

"I need to pay for my share."

"No you don't, it's a work meal," Ben insists.

"I don't work for you!" I say, eyes wide.

"Not yet, but we might want some promo photos doing at some point. We'll call this a fact-finding meal."

Sean steers me towards the door. "Hang on, we haven't said bye yet." Sean rolls his eyes as each one in turn comes and gives me a hug.

"Have you all quite finished?" Sean pulls me towards to door, his face unamused, as I wave goodbye.

Out in the street, dusk has set in and the sky is an orangey-red. I didn't realise we had been there for so long. Sean turns to me. "You okay? I know they can sometimes be a bit much."

"I'm good. I loved being around them, they're fun."

"Well... now I want you all to myself. It's about a mile and a half back to mine. Are you okay to walk? Or we could get a cab – you've been walking all day."

"I can walk." He grabs my hand and pulls me up the street. "You're breaking one of the rules Sean." I smirk.

He immediately drops my hand. "Sorry."

"Just because you've had a few to drink, doesn't mean the rules go out of the window." I say, jokingly.

"I haven't had a few to drink." He says matter of factly.

"I saw you drinking bottles of beer all afternoon."

"I had one beer, then I went onto alcohol free."

"How come?"

"Well if you're not drinking, I'm not drinking."

"I don't mind, you know. Just because I don't, doesn't mean you can't."

"I know. But I wanted a clear head."

"In case I took advantage of you?"

"Again? Maybe." He laughs. "Or maybe because I wanted to take it all in." We fall silent for a bit, I don't know what's running through his brain right now, but mine is a jumble of all kinds of thoughts.

I feel like we've been walking for miles. "How much further is it? I'm exhausted."

"I did warn you. It's about another mile."

"You didn't warn me that it'd be all uphill!"

"Come on then, get on." He squats down and points over his shoulder. I give him a look of horror. "I'll give you a piggyback."

"No way, I'm way too heavy!"

He rolls his eyes. "Shut up, there's nothing to you. I probably bench press twice your weight."

"Whatever. You've been warned. And only because I feel like I couldn't walk another step." I wrap my arms round his neck and do a little jump onto his back. He catches my legs and bumps me into place. As he stands straight up with ease I see the world from a whole different perspective.

"Comfortable?"

"Hardly! Wow is this the way you see the world?" I joke. "The air is so much thinner." He pretends to drop me and I let out a screech.

"Cheeky." He smacks my bum and I yelp again. "I was thinking we could have a bit of a touristy day out tomorrow. Grab some lunch and then we could head out again. I can show you a bit of Edinburgh night life in the evening."

"Sounds good."

He stops still. "I don't think we'll get through that door. Can you walk now you've had a break?" I look up and I realise we're standing outside his building.

"Yep! I've had a nice little rest." He lets go of my legs and I slide down his back until my feet reach the floor. He takes hold of my hand, but this time I say nothing. He pulls me through the foyer towards to lift. I feel the nerves flush through my body as we wait for it to arrive.

The ping brings me back to earth. The doors open and we step in. But before the doors close Sean is towering over me. He bends down as his mouth meets mine. It takes me a bit by surprise and I pull away to try and catch my breath. "Breaking rule two again…" I say.

"I thought we were having sex in the lift."

He smiles as he sees the shock cross my face, but I'm spared any more as the lift opens on his floor and we both step out and head to the front door. The atmosphere has changed. It's like he wants to say something but doesn't know what the reaction will be. He unlocks the door, opens it and enters, passing through the hall and into the living area.

He makes his way over to the sink, gets a glass from the top cupboard and fills it with water from the sink. I watch every move he makes. He turns to me and lifts the glass as if silently asking if I want one. But I shake my head. I need to know what he's thinking, but if I ask him outright, he's likely to fob me off. Instead I ask, "where am I sleeping?"

He looks at me for a few beats and then answers. "I was hoping you would stay in my bed... with me. But if you'd rather not, that's okay, the spare room is ready."

"Okay."

"Okay what? My bed or the spare bed?"

"Your bed." The tension leaves his face.

"I thought you were having second thoughts for a minute."

"And I thought we were gonna have some open communication, because you just shut down on me there."

"Sorry, I was overthinking." He stalks over and wraps his arms around me. "Can I kiss you now?"

"I suppose."

He puts his hand round the back of my neck and pulls me into a chased kiss. He pulls away and looks at me, licking his lips, like he's hungry for me. At last he moves in for a deeper, toe-tingling kiss, as I feel the lust rise up through my body.

I pull away. "Wait. I can't, I'm disgusting. I've been fleeing round all day and I'm really sweaty."

"Shower then?" His eyes turn mischievous and he pulls me back through the hall and into his bedroom. We pass his bed and go straight into the bathroom. He finally let's go of me and starts to strip off. I just stare at him, not quite registering what is happening.

"What are you doing?"

"We're getting in the shower."

"Together?"

"Oh yes," He says with a grin, then frowns. "You can't be self-conscious? I've already seen you naked."

"I know, but I was delirious at the time. I haven't seen you naked."

"You've seen the best bits." He's fully naked now. He turns and steps into the shower, turning it on in a swift motion. Oh my god, I had not seen the best bits until now. He has the roundest, most peachy bum, on top of those thick, hard, gorgeous thighs. You know those posters you had on your bedroom wall when you were a teenager. The ones we used to drool over as we imagined the perfect man. They are nothing compared to this sight. I'm dumb struck and possibly dribbling now. "You're not in the shower Hannah." His tone is firm and, as if I can't do anything other than what he commands, I start to undress. I don't want to I take my eyes of his perfectly sculptured body.

Kicking my clothes to the side, I step into the shower as he turns towards me. He moves us both round so I'm fully under the water. "Let's get you washed." I actually have no idea what I'm doing. Who is this person I have become? Taking showers with fit men, being all naked. I have never showered with someone else before – I've never felt the need. But this man is something else.

He takes a bottle of shower gel, squirts some onto his palm, lathers it up and places both hands on my shoulders. Shoulders that are nearer to my ears than they are anything else. I think he feels my apprehension and is going slow. He gently rubs his hands up and down my arms to try and ease some tension, before pushing them over my shoulders and down my back. The whole time his eyes have never left mine and the heat is rising between us. As he strokes down my back for the second time, he dips his head and kisses me on the lips.

I'm so taken by the tingling on my lips that I barely notice him soaping my breasts until he touches my already very hard and very sensitive nipples. I gasp. "This okay?"

"They are sensitive."

"They are amazing."

"They are annoying."

"Shut up and turn around. Hands on the wall."

"Bossy."

"Do you need your hair washing?"

"No, I did it this morning." He lathers his hands up again and washes my back, then pulls my hips back towards him so I'm stretched to the wall.

"Legs apart." I do as I'm told, which is completely unlike me and with one movement his hand slips between my legs and is washing that very intimate part of me. I let out a moan as his fingers dip inside me. I can't believe I'm actually about to have shower sex. He pulls his fingers out and presses his body up against me and kisses my neck. I can feel how hard he is as his breath hitches with each touch of his lips. "Hannah, do you want this?" I nod in agreement. "I need to hear you say it."

"I want this." And without hesitation he pushes forward and pulls me up, his arms holding me round the waist, as he moves and slides inside me, filling me up. He better not ask me anything else because I can no longer function. The pleasure of his slow measured movement is building throughout my body and I can't stop the moans from coming out of my mouth.

"Hannah, what are you doing to me?" He pulls away and whips me round to face him. He keeps me upright with one arm around my waist. But before I've found my balance he's scooped me up, wrapping my legs around him. I squeal as my back hits the cold, damp tiles on the wall.

His lips crash down on mine at the same time as he pushes inside. I'm overtaken as my climax builds with his rhythm. I feel completely full, completely surround by him. I can feel I'm on the edge and just the slightest thing will push me over. He must sense it too because he pulls his mouth away from mine and kisses down my chest until he reaches my nipple. He sucks it into his mouth. In that moment I'm completely overcome. The orgasm sweeps over me and I see stars. He's not far behind as he groans into my shoulder.

With me still in his arms he slides down the wall and sits us on the floor of the shower. It's still gushing water everywhere and our foreheads are pressed together. We sit catching out breaths for what seems an age, until he says, "we better move or we'll be stuck here forever."

"I'm not sure I can, I've lost feeling in every muscle." He lifts me off him and places me on the floor as he tries to get up. Eventually standing straight he turns the water off. Grabbing a towel with one hand he helps me to my feet. "Sorry I was meant to be getting you clean, not dirty again." He wraps the towel round me and pulls me close, kissing me on the nose, before wrapping another around his waist.

"I think I'll let you off."

"Let's get into bed before I collapse."

"I need my bag with my pyjamas in."

"You won't be needing them." He guides me out of the bathroom and around the side of the bed, lifting the covers to usher me in. I think we can safely say I'm not gonna be getting any sleep tonight.

Chapter Twenty

Sean

As I start to come round, my body feels all kinds of tired, but the most overwhelming feeling currently is something covering my body. I'm lying on my back, one arm behind my head. And I'm half-covered in a warm, soft weight. I start to prise my eyelids open and see her blonde hair across my chest, one arm and one leg over my body, her seriously amazing bum just out of the covers.

My mind goes back to last night. I have slept with quite a few women, but this woman is something else. She's just so unapologetically Hannah. In the past few years I've had the same set of women that I hook up with, and looking back, they were all carbon copies of each other. Fake lashes, fake nails, fake personalities and fake tits. They all looked the same way and acted the same way, like they were all playing a role. Mainly a role from a porn movie, with their over-exaggerated thrusting and moaning. And for a bloke in his late twenties, that's the ultimate dream. Until it isn't. And I think I've come down to earth with a bump.

Hannah is completely different. She's a little self-conscious about her body, and God knows she doesn't need to be. But that goes out of the window when she's in the moment. She gives out little gasps and moans that show me how she likes something. She's not performing, she's just feeling and it's like a revelation. I've never really realised how fake these other girls really were until I came across the real thing.

I nearly lost all feeling in my body in the shower last night. The climax that came over me was something I'd never felt before and all because of the way Hannah moulded around my body. But I couldn't get enough and I had to have her over and over again until we were so exhausted that sleep took over. Just being with her, waking up with her, is something else. Hannah is the kind of girl you fall in love with.

Jeez, where did that come from? The panic starts to rise up from my stomach. I really can't be feeling this way, we're only meant to be friends and I vowed to myself I would never get myself in that position again – a position where I could get hurt and lose everything.

I try to inch myself away from her – emotionally and physically – and slip out of bed without waking her. I'd love to continue our session this morning but I need to put barriers up and separate last night from today, or things will get messy. I pull my boxers on and head for the kitchen. Today is going to require a lot of coffee.

About half an hour later I spot Hannah over my phone and look up. She's even more beautiful every time I see her. "Morning beautiful. Coffee?"

"Hello Handsome." She smiles. "Coffee would be amazing." I turn and grab a cup and place it under the coffee machine, press the button and the coffee beans ground around, filling the silence.

I place her cup on the worktop as she takes a seat on the stool. "What's planned for today then?"

"Well, I thought we could go to the National Museum of Scotland."

"Sounds fancy."

"It's a nice, fun place. Then maybe we could go to a gallery of your choice. We could have lunch out, then later I could take you to see the Edinburgh night life in all its glory."

"Sounds fun."

"Get yourself dressed and we'll head out."

"Will we be coming back before tonight or do I need to dress for all occasions?"

"We can play it by ear, aim to stay out but we can come back if we need to."

"Can I have a shower?"

"Yes of course."

About 45 minutes later we're ready and head off to do some sightseeing. The first stop is the Museum of Scotland. I used to love coming here as a kid. We walk through the entrance and the look of awe across Hannah's face makes her look even more beautiful.

We explore all the different rooms and exhibits, my favourite being the full-scale dinosaur. Hannah seemed to love the fashion bits. We spent all day hand-in-hand, exploring and chatting. Everything seems so natural.

We visit the portrait gallery and look at all the massive paintings. Well Hannah does. All I can do the entire time is watch her. As she takes in every detail of the paintings, I take in every detail of her. I've never before wanted to spend all my time with just one other person and it's brilliant. But bloody scary. When I'm with her, I don't want to think about anything else, except the here and now.

We stop off for a bit of lunch and then carry on our walk around the city before deciding we'd head back home to have a rest and get changed before heading back out for the nightlife. So we make our way back to the flat.

Chapter Twenty-One

Hannah

We've had a lovely day out. Sean has shown me the sights, we've had an amazing meal and now we are in the smartest bar I have ever been in. It's a world away from the Dog and Swan, with its high ceilings and posh décor. I'm glad I brought something a little more nightlife-y to come out in.

I look around at the colourful shelves with hundreds of different bottles of booze and styles of glasses. The place is really busy, but not with the same vibe I'm used to. There's no indication that it could kick off at any moment. The place even smells different, of expensive perfume and sweet alcohol rather than stale beer and the men's toilets.

Sean spoke to the woman at the door who escorted us over to a high table with stools around it, and as I haul myself up onto one, he orders drinks. I'm not very adventurous with drinks, so

I like that he takes the lead. He sees a few people he knows and gives them a little wave, but instantly focuses back on me.

"Have you had a good time?"

"Yes, I really have. I has taken my mind off everything."

"You didn't really tell me how this thing with the gallery will work."

"Well it's a three-month thing initially. The gallery has a sponsored opening for an artist. The lucky artist will learn how the gallery works and work within it. They pay for your accommodation and you get to hold an exhibition in their gallery."

"So you'd be away for three months?"

"Initially yes. Then they'd see how it goes."

"Have you thought about how you'll support yourself? London is an expensive place."

"I have some money saved for this kind of thing and I can still sell my prints online while I'm there, just nothing from the exhibition."

"Sounds like a great opportunity." But his expression doesn't fit his words. Like he's a bit lost.

"Tell your face that."

"Sorry. I will be thrilled if you get it, I'll just miss you, that's all."

"I haven't got it yet. And it seems less likely now. They had thousands of applications so it's probably not going to happen. You are stuck with me a while longer."

"I love being stuck with you." He looks over my shoulder and his face drops. "Oh god."

"Sean?" I turn around to see a long-legged, slim woman, her blonde hair curled over her shoulders and down her chest in ringlets. She flutters her thick eyelashes. I'm not sure whether it's to look more attractive or whether the sheer weight of them are pulling her lids down. I've got to say she smells amazing. She totters past me and kisses Sean, who by now looks embarrassed, on the cheek. "Are you going to introduce us?"

Now she's in front of me I have a better view. Her legs go on for miles and her dress is so tight it leaves nothing to the imagination. I'm so envious of a body like that. All in proportion and balanced.

"Cheryl, this is my friend Hannah. Hannah this is Cheryl."

"Hi." I give her a warm smile that she doesn't even try to return.

"Hmm…" She looks me up and down. "Back so soon?"

"Business meeting." I have a feeling these two have a history, but he's being very abrupt.

"Well, maybe I'll see you later then?"

"I don't think so." She gives him a little grin and saunters off.

"Who was she?" I ask.

"Just someone I used to know."

"A friend?"

"Not really." He takes a drink and shakes his head. It seems to snap out of his mood. "So, that there London. It'll be fun if you do get it. What's your plan if you don't?"

"No clue. I'll just keep doing what I'm doing, I suppose."

"I mean, five years down the line would you want your own gallery or to travel the world taking photos?"

"You've a lot more faith in my abilities than I have."

"You just need to stop and have a think about what you want for your life."

"Maybe. And on that note, I need to pop to the bathroom." I jump down off the stool and head to the back of the bar. I push through the door into the toilets and come to an amazed halt. The place is more like a boudoir than a convenience. Huge, gilded mirrors and shiny surfaces. As I'm washing my hands, I feel a presence behind me and look up into the mirror. The woman from before is standing behind me.

"So you're the new one?" The venom in her tone is evident.

"New what?"

"I wondered why he was keen to leave last week when we hooked up."

"What are you talking about?"

"You're not really his type." She gestures her hand up my body, "all rough round the edges. He'll get bored of you in no time and be begging me for more." It's like she's having a conversation with herself.

Who the hell does this woman think she is? I don't stand for this kind of shit from anyone. "Is that so? I didn't think he went for fake. He usually likes his things limited edition, unique."

"But he doesn't usually like them fat and geeky. Even he has limits. Why don't you just get back to your back water and leave the adults to play?"

"Fuck off Barbie."

"It's Cheryl." She says with no note of irony.

"Whatever!" I turn and walk out of the room, reeling from the confrontation. So, Sean was with her the other week? He didn't mention it. Was this before or after the exclusivity conversation? Plus, who would want to hook up with her? The self-doubt creeps in again because who would want to be with me? I walk over to our table and Sean's face falls as soon as he sees me. "What's up?"

"I don't feel too good. Can we go home?"

"Yes sure, is there anything I can do?"

"No." I walk past him, straight out of the door and onto the street. He catches up in no time and hails a cab. And just like in the films, one turns up straight away and he opens the door for me.

We sit through the entire journey in silence and reach the flat within minutes. He pays the driver and we head up to the flat.

"Is everything okay?"

"Fine."

"We all know fine doesn't actually mean fine." I just shrug at him as we make our way into the living area.

"I think I should sleep in the spare room tonight." Emotion devoid from my voice.

"If that's what you want." He looks confused. Well that makes two of us.

"Yes. I'm actually really tired. I might go to bed now."

"Okay."

I turn, head to the bedroom and close the door after me. I don't know how I'm meant to feel about all this, but I just can't sort these millions of thoughts buzzing round my head.

There's a gentle knock on the door. Sean opens it and puts his head round the door. "I brought your bag and a glass of water."

"Thanks." He puts my bag inside the door and the glass on the bedside table before he turns to leave. He hesitates at the door. He turns to look at me as if he wants to say more but thinks better of it. He leaves and closes the door behind him.

Several hours pass of me tossing and turning, regretting not speaking to Sean about it. I finally bite the bullet and get myself out of bed and make my way to Sean's bedroom. I open the door and peer in. The blinds have been left open slightly. The light that streams in highlights his amazing body. He's lying in bed with one arm over his head, his muscles standing out in the shadows. His chest rising with his even sleep breaths.

I make my way over to the bed before I change my mind I lift the covers that are pooled over his waist. I slide into bed and put my arms around him and snuggle in.

"Hey!" he says, sleepily, leaning into me.

"Hey."

"Feeling better?"

"No, not really."

"What's up?"

"I got a bit in my head."

"Do you want to talk about it?"

"I had a visit from your mate in the bathroom."

"Mate?"

"Barbie."

"Ah. What did she say?"

"She said you hooked up the other week." He seems to tense a little, so I gather there is some kind of truth in it.

"That was the intention. But it just felt wrong."

"So you didn't hook up?"

"No. I went round and changed my mind almost immediately."

"How come?"

"I think I was only really there because I was wound up. I wanted to escape my own head. But she was just not what I wanted or needed. So I left."

"What did you want?"

"You."

"Oh…"

"Let's talk more in the morning. I can't form words right now, I'm so tired."

"Okay." I smile knowing that even before we got close, he chose me.

"Close your eyes and stop thinking."

"Okay." I do as I'm told and fall fast asleep.

Chapter Twenty-Two

Sean

I haven't seen Hannah in a few days. Even though we had that little incident with Cheryl, I thought everything was fine. The drive home was quiet, but I put that down to us both being tired. I think the weekend has rattled us both in different ways. But we've messaged and seen each other since, so I thought it had all blown over.

We even went out to see a film in the week. We had a nice time, or at least I thought we did. We came out and bumped into Woody and after that Hannah seemed to go quiet. And we haven't spoken since. But now I need a distraction. I'd usually message Hannah but that seems off the cards right now. I pull my phone out and message my friend.

> **Me**
> You up to anything? I need a distraction

> **Jonathan**
> Xbox. I've had a row with Lizzie and I'm back at the flat. Come over, we can be miserable together.

> **Me**
> On my way.

I get to Jonathan's flat and knock on the door.

The door opens. "Alright mate. You don't look the best." Jon looks worse than I feel.

"Thanks."

"No offense," I say, holding my hands up.

"Actually some taken, this is me at my best." He laughs. "Come on in, you want a beer?"

"May as well."

Jonathan's place is the ultimate in-between pad. The ones that newly divorced men get when they leave their wives. Nothing matches, there's no kind of design to anything – it's just an existence. Somewhere to eat and sleep. Which is funny because Jonathan has been separated from Lizzie for a few years now. The flat is big enough for him to have the two kids stay over but is a world away from luxury. Like it was never meant to be permanent. I wonder why he didn't find somewhere else, move on.

"So what's up with you?"

"Dunno, I feel a bit... I'm actually not sure. Why are you hiding away in here playing with yourself, so to speak?"

"I've fucked up and I'm not sure what to do." He heads to the fridge and pull out two bottles of beer and hands me one before he points over to the sofa.

"Okay, spill." I move to sit down.

"Me and Lizzie fell out. I thought she was being over dramatic about something, but it turns out she was right."

"You better start from the beginning."

"So there's this colleague at work and we get on really well. She's on the other team, so we don't work with each other permanently. She sometimes comes out for a drink after work with everyone. We get on, as friends."

"Seems fine."

"Lizzie has a bit of a bee in her bonnet about her. She says that Helen wants to be more than friends. So when Helen started to turn up at football, Lizzie wasn't happy. But she came to see everyone not just me, so as far as I was concerned, she was just seeing things that weren't there."

"Was that the other week when Lizzie gave you the silent treatment on the way home?"

"Yes."

"And this Helen, was she the one that was all bouncy on the touchline?"

"That's her."

"Yes mate, she's definitely got a thing for you."

His face drops. "You could see it too?"

"She did keep touching you. Does she know how things are with you and Lizzie?"

"I don't even know how things are with me and Lizzie. But as far as people at work know, we have kids together and we are amicable. The footy lads know more but it's not common knowledge that we are on and off."

"So Lizzie is unhappy about her being around?"

"No, it gets worse. Helen messages me every so often, not about anything really, just memes and work stuff. But the other night she messaged asking for help with a leaking tap, could I go round."

"And what time was this?"

"Nine. I was at Lizzie's and we were going to watch a movie but couldn't find anything. I said I was gonna go to Helen's to fix this tap and she went off it. We had a massive argument and I told her she was seeing things that weren't there. So she basically told me if I went over there, I wasn't to come back."

"Don't tell me you went."

"Yes. I just couldn't see what the fuss was about. And I didn't like to be told what to do."

"So what happened?"

"I went round and she answered the door in almost sleep-wear. Nothing revealing, just a bit familiar. Like a vest and shorts, with a big baggy cardigan thing over."

"Tell me by then you were getting some alarm bells."

"Well a few, but I thought I'd just fix her tap and leave."

"Actually fixing her tap or is that some kind of euphemism?" He gives me the *not funny* look.

"So I go in and fix the tap. It was really simple. A few more alarm bells went off, cos she's a capable woman, good detective, she could have just YouTubed it. But then she leans in, asks how she can repay me and tries to kiss me."

"Shit. What did you do?"

"I freaked out and legged it. Mumbled something about being with Lizzie and ran out the door."

"And you haven't told Lizzie?"

"I don't know how to."

"Grovel. Women have a sixth sense for these kinds of things."

"Yes, but I don't even know how to start that conversation. Plus I don't even know what we're doing. Are we together, are we just casual, what?" He gives a big sigh.

"I don't know what to say mate."

"How about you tell me your woes. Maybe that will make me feel better."

"I don't know where to start with that either." I take a deep breath and start to explain. "The short version is that me and Hannah started a *friends with benefits* arrangement. And one of us has caught feelings."

"Oh. I take it she wants more."

I just look at him for a minute because I haven't even admitted it to myself yet. "No, me!"

"Oh! Is this a bad thing? Does she not want to?"

"She does want more too, I think."

"Okay, I feel like I'm missing something here. What's the issue?"

"I swore I'd never be in a relationship again."

"Things change."

"Not this drastically. I don't really want to go into the details but I just can't give more."

"Looks like we're both screwed then. Can we just not talk anymore and play a game?"

"Fine by me."

Chapter Twenty-Three

Hannah

This last week has been, for want of a better word, boring. It's been the same old routine, every day. Work in the café, go home for something to eat and then back out to the dark room, with sprinkles of trips to the Post Office.

The only saving grace was that I went out to see a movie with Sean. All in all it was great, a bit of an action movie but it didn't matter, it was a good distraction. The problem was it left a little bit of a bitter taste afterwards. He did make up for it after we got back to mine but that makes things even more confusing.

As we were leaving, we bumped into one of Sean's football friends and his girlfriend. I think his name was Woody or something. Anyway, everything was fine until the whole conversation turned to *No, we're just friends*. And I know it shouldn't annoy me, but he's not acting like *Just Friends*. I'd actually rather him say *We're friends, but we actually sleep together too but we're not in a relationship.* At least it's the truth. And I know we decided to keep the whole thing quiet, but that, with also being exclusive, is starting to be a bit tricky.

His work mate Liam keeps coming into the café and chatting me up, asking me out, and I keep having to find excuses. I mean no should really mean no, without having to give a reason, but some men can't seem to work that out. Just because you're available, doesn't mean you will automatically want to date them.

In fact, I need to knock that on the head once and for all, so I message him to sort it himself.

Me
> Hey

Sean
> Hey

Me
> Can you either tell Liam that I'm not interested or that we're sleeping together?

Sean
> Why? What's happened?

Me
> Because we're *just friends* he thinks it's okay to keep asking me out and won't take no for an answer

> **Sean**
> I'll sort it.
>
> Are you okay?

> **Me**
> Fine

> **Sean**
> Fine

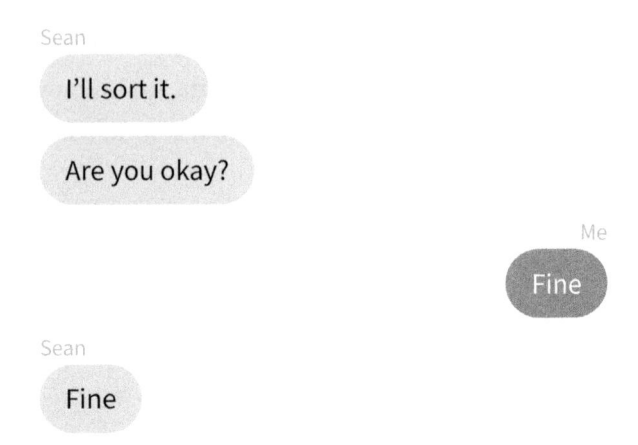

My phone beeps again and I think it might be Sean trying to delve for more on what's gotten into me. But it's not.

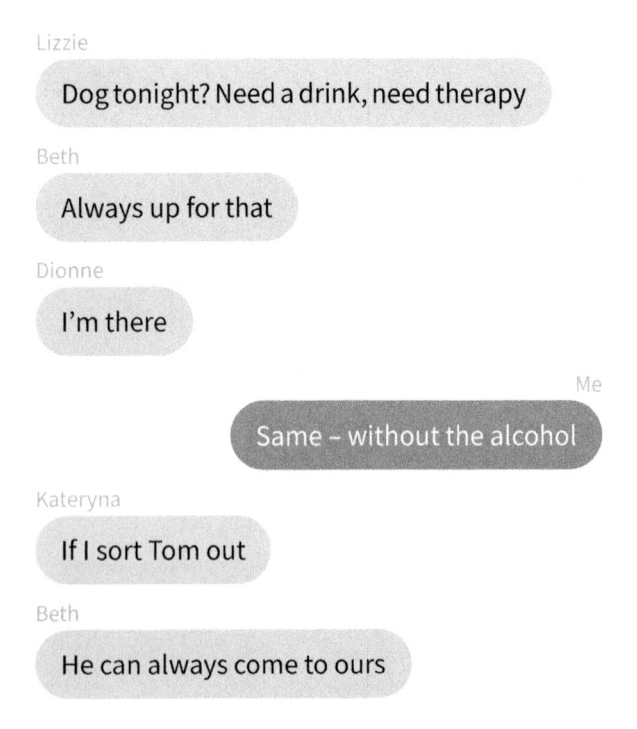

> **Lizzie**
> Dog tonight? Need a drink, need therapy

> **Beth**
> Always up for that

> **Dionne**
> I'm there

> **Me**
> Same – without the alcohol

> **Kateryna**
> If I sort Tom out

> **Beth**
> He can always come to ours

Kateryna

Think he sleep at friends. I'll see

At least it's not just me having a mind melt. My phone beeps again and I pick it up, thinking it's a continuation from the girls. But no.

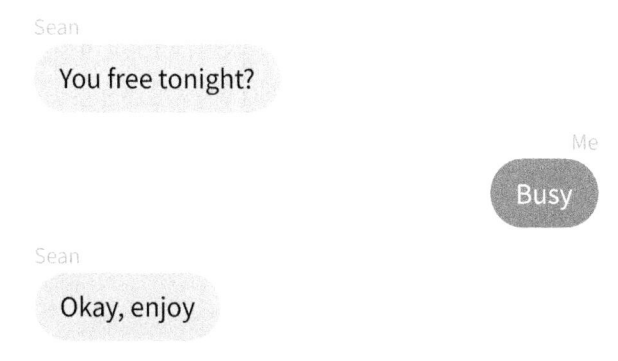

Sean

You free tonight?

Me

Busy

Sean

Okay, enjoy

So we're at that point then. He hasn't even asked what I'm doing. Maybe I am just wanted for a hook up. This has all got as bit much.

The Dog and Swan, how I love this place. I push through the door and see the girls in their usual spot and head over, waving at Mitch behind the bar as I go. We do our usual hugs, and everyone takes their seats again.

"Mitch has got these new fruity mixers that I thought you might like to try." Lizzie points to the drink already on the table. It's so lovely that the girls have taken on board my alcohol-free life, I often need to just keep reminding people. My mother is the same. She constantly asks if I want a glass of wine, and when I say 'no I don't drink' she just scoffs.

"Thanks."

"How was Edinburgh?"

"It was really nice. Did loads of sightseeing. Oh yes, and I met the boys, which was hilarious."

"Oh I'd love to meet up with them again soon." Beth sighs.

"You just want another bender in Edinburgh."

"True. Did you go to any nice restaurants?"

"Oh yeah, we went to this bar that was way out of my league. They must go there often though. It was so far from this place it was unreal. It was called something like Crystals or something."

"Oh my god, that's where we met the boys." Beth bounces with excitement.

"It really is something else," Lizzie says.

"Yes, it was lovely. Except I got cornered in the bathroom by one of Sean's old flames and she was a bitch."

"What did she say?" Lizzie eyes widen.

"She called me fat."

"Bitch."

"And geeky."

"She didn't!" Beth puts her hand over her mouth.

"Yes. But I'll take geeky cos that's a compliment. Oh and I'm not Sean's type, he'd get bored of me and go back to wanting her. Or something like that. Even though Sean had told her we were friends."

"Are you just friends?"

I shrug. "I don't really want to answer that question to be honest."

"You know she didn't have a thing with Sean, she was just a distraction," says Lizzie.

"I don't really care, it was just, why would you confront another woman like that?"

"Jealousy." Beth pulls a face.

"What does Barbie have to be jealous of?" I ask.

"Clearly you, you're gorgeous."

"Anyway, I don't want her to take up any of my mental space. I've already voodoo dolled her, so we're good."

"Come on then, spill!" Dionne looks to Lizzie, the whole reason the meet up was called.

"Oh well. I've had a falling out with Jon."

"Oh no! What happened?" Beth looks concerned.

"He went round to fix a colleague's leaking tap."

"Right, that doesn't sound too bad," I chip in.

"For context, the colleague is a woman who fawns all over him, messages all the time, has no boundaries what so ever. And because me and Jon are not officially back together, she thinks he's fair game. He also can't see what's happening. So we argued about it and he went anyway."

"That's not good."

"No. I wouldn't be surprised if she opened the door to him naked."

"You don't really think that would happen?" Beth looks shocked again.

"She's even started to come and watch him play football."

"Could she be there to watch the others?" I play devil's advocate.

"That's what he said, but I don't believe it for one minute. She like bounces up and down on the spot when she sees him walking over to her."

"Ah shit, she has it bad."

"Yes, but there's no telling Jonathan."

"How did you leave it?"

"I told him if he went, bearing in mind it was nine at night, he wasn't to come back."

"And?"

"He went and didn't come back."

"And how do you feel about it?" This is definitely an adhoc counselling session.

"Honestly? I'm devasted." I've never seen Lizzie upset, tears pooling in the corners of her eyes.

"You don't think anything happened, do you?"

"I don't know, but he made the choice and it wasn't me. But because we didn't decide whether to get back together properly or not, he has every right to find someone else."

"But did he know what he was choosing between?" I question.

"What do you mean?"

"Well men can be particularly stupid at times. Did he think he was choosing between you and her romantically, or did he choose between staying with you to watch TV or helping a friend out?" I try to reframe the situation to give a bit of perspective. "I mean, even though we can all see how this woman is acting, maybe he really can't see it. Maybe for him it would be the same as one of the lads asking for help if their car broke down."

"Can you lot stop being so reasonable and let me wallow?" Lizzie folds her arms across her chest and slumps in her chair.

"Yeah, sure. He's a dick, he doesn't deserve you."

"Idiot."

"You know I know people who could get him killed. Or even better, her." She says in a hushed voice and I totally believe her.

"It always goes one step darker when Kat's involved." Beth laughs.

"Can someone else cheer me up with their times of woe? Dionne, how's Seb?"

"He's a prick. I think I'm gonna quit."

"That's more like it." Lizzie responds, happy in some way that its not just her.

"No, you love working there," Beth pleads. She looks concerned again. Beth is definitely the maternal one of the group.

"Okay. Maybe just go back to my old job."

"Yes, we need you. Those guys on team are useless." Kat nods her head as if it's been agreed.

"I just can't work with his demands."

"Is that work demands or sex demands?" Lizzie asks.

"Both."

"Well, Jonah has asked to take up snowboarding." Beth changes the subject.

"Ah…"

"Yes. So not only do I have to shell out for expensive kit, but also, I'll probably need to take insurance out on him."

"Whose idea was that?"

"They had a taster session with school."

"A bit random."

"I'm pretty sure the school is getting some kind of kickback from it, in one form or another."

Everyone nods in agreement. The conversation carries on about every day comings and goings of life, until it's time to call it a night.

I step out into the cold night air, arm in arm with Dionne. Her house is close and mine isn't far from that, so we've decided to walk.

"Do you want to tell me what's happening with you and Sean? I could mind my own business, but I just don't want to."

"It's complicated."

"He's a bloke, it's always complicated. I know he likes you."

"How?"

"Because of his moods. He was different when he came back from Edinburgh. More relaxed. Unlike the time before. His little face lights up when you text, aww." She pulls a soppy face. "When you're around it's like he has love heart eyes."

"Oh stop. That's ridiculous. We are in a *friends with benefits* situation. He doesn't want a relationship, and I thought I could handle that. But the amount of times he says, we're *just friends*, while knowing we're not just friends is really winding me up. And it shouldn't, because it was me that wanted to keep it quiet. But he acts like we are in a relationship until we bump into someone we know. I know it seems totally hypocritical of me to want both."

"Then you've got to ask yourself, what are you willing to put up with? Does it upset you so much that you'd rather not see him anymore?"

"I don't know."

"How would you feel if he started dating someone else?"

"Murderous. Only because he said he didn't want a relationship." Okay maybe not ONLY.

"Okay, what if you called it off and he went into a *friends with benefits* thing with someone else?"

"It actually makes my skin crawl just thinking about it."

"So maybe you need that conversation with him."

"Maybe, but he won't change his mindset. So what do I do then?"

"I really don't know. What's best for you? Do you completely throw in the towel or do you keep going round in circles of non-commitment?"

"Hmm." Those thought have been running round my head too.

"Don't listen to me, what do I know? I'm getting strung along by a player."

We arrive at the end of her road and she gives me a hug. "Do you want me to get Sean to walk you home? Give you a chance to talk?"

"No, I need some thinking time."

"Okay, message me when you get in." I give her a little wave and carry on in the direction of my house.

My mind whirls with all kinds of questions, all kinds of situations and possibilities playing out in my head, but I'm coming up with no answers. I've zoned out and am on auto pilot, until the sound of footsteps behind me filters through my thoughts. The steps are getting quicker and the keys that were in my pocket are now in my hand, ready to be used to defend myself.

I wish I had gone to self-defence classes with Verity. I turn quickly before they can get too close. At least if I know what

I'm up against I might have a chance. A familiar figure closes in on me.

"For fuck's sake Drew. Why are you creeping up on women?"

"I'm not creeping up on women, I wanted to talk to you." From his demeanour, I think its more than just a talk.

"Could you not have called?" I try to dismiss him.

"This wouldn't have translated." He shoves me against the wall, which takes me by surprise. "You, Hannah Spanner, have got me in some deep shit with Dad." Even in the dark I can see his face is flushed, his eyes have taken on a dark edge, and in all honesty, I am scared of what he might do next.

"You got yourself in trouble." I try to sound confident and not give him the pleasure of seeing me panic.

"Now I have to pay him the money you demanded, and he's put off my promotion at work."

"Fucking grow up Drew." His eyes narrow and I can smell the beer on his breath. He raises his arm as if to grab my jumper, but before I can react there's motion to the side of me and Drew is on the floor.

Sean stands over him, panting. He looks like he might actually kill him. "Never fucking touch her again," he growls and lays a warning blow with his foot into Drew's stomach.

"Who the fuck are you?"

"I'm a friend of Hannah's."

I pull at Sean's arm to stop whatever carnage might happen if Drew decides to be brave. "Get lost Drew," I say for his own sake, and he scrambles to his feet and makes off down the street.

"You know him?"

"I think the question should be, why are you here?"

"Good job I was."

"That was my step-brother. He's a dick, but he's generally harmless. You didn't need to wade in. And why were you following me?" Although relieved that Drew has gone, a sudden rage starts to swell up.

"Dionne came home and said you decided to walk home, so I wanted to make sure you got there safely."

"Why Sean? We're *just friends*."

"That's what friends do." I roll my eyes that he just can't see what I'm getting at.

"Just go home. I don't need a knight in shining armour."

"What's got into you?"

"Perspective." I turn and start walking up the street towards home. But he doesn't go home, he just watches me as I walk away. I have no doubt he'll follow me at a distance to make sure I get home safe. That's just what he does.

Chapter Twenty-Four

Sean

What the fuck just happened? I watch Hannah walk up the street and into her house. I expected her to come back with Dionne, but when Dionne walked in alone, I was concerned, so went to make sure Hannah got home safe.

When I saw that guy push her up against that wall, I just lost my shit. But he was her step-brother. Why would he be threatening her in the middle of the street, late at night? And then she didn't thank me for my intervention. I've obviously done something to piss her off, but I have no clue what.

She must have a problem with me saying we are friends, because her face turns to thunder when she hears it. But that's what we agreed, and it was her who wanted to keep it a secret, so I'm clueless as to what I've done wrong.

I get back to the house, let myself in and throw myself on the sofa.

"What's happened?" Dionne says from the kitchen. "What did you do?" She narrows her eyes at me around the door.

"Why do you assume that it's me that's done something wrong?" She shrugs. "I went to make sure Hannah got home safely, only to find her step-brother pushing her up against a wall. Although I didn't know he was her step-brother, and I waded in."

"Ah Drew. He's an idiot."

"Well she didn't seem very happy that I intervened."

"It's a funny situation. He bullies her and she doesn't say anything because her parents never believe her. He's the golden child in the family."

"Well now I'm in the dog house for doing the right thing."

"The right thing?"

"Helping a friend out."

"Oh yeah because you are *just friends*."

"What's that supposed to mean?"

"Absolutely nothing." She says folding her arms over her chest, like I'm supposed to understand what the hell she means.

"You know what? I give up. I don't understand women at all."

I get up from the sofa, give Dionne the death stare and go upstairs. Maybe a shower will help me relax a bit. But before I do, I drop Hannah a message.

Me

Sorry if I overstepped. I didn't mean to upset you. Please forgive me

Forgive me for something I don't even know I'm doing. How am I supposed to navigate this?

· ❤ · ❤ · ❤ · ❤ · ❤ ·

Hannah never replied to my messages, or the other 20 or so casual ones I sent after that. I really don't know what to do. I've been distracted at work again. The guys down here must think I'm incompetent. All I seem to do is glaze over and stare into the distance. I catch someone walk past my office from the corner of my eye. "Liam!" I shout after him.

"Yes boss."

"Hannah." His face lights up. Does my face light up when I think about her? "Leave her alone."

"What do you mean?"

"You going in asking her out every other day is border line stalking."

"Wh-what?" His face drops.

"You're making her feel uncomfortable."

"I didn't mean to." He looks genuine for once.

"Looks like we're both doing stuff to piss her off at the minute."

"So what's with you two?"

"None of your business."

"Like that is it?" He smirks.

"Like what? Now you're starting to piss ME off."

"It's obvious that you two are into each other." He can't possibly see that. And how can he tell Hannah is into me, because I sure can't?

"And yet you still ask her out."

"I thought it might be funny to see your face when she said yes." He smirks.

"That's never gonna happen. Get back to work before I fire you."

"You love me too much to fire me," he says with the cheekiest of smiles. I narrow my eyes at him and he gets the hint. He leaves with a little chuckle. Then a thought occurs to me.

"Liam," I shout out. He has only got as far as the coffee machine.

"Yes boss."

"Have you been to the coffee shop today?"

"Erm, maybe." I give him the look and he gives up the information I'm after. "She's not in today. She's at home packing, is what the other one said." He shrugs like he doesn't know what that meant.

"Packing?" That settles it. I'm going to have to go round and see what's going on, since I'm getting no other answer.

The journey takes no time and I'm parked in her unusually busy street. I get out of the car and make my way to her house. As I get nearer, I hear raised voices and wonder if it's the step-brother again. I knock on the door and someone from inside shouts something inaudible that I take to be a sign to go in.

"Hannah?" I make my way into her living room where she is standing, clearly upset with an older couple. From the similarity between the two women, I presume it's her mother.

"Who the hell are you?" asks the man. He has a slight build and is wearing a designer suit that's very dated.

"Oh are you Hannah's boyfriend?" The woman's face lights up and she claps her hands together. She's defiantly not how I would have imagined Hannah's mum to be. She's dressed in a woollen skirt and jacket, with a string of pearls round her neck. Her hair is styled and wouldn't move a millimetre with all the hairspray that looks to have been used. She seems old before her time, with no hint of Hannah's creativity in her dress sense.

"I'm a friend of Hannah's," I say, purposely avoiding the phrase *just friends*, and her face drops. Just like Hannah's when I say *just friends*.

"Maybe you could talk some sense into her then," she says, while Hannah has her hands on her hips and a face of thunder.

"About what?"

"About this stupid idea of going to London to take pictures." The man's tone is full of distain.

"What? You got the intern gig? That's amazing news."

"What?" The man looks at me like I'm stupid. I move towards Hannah to give her a hug and congratulate her, but she puts her hands up to stop me.

"Look, I don't need any of your permission to live my life. I'm going to London and you've got no say in it." It baffles me why her parents aren't supporting this amazing opportunity for her.

I jump to Hannah's defence, thinking it may help my cause. "Hannah is an amazingly talented photographer, and this is a great opportunity for her." Hannah just glares at me. Not helping then!

"How are you going to fund it? Don't think we'll bail you out." The man is clearly on his soapbox.

"Well, it's none of your business how I fund it. And you never bail me out."

"We bought you this house," he says, defiantly.

"No, you gifted me the deposit and I pay the mortgage myself."

"Why can't you be more like Drew, settle down with a decent, well-paying job?" This is the woman, and now it starts to make sense.

"Look, I don't know why you put Drew up on a pedestal. He was given that job, even though he isn't qualified or has any experience whatsoever. His colleagues continuously bail him out and every time he wants anything, Daddy hands it to him on a plate.

"Drew is an obnoxious prick, who constantly harasses me at work, because nearly two decades ago, we took his fathers undivided attention away from him. And the both of you are either blind or stupid not to see it." I have even more admiration for her.

"Hannah, that's quite enough."

"Yes, I absolutely agree. Please get out of my house."

"You can't speak to your parents like that." The man stands tall.

"I just did, please leave." She points to the door and they scuttle out, mumbling about disrespect and other such parent rantings. "And as for you!" She turns on me, pointing a finger. "I don't need to be defended by you. You are not some kind of hero of the hour."

"I'm not trying to be, I'm trying to be a friend."

"But we're not friends are we Sean?" She's really shouting now. "We're sleeping together, something you like to describe as *just friends*. Well here's a news flash, you say you don't DO relationships, well that's bollocks because we are in a relationship." She gestures between us. "And you're also in a relationship with Megan, Dionne, Ben, Jonathan and everyone else. Each one of those relationships could turn sour, but with ours you won't even entertain the fact that we could have something together." She takes a breath, but before I can interject, she continues the rant. "But let me tell you this Sean Hutchinson, I am no one's dirty little secret. So this, whatever *this* is, is over. Get out!"

"Wh-."

"Get out!" She screams, face flushed.

I stare at her for a few moments and the fire in her eyes tells me I'm no match for her anger. So I turn to leave, closing the door behind me. I walk back to my car and sit there, stunned by what just happened. I mean where the fuck did all that come from?

Chapter Twenty-Five

I really don't know what to do for the best. It actually pains me to know that Hannah thinks she's my dirty little secret. It was her that wanted to keep everything quiet and I was very clear about not wanting a relationship.

And I've been an absolute nightmare to live with over the past few days, I kind of feel sorry for Dionne.

I'm sitting on the sofa, mindlessly scrolling through Netflix, trying and failing to find something to fill the void. Actually I'm not really trying at all. My head is too full of whys. Why did I start up something with Hannah? Why did I let her get under my skin? Why does she think I'm the devil? Why won't she talk to me? Why the fuck did I come here in the first place? Why don't I just move back to Edinburgh to my old simpler life?

I hear the key in the lock and Dionne steps in. "Hi honey, I'm home." I don't answer back I'm not in the mood. "Still in a delightful mood I see," she says, as she closes the door behind her.

"Hmm." I have taken to using noises rather than words.

"Have you spoken to Hannah?"

"Why would I?"

"Because you're sleeping with her maybe." I sit up straight, realising that Dionne knows more than I thought about our situation.

"WAS sleeping with her. She told you?"

"Well, it was pretty obvious."

I narrow my eyes at her. "Well, she called it off."

"I thought you'd still go to see her off." Confusion crosses my face.

"What?"

"She's getting the train to London this morning." Oh god. I feel like I might vomit.

"What time?"

"She's on the 10:35 to Kings Cross."

"Shit!" I jump off the sofa and grab my keys. I have 20 minutes to catch her before she leaves.

I drive like a maniac, trying to get to the station in time. But the amount of traffic lights and road closures are ridiculous. I belt it up the hill and abandon my car in the station car park.

I sprint through the ticket office and onto platform one.

But the train has just pulled out of the station and I watch as the end carriage disappears into the distance. She's gone. Fuck!

Chapter Twenty-Six

Lizzie

Things are still pretty bad with me and Jonathan. He didn't come home after our argument and we haven't really spoken since. So when I got a message from him asking me to take him and Sean to football, I was more than surprised. I really wanted to tell him to shove his football match, but I couldn't let this situation fester much longer.

I pick him up from outside the flat and he's acting as if nothing has happened. He just opened the boot and dumped his kit, then got in the passenger side. He gave me a curt hello and I set off to pick up Sean. We pull in outside Sean and Dionne's and he breaks the silence.

"Liz."

"That's my name."

"I've got something to tell you." My heart sinks. This sounds bad. Has he decided to end it all just before his mate gets in the car, so I don't make a scene?

"Go on."

"You were right about Helen."

I bloody knew it! "It's a chore being right all the time." This time I really do hate it.

"When I went to hers, she tried to kiss me." I feel all the blood drain from my face.

"And did you kiss her back?"

"God no. I left. I wouldn't kiss anyone else when I'm so obviously in love with you."

I jump as the boot opens and Sean throws his bag in. "This will have to keep until later," I say, as Sean gets in the back and slams the door.

"Hmm."

"Good morning to you too, ray of sunshine."

"Can we just get on with it?" Sean's tone is not one I've heard from him before and I look to Jonathan. He raises his eyebrows, I start the car and head off to the playing fields.

We pull up at our usual parking spot and Sean bundles out of the car without any acknowledgment or thanks, grabs his bag from the boot and walks over to the rest of the team. "What's going on there?"

He shrugs. "Can we finish our conversation when we get home?"

"Sure."

Luckily, spring has sprung, and it's not minus four anymore, so I can stand on the touch line and still feel my fingers and toes. The boys are all on the pitch warming up and getting in position for the start of the match. The whistle blows, and I think of what's just been said. Obviously in love with me? Not very obvious, not even as obvious as how much that woman was hitting on him.

I look up and down the pitch and speak of the devil. There she is, although not so jumpy and excitable. She sees me and looks suitably embarrassed. She turns away, and I focus on the football.

The next thing I know, there's someone standing next to me. This is all I need. I don't like people at the best of times, let alone people who try to cop off with my fella. "Is it Lizzie?"

"Yes."

"I'm Helen."

"I know."

"I don't know if Jon told you what happened." Jon now, is it? Still with your over familiarity.

"Not much. But I warned him and he didn't listen."

"I really wouldn't have pursued him if I'd have known you were together."

"You've seen me here. I wouldn't be standing here freezing my tits off just because I've pushed his kids out of my-"

"Well I see that now. I'm sorry."

"I don't blame you really." And I don't, I actual feel for the woman. "He's a good-looking bloke and he hasn't made his feeling towards me very, how do I say it, forthcoming. To me or anyone else."

"I just wanted you to know I'm not the kind of person to take another woman's man."

"Helen," I turn to look at her face on. "you're obviously an intelligent, strong woman, why are you pursuing men like that anyway? I'm sure there's plenty of eligible men out there desperate to date you."

"I don't know. I've had my confidence knocked. My ex ....well I'm sure you can imagine."

"Well, I'm glad you cleared the air." I look over to Jonathan but he's not noticed our conversation and Helen takes that as her cue to leave.

The match goes by pretty uneventfully and there's about ten minutes until the half time whistle. Sean is brought down and the referee doesn't see if, so Sean makes a massive fuss about it. But then I see Jonathan and my senses are heightened. I know that look he has. It's usually the one he gets just before something big goes down. He's making eye contact with some of the other players in some kind of silent conversation that's running between them.

I try and push it out of my mind and concentrate on the play down the other end, but then raised voices draw my attention back to where Sean has an opposition player by the neck of his shirt. His face is red and he's practically foaming at the mouth. The team see it at the same time and run to pull them apart, but Sean's arm comes back and punches the guy in the face. He crumples into a heap on the floor.

Sean is bent over him, seething, shouting in his face, while Jonathan and Woody try to pull him away. Even Titch the goal keeper is getting involved, holding Sean back by the arms while Jonathan is in his face trying to calm him down. The referee blows the whistle, runs over to Sean and shows him a red card. Sean shrugs the guys off him and stalks off the pitch.

Shit, I walk down the touch line to meet him as he exits but he turns and heads for the car. I have to jog a little to catch up with him and I hear the whistle for half time behind me. "What was all that about?"

"Nothing."

Jonathan has come off the pitch and is catching up with him. "Mate, what's going on?"

"Is this about Hannah leaving? It's obvious you've been seeing each other," I say.

He stops abruptly and turns towards us. "That's none of your business."

"You can't take your anger out on the pitch."

He points between the both of us and glares at us both. "Don't you two try telling me what to do about my relationship until you've sorted your own shit out. Just fucking get over yourselves. You're both so in love with each other, it's sickening. Just get married and put us all out of our misery."

I'm stunned by his outburst, as I watch him pick up his bag from the side lines and starts to make his way out of the park. "Where are you going?" He doesn't answer, he just keeps going.

"I better get back to the match." Has he not just heard what I heard? Is he not concerned that his friend is having some kind of melt down?

"Should I follow him?"

"No leave him to it."

Jonathan turns and walks back over to the other guys waiting for him on the edge of the pitch and I pull my phone out to make a call.

The video chat rings and eventually two faces fill the screen.

"Guys, we have a problem."

Chapter Twenty-Seven

Hannah

London is definitely not what I expected. Not the place so much, but the set up with the gallery. The gallery is a modern building in the heart of Soho. It's a light and airy building with a shop connected, and downstairs is all the art studios and dark rooms. My kind of heaven.

As far as work is concerned, I have basically been getting endless coffees for everyone, which is ironic in itself, but also a lot of phone answering and being a general dogsbody.

The internship came with accommodation in the form of a very run-down shared house with more people than bedrooms and a front door that seems permanently open. There is some form of party or gathering every night. I don't know when these people sleep and which of them actually lives here.

The hustle and bustle of the place is 24 hours, so sleep hasn't been easy to come by. And although the first few days of work took my mind off the tall handsome man back home, the nights have been next level abysmal. Thoughts of him have been going round and round my head and I've been going over and over it in my head. Still I come up with no answers.

I flip flop between different standpoints. Maybe I shouldn't have shouted at him the way I did. Maybe I shouldn't have taken him up on his offer in the first place. Maybe I should have been a bit calmer with it all. But I've been kidding myself that I could keep it casual, it's just not me. The way he made me feel had my mind blown and I just couldn't say no.

There're two different sides to it. The sex was amazing and I can honestly say I have never felt like that with anyone before. It was like he just read my body. He was gentle yet firm, knew where to touch me and what to say. And I wonder whether I will ever feel that way again. I mean, was it just him, or have I been going for the wrong types of men?

The other was the emotional, friendship side. I thought, well probably hoped, that the way he looked at me meant something more. The way our eyes met before we kissed made me feel like I was his everything. I thought maybe those feelings for me could outweigh the other feelings. Outweigh the reasons that made him reject the chance of a relationship with anyone. He made me feel special, but by all accounts, he made everyone feel special. It seems a bit irrelevant now, because I'm down here and he's up there. And there's been no contact from him. I didn't really expect there would be, but I hoped.

At least I've made a few friends since I got here. Toby is my main friend. He's my tour guide and lunch partner. He graduated from intern to full time member of staff when I joined. Although I'm not quite sure what he does, exactly. We go for lunch together just about every day, and when I say lunch, I mean we get some bread and ham from the local Tesco Extra round the corner and make up sandwiches in the gallery's tiniest of kitchens, then sit on a park bench and people-watch.

Then there's Lottie, she is the niece of the gallery owner and is in art college. She often comes over to help out. She's just 18 and I thought, being a 32-year-old spinster with a smart mouth and a lack of tolerance, we'd have nothing in common. But she has an old head on her shoulders and she's very down to earth. Plus, she knows all the cool places to hang out. And next week we all have the privilege to work as waitresses at the next exhibition opening night. Sounds really fun, not! But I suppose I need to get used to these kinds of things.

As for the friends I've left behind, I've had a few messages from the girls. But nothing really mentioning Sean. Oh, apart from a weird one from Dionne when I was on the train coming down here, asking whether I'd seen Sean at the station. It would have been nice but I properly scared him off the last time we spoke. My parents had wound me up so much I couldn't think straight and it all just came flooding out. And I basically ran away without saying goodbye. I think letting me leave without a goodbye spoke volumes.

London is something else. I both love it and hate it in equal measures. I love the vibrancy of it all, the culture. We're surrounded by theatres and galleries. There are a few pubs and bars that just seem to be full of artists and musicians, whatever time of the day you go in.

I don't like the rush of everything though. Everyone has to be somewhere, and god forbid you get in their way. There's no conversation in cafes or shops. It's just not something I'm used to. It's not my first time here, but when I've visited, I'd been part of the busy. Part of the crowds of tourists and the rush of getting places and seeing things.

Toby has said he'll take me sightseeing on our days off. That is if we can get a day off together. But it will be nice to see the sights from a different point of view, from a slower place, when we don't have to rush to an event or so we don't miss the train home.

And there it is again. Home. I wonder if having this adventure will mean I never really settle when I get back. My two lives are like polar opposites. And then there's the people. My friends, new and old. For people that I have only known for a few months, they have become very important to me. Each one of the girls has messaged me independently as well as in the group, to ask how I'm doing. They want to know about my new life.

Cynthia and Sally have been in touch regularly as well, wanting to live vicariously through me. Also Cynthia is still complaining about the coffee machine.

There are still two people that I have had no contact from, one I'm desperate to hear from, the other not so much. There has been deafening silence from my mother since the argument. I suspect she is waiting for me to fail and come home with my tail between my legs. And even if this thing went pear shaped, that wouldn't happen, I wouldn't give them the satisfaction.

I find myself pulling my phone out when I've seen something funny, or done something new, to message Sean, then I realise I can't and I have an acute pain in my chest. There's been more than one occasion I have nearly burst out crying at the fact that I can no longer speak to him. I took a walk round Hyde Park with my camera and saw two ducks having an argument. I had to stop and sit down to catch my breath, the pain was so immense.

In some ways, I wish I'd never met him. That way there would be no pain, no crying myself to sleep. But then I wouldn't have experienced what I had with him. I really want to ask Dionne what he's up to but that would put her in the middle and I don't want that.

I'm with Toby and we are currently having our usual lunchtime on the bench in the park, although today must be a special occasion because we splashed out and bought a pot of sandwich filler – tuna and mayonnaise, with the sweetcorn picked out so not to ruin it.

The sun is shining and it's a crisp day. Toby sits and tilts his head back towards the sky. He's a really good-looking man, and I know it's not just me who thinks it. The number of women that take a second look is verging on ridiculous. He looks the epitome of style and masculinity. He's the kind of guy you'd take to an event to make people jealous. But I'm 100 percent not his type. He's currently lusting after an Italian artist called Luigi. Although we don't know his actual name.

"Hannah, can I ask you a question?" He looks towards me and gives me sad eyes.

"I suppose."

"Why were you so sad when you first got here? Where you homesick or something?"

"No, definitely not homesick."

"So what then? Someone you left behind?" I don't answer him and he sits up straight as if I have got his full attention. "It is, isn't it? A man?"

"Yes. I was kinda sad about someone when I first got here. Not that I had any right to be, we weren't together."

"I can feel a story coming on."

I roll my eyes. "You don't want to hear my tales of woe."

"No, I really do. It makes me feel so much better about my life."

"Thanks." I laugh. "I don't know where to begin."

"It doesn't really matter, just spill."

"Okay." I take a deep breath because I actually don't know what I'm gonna say, the words are fixed behind a dam. Once I open those flood gates, who knows what will come rushing out? "I met this guy and he was gorgeous and he happened to be a friend of a friend. We kept bumping into each other. One thing led to another but he told me he didn't do relationships. He wanted a *friends with benefits* thing with me. I refused and we decided to be friends, but he was doing all kinds of nice boyfriend things and I eventually said yes to the benefit side."

"Sounds like a good plan so far."

"Except I wanted to keep it quiet, so he kept describing us as *Just Friends* to people and I hated it. It was like I was in two relationships. The one when we were alone, and the one when we were with people."

"Isn't that what you both wanted though?"

"I thought I could handle it, but it ended up winding me up so much that I called it off in one big crazy rant."

"And how was it left?"

"Like that. The last time I spoke to him was me telling him to get out."

"And do you regret breaking it off?"

"We couldn't go on that way, but I didn't realise how much I would miss him."

"And there's no way back?"

"I'd always want more, and he never would. So no."

"Do you know how he feels about you?"

"I thought he might feel the same. The way he acted made me feel special. But it seems like that's just the way he is. He goes above and beyond for everyone. Great boyfriend material, but he doesn't commit."

"Shame. You deserve someone nice."

"I think I do. I definitely deserve someone who can give me the sex he did."

"That good?"

"Better!"

"Oh my god, I'm so jealous."

I look at my watch and realise it's time to get back to reality. We pack up our lunch things and head back to the gallery.

Chapter Twenty-Eight

Sean

I really don't know what's going on in my head right now. I'm usually the one who calms things down, but I've got so much rage burning inside me. I'm totally out of control. I walk the three miles back to my house, still in my football boots, in a total daze.

I'm so angry, mainly with myself. I keep going round in circles. If I feel this shitty for not being with Hannah, then maybe I should be with Hannah. But then feeling so bad about not being with Hannah proves the point I have made with myself. I should not be in a relationship in the first place. It only causes heartache for both sides and I'm not sure whether I'll be any good at it. The last thing I want to do is hurt Hannah, but it looks like I've done that already.

I did say my head was a mess of contradictions.

My phone pings in my bag and I search around, wondering which one of my friends it will be, having a go at me for my behaviour. One thing I do know is it won't be Hannah.

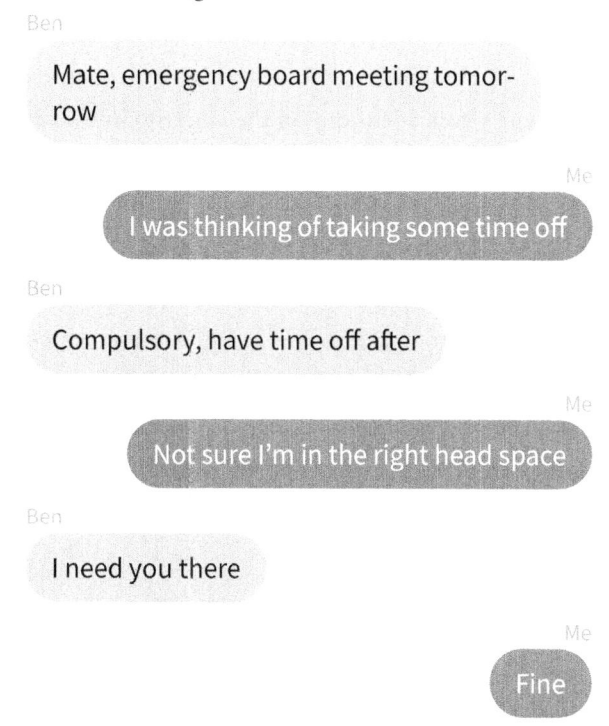

Ben: Mate, emergency board meeting tomorrow

Me: I was thinking of taking some time off

Ben: Compulsory, have time off after

Me: Not sure I'm in the right head space

Ben: I need you there

Me: Fine

Well at least it's a good excuse to get out of town. I'm not sure I can bear seeing everyone's disappointed face when they find out I kicked off. I arrive at my door and toe off my boots. I go straight in and upstairs to shower and pack.

There's no sign of Dionne, so I leave her a note.

Gone Home for a bit

Sean x

It's taken no time at all to get to my flat. A mixture of loud music and being on auto-pilot. I put my key in the door and open it. Stepping in I realise what a colossal mistake I have made.

Even though my cleaner has been in and cleaned, the place still smells of Hannah. That mainly vanilla smell with a slight floweriness. The flashbacks of her being here are gonna drive me insane. There's even a lens cap on the worktop in the kitchen that must have fallen out of her bag. It's probably been kicked under something and my cleaner has retrieved it. I stare at it for a ridiculously long time.

What do I do? I pace up and down the living room floor from end to end, trying to work out how I get this woman out of my head. The gym. It's the only thing I'm going to be able to do to distract myself. And if I do enough, I'll be exhausted and I'll sleep, no problem. So I change and head to the basement, where our onsite gym is, and start a brutal routine.

· ♥ · ♥ · ♥ · ♥ · ♥ ·

I've never hated Monday mornings before. I love my job, so why would I not want to get up and go in. But today is a totally different matter. Although I spent two hours in the gym last night, I didn't get much sleep. I came back and had a shower, cue flashbacks of Hannah in the shower with me. Then I couldn't bear to get into my own bed but remembered Hannah had slept in the spare room too, I ended up tossing and turning on the not-as-comfortable-as-I-thought sofa.

I wonder if they still have exorcisms of homes? Or, what was the thing that Megan said, where they set fire to some twigs and waft the smoke round the room. Anyway, I need something.

I push through the doors to Ambrose Holdings and wave to Stacey at the desk. She just points to the conference room and I'm glad for the lack of small talk. As I walk down the corridor a wave of unease sweeps through me. I have been so caught up in my own head, I never gave a thought to what this meeting was actually about.

As I open the door, the oval table has three people seated around it, a lot less than I expected. The chatter stops as I enter the room. Something's off. There's Ben and Joel, but also Piers and he doesn't even work here. Their faces are etched with sadness and it suddenly hits me.

"This isn't a board meeting, it's a fucking intervention."

"Sit down." Ben says in a stern voice he only uses for business.

"Not until you tell me what's going on."

"We're just a bit concerned about you." Joel says, and it's unlike him to speak up first, so I take a seat at the end.

"Nothing wrong with me."

"Punching someone at the match is nothing?" asks Piers.

"He was goading me."

"From what I heard you were looking for a fight."

"Who's been telling tales?" I roll my eyes, annoyed that they've all been chatting behind my back.

"Does it matter?"

"Do you want to talk about what's been going on?" Joel wants to talk about feelings, that's just not normal.

"No, not particularly."

"Is this about Hannah?" Ben asks.

"What about Hannah?"

"That you two were seeing each other and now you're not."

"And that's given you some kind of personality transplant," Piers adds.

"We weren't seeing each other. I don't do relationships."

"She must have one hell of a pussy!"

"Fuck off Ben." I jump out of my seat, ready to punch him in the face.

"Calm down, it was just a test. Didn't you say exactly the same thing about Emma?"

"It's different." Touché!

"How?"

"It's complicated." I sag down in my seat.

"It's pretty much anything but complicated. You like her, she likes you, you're clearly good for each other. But YOU have it in your head that avoiding commitment will stop you from getting hurt."

"Do you think all those people who have lost someone would say they'd not do it again because, in the end, the pain of losing them was too much." This isn't the first time Ben voiced these concerns.

"Maybe." He rolls his eye.

The door opens suddenly. "What have I missed?"

AMELIA FUCKING PRESCOTT! I can't stand this woman, we've never got on, so why is she here? Joel thinks we don't get on because we've always been fighting for Ben's attention. I think it's because she's a smart arse and she thinks she's funny. I try to avoid her, but she's Ben's *other* best friend.

"What the fuck is she doing here?" I point my finger at her.

"I thought we could get the female point of view." Ben says.

"And how many men have you dated Ami?" My tone is hostile.

"Enough to know a prick when I see one." She narrows her eyes at me. I don't see how she'll have a better view on anything, since she's gay. She takes a seat next to Ben.

"How did you leave everything with her?" Ben starts back up with the interrogation.

"She basically told me to fuck off. Said she was no-one's dirty little secret." They all grimace. "It wasn't me who wanted to keep it a secret." I say in my defence.

"And you can't see yourself being in a relationship with Hannah?" I shake my head and stare down at the table. But in all honesty, I have thought about it and I have seen myself with her, every time I close my eyes. But I can't let myself go there.

"Why are you letting an experience from 10 years ago, dictate what you do now. We were very different people then." Ben's tone has softened slightly.

"Just leave him alone. It's his life, if he's decided not to be in a relationship then that's his choice."

Well, that was unexpected from Ami, she's never usually on my side for anything. "Finally, someone who can see my point of view."

"And in 10 years' time, when she is happily married with kids, and he's scrolling through pictures of the two of them while he sits alone in his bachelor pad with a receding hairline, that's his choice." And there it is.

"Fuck you all! This meeting is over."

"Sit back down. She didn't mean it."

"Yes, I did." Ben glares at Ami, probably regretting her invitation.

"No I'm taking some time off, so I don't have to be around you lot anymore."

"Fine. Take some time to consider your next move."

"What next move?"

"Well if this is going to continue to affect your work, then we'll need to have a rethink of roles." Ben gets all business-like again.

"It isn't affecting my work." Sudden panic rises up through me, he can't be suggesting what I think he is?

"With your temper, I'm worried it might bring the company into disrepute." I shake my head. "Sean mate, you wanted to sack Liam for asking Hannah out."

"No I wanted to sack him because he's a smug shit! You can't actually be threatening to sack me. I've been here from the start." Ben just shrugs.

"Fuck the lot of you." I storm out of the room and out of the building, trying to work out what the fuck just happened.

I walk into the city centre and just keep on walking. Past all the shops, all the tourists, trying to get a grip of what was said. My best friend wanting to fire me. My job is everything to me and we've been together since the start. He's blowing this totally out of proportion.

After about three hours walking in a circle, my stomach growls at me and I decide I'm gonna have to eat before I pass out. I step into a sandwich shop and pick something from the fridge so I have as little human contact as physically possible. I pay and head off to find myself a seat in Princes Street Gardens.

My phones pings in my pocket. I'm reluctant to see who it is, but curiosity gets the better of me.

Ami: If you want to chat without a fairy-tale rose-tinted perspective, I've got the day off

Me: Slacker

Me: What are you gonna tell me that the rest haven't?

Ami: I'm not gonna tell you anything, I'm gonna listen

Ami: But whatever

I sit and think about it for a while. Maybe I need someone who'll give me an alternative, unfiltered perspective.

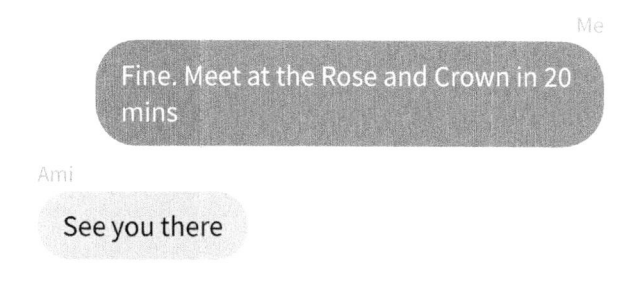

Me: Fine. Meet at the Rose and Crown in 20 mins

Ami: See you there

This could go one of two ways. It could be an epiphany or a complete disaster.

Chapter Twenty-Nine

I sit at a table waiting for Ami to arrive, wondering what insights she might bring, and hating myself for letting her convince me to hear her out. "Alright loser?" And here she is. "What are you drinking?"

"Pint for me." She heads off to the bar.

When she comes back, she places my pint down alongside her glass of what looks like a gin and tonic. "Can we just curb the insults for today please. I don't have the emotional energy for it."

"Sure thing, handsome." I roll my eyes as she grins back at me.

"What's Ben told you?"

"Just that you were seeing someone and now you're not and have become a bit unhinged."

"Unhinged is a bit far?"

Amy shrugs. "I always thought you were a bit already, so it's not news to me. But anyway, this woman?"

"Hannah."

"You like her?" I nod. "Then what's the problem?"

"I always said I didn't want to be in a relationship with anyone again."

"Again?"

I pause weighing up whether I should tell her the story or not, but what have I got to lose. I'll give her the quick version though. "In my twenties I got badly burnt. Swore off giving in to another woman."

"And you've got this far and never wanted anyone to be more?"

"I've never liked anyone that much before. I realise now I only ever picked women who I could detach from, mainly because they were pretty fake."

"Like Barbie or whatever her name is?"

"Ha, Cheryl. Funny that's what Hannah called her." I smile as I think about her, of that weekend, and then I feel myself come back to earth with a bump.

"They met?"

"She confronted Hannah in the bathrooms when we were out. Talked shit to her. Really rocked her confidence."

"Bitch." I smile in agreement – which has to be an alien concept where me and Ami are concerned. "Have you ever imagined what life would be like with Hannah, if you were open to a relationship and didn't have this kind of pact with yourself?"

"A bit." I lie, I've thought about it constantly.

"And in that life, how would you feel?" I just shrug. "Okay... How would it make you feel if Hannah found that life with someone else?"

"Physically sick."

"I can understand you putting up those barriers." I look of understanding crosses her face, and she fiddles with her glass.

"It's irrelevant now anyway. She doesn't want anything to do with me." I sit back in my chair, resigned to the fact that I well and truly blew it.

"Why?"

"Because she said she didn't want to do it anymore."

"But do you know which part she didn't want? Was it the being together part, or the sneaking around and not being honest with everyone part?"

I stare into my pint. "I think I preferred it when we were arguing."

"It's okay, normal service will resume shortly."

"And she left without me being able to say bye."

"And how does that make you feel?"

"Is this a therapy session?"

"Maybe."

"It makes me feel a little bit broken, like something inside of me is missing." I try and hold myself together, because just simply talking about her makes my heart ache. I look down at my empty glass as a distraction. "Another drink?"

"Yep, mine's a rhubarb gin and lemonade." I head off to the bar to get served.

I place the drinks on the table as Ami is looking at something on her phone. She quickly puts it away when I arrive. "You're not reporting back, are you?"

"No. You're not the only one with girl trouble."

"You have to tell me now. It'll make me feel better."

"Maybe after a few more of these." She clinks her glass on mine. "Tell me about work."

"Well I might not have a job by the end of the week, it seems."

"Of course you will. Ben wouldn't cut you out. It's just his way of shocking you into action."

"Sounded pretty convincing to me."

"They're just worried about you, and everyone knows how much you love work. It was more about where you're gonna be. Are you staying in Edinburgh or are you going back to England?"

"I really don't know. I think this whole thing started because I felt a bit lost. I do like it in Winford. I have a few friends, even if Megan is still away. I play football. The guys at the office, on the whole, are okay. But it's a total change from here."

"But Hannah is there."

"She's not though. She's gone to London. It's only for three months, but I doubt she'll be back permanently."

"Why not?" Stirs her drink and leans forward with questioning eyes.

"Because she's so talented, they'll either want her to stay or she'll find something similar elsewhere."

"Hmm."

"What are your words of wisdom now?"

She looks at her glass. "I think we need something to soak these up." She turns towards the bar. "Matty, have you got any food on?"

"There's some kind of vegetable cobbler thing or steak and ale pie." The barman shouts back.

"Two steak pies then," she shouts over. "God knows what's in the vegetable cobbler."

"You surprise me. I didn't have you down as a steak and ale pie kinda girl. More like the quinoa salad, roasted veg and halloumi kind."

"I'm just the gift that keeps on giving." She grins at me. Maybe I have Ami all wrong. "Anyway, you're gonna need to work out what you want your life to look like."

Oh god, back to this. "I just don't know."

"I mean, for example, would you rather be out drinking and partying, having all kinds of fake women hanging off you. Or would you prefer to curl up on the sofa with Hannah?"

"I think you know the answer." It must be obvious by now.

"This pact has kept you safe from those relationships that would have never gotten anywhere. But it might now keep you from your soul mate."

"Do you believe in soul mates?" Who even am I?

"I think there must be such a thing. I mean, sickening as it is, look at Ben and Emma."

"I never believed in it until now. I didn't believe in love at first sight either."

"So you are in love with her?"

No one has asked me this before and a dawning realisation hits me. Panic rises through my chest and into my throat, and I only just manage to get the words out. "I think so."

"So what's stopping you going and getting her back and opening up to a relationship?"

"Well, there's the big question of *does she feel the same way?* And I couldn't do it now and have her distracted from something she's worked so hard for."

"Well there's only one way to find out."

"And how do I get rid of all this baggage I have in my head about relationships?"

"I really don't know. See a therapist?" I look at her in the eyes. Is she joking or not? "Think about it. You did this to stop yourself from getting hurt, but now you're hurting even more by continuing."

"Maybe."

"Think about what you want. Take some time off, so you can make a plan on what's next." Damn it, this woman is too logical and I feel myself agreeing with her.

The moment is broken by Matty putting two plates of food on our table in front of us.

Chapter Thirty

Hannah

Today we are going on an adventure. Well not really but me and Toby have managed to get a day off together and he's taking me on a photographic tour of London. I thought when I got down here I would be doing a lot more photo taking than I have been. But time just seems to drift away between making coffee and running errands.

I got the idea for my next collection when I was in Edinburgh. Just the thought of that weekend bring both happy and sad feelings back. London, like Edinburgh, has a great mixture of old and new, so I'm taking shots of how they compliment each other. First stop, the London Eye. Lottie got us free tickets, so we can take shots of the Eye with the older buildings as a backdrop, and then work out where we go next, from what we see from up high.

My phone pings with a message.

Beth

I may kill my husband. Anyone wanna be my alibi?

Lizzie

I've got a shovel. You need help digging?

Dionne

You've been with me all day

Kateryna

I know someone, but also can headlock

Beth

I may need a new patio

Me

Here for support (from a distance)

Beth

Ah Hans. How's it going?

Me

Just heading out for some sightseeing

Dionne

Say hi to the gorgeous Toby for me

Lizzie

Send pics, we need proof of life

Me

Miss you guys

At that point Toby comes out of the gallery, messing with his camera bag. "Tobes! Pic for the girls?"

"Always." He puts his arms around me as we take a cheesy selfie and I send it to the group chat. "Right lets get going, we've a lot to fit into our only day off since time began."

"I though this was gonna be leisurely sightseeing?"

"No such thing in London." I huff at the thought of the manic day ahead and link arms with him as we make our way to the tube station.

Chapter Thirty-One

Two Months Later

I don't think I've ever been so nervous in my life. Everyone is buzzing around making sure everything goes without a hitch. Me? I'm just standing in the middle of the gallery, frozen with anxiety, unsure about what to do for the best. It's the opening night of my exhibition and the doors open any minute.

I'm wearing a silver halter neck dress and heels, which is a first for me. The armour of my baggy sweatshirt has gone and I'm totally out of my comfort zone. Toby took me shopping yesterday. He had a friend in a boutique, not far from the gallery, who got me a ridiculous discount on the clothes, and in return, I agreed that they could use some of the photos of me from the night.

Toby's job tonight, unlike when we are usually here, is to show guests around the exhibition and generally calm me down. Which is going to be a job in itself. He's had me doing breathing exercises about five times already and we haven't even started yet. It's at this point I wish I did drink.

A tap on my shoulder makes me jump. "There's nothing to be nervous about. The place looks amazing. Your work is just next level and I think there's going to be a lot of interest." Toby squeezes my shoulder. "You've got this." I totally don't got this. The imposter syndrome is bearing down on me, glaring at me, saying you don't belong here, you're not good enough, who would take you seriously?

I push the thoughts away as the first person walks through the door. It's the gallery owner, John. I'm surprised because he doesn't usually come to these things. He sees me and makes his way over. "Hannah, what an amazing job you've done. These photos are so impressive. I'm glad you chose to come and work with us."

"Thank you." It's all I can muster.

"We'll catch up later, enjoy." I smile as he turns away and heads to talk to the rest of the staff.

I shake my hands out in front of me, hoping it will shake away the nerves.

The door opens again and a few people wander in, picking up a glass from the waitress at the door, then make their way round the photos, pondering each one. And as the minutes go by, the gallery fills up. I need to start mingling or something, rather than stand here looking out of place.

"Hannah." I recognise that voice. I turn to see my friends from Winford, grinning at me.

"Oh my god, you came?"

"Of course we came," Dionne says, greeting me with a wide smile.

"Especially because we are now friends with a famous photographer." Beth is excited, I can tell.

"I knew her when she was talking photos of a non-league football team," Lizzie jokes.

"Can I have your autograph?" Dionne says, with a straight face.

"Kateryna is sorry she couldn't make it. Tomasz has some awards ceremony, but she sent us with this." Lizzie hands me a bottle bag.

"It's not vodka, is it?" I open the bag and pull out a glass bottle with a stopper, obviously homemade, with a handwritten sticker that says *Congratulations*. "What is it?"

"No idea, but she assured us it isn't alcoholic and said it had special properties. I didn't want to ask anymore."

"Anyway, we just wanted to say how proud we are of you." Lizzie hands me a card and then does a very unLizzie thing and pulls me in for a hug. Beth and Dionne join her. "Don't read that now. Find a time when you're safe to ugly cry."

"We thought it would be nice to take you out for dinner to celebrate too, once the excitement has calmed down."

"Sounds great." I could really do with a Dog and Swan girl catch up right now.

"Now show us your amazing work."

"This way." I gesture towards the first group of photographs.

"Wait, I need to take a photo. Hannah, stand in front of the sign." Beth points to the sign that reads,

Healing
By Hannah Spencer

We walk round the gallery and I explain the meanings of the photographs and how they fit in with the theme, until we get back to the start. I notice two more people I recognise. Cynthia and Sally are standing talking to the gallery owner. How are they even here?

I rush over to them. "What are you doing here?"

"Didn't you know, we are very cultured and like to come to London to see the art and what not." Cynthia says with not a hint of irony.

"Hannah!" Sally screeches and jumps up and down, eventually pulling me into a hug. "We are so proud of you."

"Yes. But you need to come back soon because the coffee machine needs cleaning." Cynthia doesn't flinch and, just as I think she might be serious, she nudges me and grins. "I'm only joking, I get Sally to do it."

I can't believe these women have come all this way to see my work. I don't think either of them have been to London before, so it's a big deal for them. "So are you staying for long?" I ask.

"We're booked into a posh looking hotel by the Tower of London," Sally explains.

"That's a bit fancy," I say. Cynthia gives Sally a devil stare.

"Erm, yes, we had a voucher. We're getting the train back tomorrow evening." Sally looks a bit sheepish.

"I'm just so happy you made it down," I say as Toby joins us, wrapping his arm around me. I introduce them to him and Sally flutters her eyelashes at him, not realising its all in vain. He offers to show them round the exhibit while I speak to the other guests who want my attention.

I see Verity walk through the door, holding hands with an athletic, handsome-looking man. She looks even better than when I saw her last and I wave her over. She reaches me and envelopes me in a hug. I've never had this much physical contact with people in one day before, but each one of them has made me feel special.

"You look amazing," I tell her.

"So do you. This is Will. Will, this is my friend and all-round amazing photographer, Hannah."

"Nice to meet you Will." We shake hands before I turn my attention back to Verity. "Can I show you your photo first?"

"I can't wait." Verity claps her hands together.

I guide them over to the other side of the room and stand in front of the huge photos of Verity, side by side. "I can't believe that was me." She looks at the photos as if she doesn't recognise herself.

"Looks like two different people," Will says as he looks up at them in awe.

"I know. One makes me sad and the other makes me happy." Verity thinks for a minute and then does a little dance and envelopes me again.

"Thanks so much for letting me show them. I know it's hard to look at the first one, but you've come such a long way. And in all honesty, I wouldn't have all this without you." I gesture to the whole exhibition. It's true. She was the inspiration behind all this.

"Anything good that can come out of it is fine by me." Will pulls her in for a hug.

"Are they for sale?" He asks.

"Yes, but you don't even want to know the price, it's ridiculous. I'm not supposed to do this but I made you copies and I've posted them back home."

"Aww that's amazing. You should be so proud of yourself."

"So should you," I say, hugging her again.

Something catches my eye and I feel my heart rate quicken. A tall figure stands looking at one of the photos, hands in pockets. I'm rooted to the spot. Words fail me as I stare at him.

"We'll have a look at the rest and leave you to mingle with your guests," Verity hasn't noticed my shock. I don't answer as she moves away. The world seems to stand still.

Toby comes up behind me and whispers in my ear. "Do you want me to go over?"

"No. I will." I manage to get my brain to engage with my feet and make my way towards him. I stop short and gaze at his profile. This man is so gorgeous. I can't put it into words, let alone capture it in a photograph.

"Hi," I say. He doesn't take his eyes off the photos of himself.

"When did you take these?" he asks without moving. I'm not sure if he's angry with me.

"The first one was at the first football match I went to. You didn't know I was there. And the second was at the park when you weren't looking." He doesn't say anything. He doesn't take his eyes away. "I'm sorry. I should have asked your permission. But we weren't really on good terms."

He doesn't say anything for what seems like an eternity. I start to shuffle my feet as the nervous tension spreads through my body.

"How do you see them fitting into the Healing theme?"

"Just the difference in them. On the second you look like you've lost something that was weighing you down. Like you are freer, lighter, less... I don't know, wound up."

"Hmm." He continues to stare, and I feel like I might be sick if he doesn't look at me or say something.

"Why are you here Sean?"

He turns to face me suddenly, the first time he's looked at me. "Why wouldn't I be here? We're friends."

"No... No, weren't not friends." He takes a minute to look me up and down.

"You look absolutely amazing. London looks good on you." Oh god, why does he have to say those things. I thought I'd put up enough barriers to stop myself turning to goo whenever he looked at me. But that look makes me feel all kinds of things. His eyes linger on my lips and I think he's going to lean down and kiss me, but he doesn't. "Hannah, I need to talk to you."

"About what?"

"What do you think?" At this point I have absolutely no idea. "Can we meet up afterwards?"

"I'm not sure that would be a good idea."

"Please." He has a look of desperation in his eyes, but I'm not sure it will do any good.

Toby comes up and puts his arm round me. Sean's face drops.

"Sorry, I'm gonna have to drag her away." I give Sean a weak smile as Toby manoeuvres me away to the other side of the gallery to meet some more people.

As the night goes on and I speak to more and more people, my nerves seem to diminish and I feel a lot more comfortable. People are loving the exhibition. The café girls have called it a night and my other friends are going out on the town. They have asked me to join them when I'm all finished, but I'm not sure I'll have the energy to be honest.

John, the owner, comes over and pulls me from my current conversation. "Hannah, I wanted you to meet Julian Lewis." He introduces me to a man in his late forties. He looks kind of professional in his suit but also has an air of flamboyance.

"Pleased to me you." He leans forward and shakes my hand, firmly.

"He has something he wants to discuss with you." John lingers between us.

"Congratulations on such a wonderful piece of work. John tells me this is your first exhibition."

"Yes, it is. I have been very nervous."

"Well, it doesn't show. I know your internship has come to an end here and I know John would love for you to stay. But I have a new gallery in Tokyo that I would love you to exhibit at. It's only just getting up and running, but I would love you to consider it."

"Wow! That's an amazing offer." I'm a bit taken a back, I did not expect this conversation.

"Have a think about it and give me a call." He hands me a card with his number on it and says his goodbyes. I stare down at the card. Is this for real?

John returns from introducing him to some other art connoisseurs with a broad smile across his face. "Was that for real?" I ask him.

"I do believe so. And he was correct in assuming that I would want to keep you here. But that is an amazing opportunity," he points to the card I still grasp in my hand, "so I will understand if you want to go for it."

"Thanks, I'll think about it."

He squeezes my shoulder, turns and leaves me to ponder. Toby comes over, fizzing with excitement like a five-year-old. "What was all that about?"

I hand him the card. "He's setting up a gallery in Tokyo and wants me to go."

"What? Do you need a colleague to accompany you?"

"I don't know whether I'm going yet."

"Why ever not?"

"There's a lot to think about." My brain has already started to go into overdrive.

"For once Hannah, think about yourself and only yourself. But also maybe me after that." He pulls me in for a hug and kisses me on the top of my head. "I'm so proud of you Han. Oh and in other news. Your man over there has been hanging around all night, just watching you. Who is he?"

"Ha." I look over to Sean, his eyes fixed on me. He looks like he's plotting. "He's the *friend with benefits*?"

"No. Fucking. Way. He is beautiful, I'd totally hit that, no hesitation."

"That's not really any gauge to how beautiful he is, you'd hit practically anything." Although he does get his fair share of gorgeous men hitting on him.

"That is not true. Mostly. Are you gonna speak to him? He came all this way."

"He's asked to talk to me after this."

"Well I can clear up everything here, you go."

"I'm not sure I want to know what he has to say to be honest." He turns me round to face Sean's direction and pushes me forward. I wasn't expecting it and I have to keep moving to avoid falling over.

Chapter Thirty-Two

Sean

I managed to sneak into the exhibition without Hannah noticing me and I've spent most of the night watching her. I don't even know whether she'll want to speak to me. Her work is incredible, I'm so unbelievably proud of her. I'm also pleased that the girls made it down and surprised her. And I may or may not have had a hand in getting the coffee shop girls down here too. It's lovely to see she has the support of her friends, because I certainly didn't see her parents here.

I've been planning this for a while. I took some time to really think about what I wanted. I even spoke to a therapist. I've kind of kept that to myself, except for Jonathan. And to say he has been my shoulder to cry on and saviour is an understatement. I think at one point it felt like he was almost on suicide watch, but I managed to pull myself back from the brink.

We've had many a night in front of the TV or the Xbox, talking crap to keep me distracted. Or I've drowning my sorrows and he's been there to pick me up off the floor. But eventually pulling myself together and we started putting a plan together, with input from a few others. I've kept the girls out of it because its not fair putting them in the middle.

And now has come the time to lay it all out on the table for her. She's the only one who can make the decision about how we go forward, or if she evenwants to have anything with me. To say I'm nervous is an understatement.

She's wearing an amazing silver dress that hugs her curves and makes her look even more gorgeous than I remember, and I didn't know that was possible. The thing that threw me a little was seeing my face on the wall. I knew she'd taken photos of me, but I didn't realise she'd put them in her exhibition.

"Hi." She's beside me now. But I can't pull my gaze from the photos. Is this the way I look to her?

"When did you take these?" I can't quite place them.

"The first one was at the first football match I went to. You didn't know I was there. And the second was at the park when you weren't looking." That makes sense. I didn't know she was at the first match, looking back I do remember someone, but they were so bundled up in winter clothes I would have had no clue. "I'm sorry I should have asked your permission, but we weren't really on good terms."

Not on good terms, if only she'd have made contact. "How do you see them fitting into the Healing theme?"

"Just the difference in them. On the second you look like you've lost something that was weighing you down. Like you are freer, lighter, less... I don't know, wound up."

Well, that makes sense. One is before her, when I didn't know I could feel something so strong for someone. The second was that day in the park. Probably the day I fell in love with her. "Hmm."

"Why are you here Sean?"

I turn to face her, shocked at the question. "Why wouldn't I be here? We're friends."

"No... No, weren't not friends." And there it is. The blow I was hoping not to receive.

"You look absolutely amazing. London looks good on you." I'm not just saying it. She looks different, like something has opened her up. Or someone? My thoughts take a nose dive again. "Hannah, I need to talk to you."

"About what?"

How does she not realise how I feel about her? "What do you think?" Has she really no clue? "Can we meet up afterwards?"

"I'm not sure that would be a good idea."

"Please." I'm not averse to begging.

Then he walks over and takes her away. I've watched every interaction they have had. I can feel the anger towards him rise up through my body and flush my skin. Is he the one that will take Hannah away from me? I'm not sure I could survive that, after everything I have struggled to come to terms with.

I've mulled about the exhibition all evening, but my eyes have never been far from Hannah. She's spoken enthusiastically to everyone about her work. She's really come out of herself. I can tell she's been nervous by the little tells that are only obvious to someone who knows her.

But the guy is picking up on them too and intervenes when he notices. At least if she does pick him over me, he understands her and hopefully won't take her for granted.

The room is thinning out and the girls have all left, each of them giving me a warning in their own way. I hesitate to reach out to her again. I don't want to push her too much. It's obvious that something important just happened because two men, who seem to be important, have spoken to her, and THAT GUY came over all excited. I watch them closely. I actually feel like I might want to throttle him. I'm sure Lizzie would give me an alibi.

He pushes her towards me, which was unexpected. I'd definitely never push her towards another man.

"Hey." She gives me a nervous smile.

"There's an all-night café open round the corner, we could go there to talk?"

"Fine. But I haven't got long and I'm really tired." I nod and place my hand on her back as I escort her out of the building.

After three streets of walking in silence we get to the café. It's a typical old-school greasy spoon, with plastic cafeteria-style chairs fixed to the floor and a Formica table top. "Do you want something to eat? And maybe a coffee?"

"I would kill for a bacon butty right now, I'm not sure their coffee will be up to your standards, so maybe a can of something." I head to the counter to order. It gives me a bit of time to gather my thoughts. I really don't know how to start this conversation.

I sit down at the table opposite her and place the cans down. I take a deep breath. "So have you got any plans for once this internship is over?"

She rolls her eyes. "Is that what you wanted to ask me? Why did you come here?"

"To see you, your exhibition."

"And how long are you staying?"

"I thought I'd stay a bit, a few weeks. I don't know. I have some business here." Why did I say that?

"So you came for business and just happened to slot me in?" She looks upset, angry.

"No! The absolute opposite. I came to see you, to tell you..."

"Just spit it out Sean." Shit. This isn't going to plan.

"I wanted to say how much I'd missed you and that it made me realise how much you mean to me."

"If I mean that much to you, why haven't you spoken to me in three months? Three months, Sean. What's happened to make you suddenly realise after all this time. Were you bored?"

"No. It hasn't taken me this long to realise. I knew straight away. I just..."

"So what? You want to get back to some benefits?" Oh god, her face is like thunder, I'm really blowing this.

"No. I want you. A relationship with you."

"But you don't do relationships, remember? You made that perfectly clear." I can see the rage in her eyes.

"Let me explain why."

She leans back in the chair and folds her arms across her chest. "Fine."

Our food number is called. I gesture that I've heard, jump up and get them and bring them back. I take a deep breath before I speak.

"When I was in my early twenties, just out of university, I fell head over heels for a girl. I thought the feeling was mutual and she moved into my flat in the space of a few weeks. Ben said there was something a bit off about her, but I thought he was just jealous of our blossoming relationship.

"She kept getting messages on her phone, but she said they were from her mum. I believed her. One day I came back early from work and found her in bed with another bloke."

"Oh god. That must have been devastating." She sits forward, empathy written all over her face.

"Oh it gets worse. Not only was she cheating on me, she never liked me in the first place. Her and her boyfriend were taking all my personal data to scam me out of thousands of pounds."

"Shit."

"So the shit hit the fan. The police were involved and, to cut a long story short, I vowed then never to get into a relationship again. She completely broke me. I totally closed off to women and relationships, I didn't trust anyone anymore and I especially didn't trust myself. How could I have not seen what was happening? So no-one got close. Until you."

"What about Barbie?" She looks at me deadpan.

"She was just a regular hook up. There were no feelings involved."

"She obviously had feelings for you."

"Well, it wasn't reciprocated."

"So now you've just changed your mind?" She eyes me suspiciously.

"No, not just. I realised I wanted to be with you more than I wanted to shield myself from heartbreak. Please tell me you feel something too."

She stops picking at her bacon and takes a breath.

"How do I know you won't just change your mind?"

"I won't." I try to touch her hand but she pulls it away. And I feel the loss immediately.

"And I should just take your word for it?"

"I've fallen in love with you Hannah. I knew from the very moment I laid eyes on you that you were special."

"Well, you're too late!" What, that guy? Her phone beeps on the table and she picks it up to read the message. "I've got to go."

"But-"

"Bye Sean." She stands up and walks out of the café, taking my heart with her. She's met at the door by that guy again, who puts his arms around her shoulder and they walk off into the night.

I sit there in shock. I never expected it to go like that, but I should have really. She's still angry with me and even laying out something that I've only really told one other person about, did nothing to win her back. I push my food away, my appetite long-gone.

I sit for another few minutes and then take out my phone and dial the number.

"All right dickhead?" Ami would usually be the last person I would confide in, but at least I'll get the unfiltered truth from her.

"Loser!" I answer but my heart isn't in the exchange.

"What did she say?"

"She said I was too late."

"Ah. And are you?"

"There's another guy here that's hanging around."

"Did she say anything else?"

"Something about not taking my word for it. She asked me how I knew I wouldn't change my mind about a relationship."

"Interesting."

"How?"

"She's saying two different things there. She's saying you're too late but I very much doubt that because she's also suggested that if she did get back with you, you might change your mind."

"But I won't."

"Let things settle. Let her take in what you told her. I wouldn't usually condone pursuing someone who has said no, but I don't think she means it."

"Then what?"

"How long are you down there for?"

"However long it takes."

"Good man. You need to do something that proves to her you're ready to have a relationship with her and it's not just talk to get her back."

"How do I do that?" This is just a total minefield. How do I convince her of that? The panic is starting to set in again.

"That's totally down to you now."

"Thanks. Speak later." She's given me a lot to talk about.

"Don't count on it!" She hangs up.

If she's right about Hannah, I need to put together a game plan to win her back. And it's gonna be a long game, by all accounts.

Chapter Thirty-Three

Hannah

I walk out of the café to be met by Toby, who as instructed, puts his arm around me as if we're together. Don't ask me why I wanted Sean to think I was with someone else and not totally besotted with him. I'm totally overwhelmed by what he's just told me.

"Are you gonna tell me what happened?" Toby asks as we walk away from the café.

"He said he's thought about it and wants to have a relationship with me."

"He does?" Toby sounds excited, but I'm unsure.

"That's what he says, but I don't know."

"What's not to know? You were devastated when he didn't want more, and now he's giving you more."

"I know. But will he just change his mind? Am I just gonna be someone to fill a void."

"There's only one way to find out."

"Well he's gonna have to make some big effort." We make our way back towards the gallery. My head is so full of questions, all on top of the excitement of the exhibition launch. I think I need some peace and quiet to able to process all this. "I can't go back to that house tonight. I may have to sell a kidney and get a hotel room."

"Oh leave it with me, I know someone."

"You always do."

He gets his phone out and dials. "Hey babes. I'm good… Could you do me the biggest of favours? … I know." He rolls his eyes at me. "Do you have any spare rooms tonight? And maybe you could give us a big discount, like, to almost free?…" There's a pause like they are checking or something. "Brilliant!" His eyes light up and he gives me the thumbs up, but his face immediately falls. "No, not like that. It's for me and a friend. We've had an odd day and the thought of going back to a shared house makes me want to vomit… yes… yes… of course." He rolls his eyes again but then lights up. "Oh my god, I fucking love you. We'll head over now."

He hangs up with a smug look on his face. "My friend got us a room. There was a cancellation two minutes ago. It's like the universe is telling us something!" He does a little weird dance on the spot.

"Where is it?"

"Mayfair."

"Are you kidding me right now?" I'm in shock.

"Nope. Let's go."

· ♥ · ♥ · ♥ · ♥ · ♥ ·

I'm back at work and on a massive come down from the last few days. Toby and I stayed at the most gorgeous hotel in Mayfair. Luckily, we didn't look our usually scruffy selves, or we really would have looked out of place. We took a hot shower each, which is pure luxury when you have to fight for a spot to use the bathroom. Not to mention the fact that there's never any hot water. I took a selfie of the two of us in hotel robes and sent it to Dionne with a *Guess where we are?* caption. We talked for a bit, but exhaustion took over and we slept like logs. We really did need the rest. But here we are, back to running for coffees and fielding phone calls. Most of my photos have been sold for ridiculous amounts of money that I can't even comprehend, but they'll stay on display for another few months.

I've been on reception this afternoon and have just taken delivery of flowers. Two bunches in fact. We hardly ever get flower deliveries so it's piqued people's interest. Both are for me. One from Uncle Mitch with a congratulations card. The other says:

> **Let me prove we can be more than friends.**
> **Let me show you what a relationship with me could look like.**
> **Love Sean x**

How is he even gonna begin to prove he can be more? And how could he possibly show me? I look up when someone else comes through the door. It's a delivery driver carrying a package. "Hannah Spencer?"

"That's me."

"Sign here." He holds out his device and I use my finger to sign. He hands me the parcel. I have no idea what this is or who it's from. Have I ordered something from the internet and can't remember? I rip the package open and find a note on top of a thick grey hoodie. The note says:

> **Don't girls steal their boyfriends' hoodies? I know you love a good chunky jumper,**
> **Love Sean x**

Without thinking I pull the hoodie up to my face to smell it. It's definitely his, it smells of him. His cologne is intoxicating. I read the note again. He's being cute, but it'll take more than a hoodie.

My stomach rumbles to indicate we're close to lunchtime. Toby finds me on reception and we are debating what delights to have for lunch when someone else comes through the door.

"Lunch delivery for Hannah Spencer." She's from the fancy deli down the road.

"That's me. I didn't order anything." How strange.

"Well it's been ordered and paid for."

"Thanks," I say, and she scuttles off.

I open the bag and we both peer in. There's a huge sandwich, a flavoured fancy drink and a brownie. "Lunch sorted, let's go," I say to Toby.

"What about me?" He pouts slightly.

"There's enough for the both of us," I laugh. "Just grab a drink from the fridge."

While I wait for Toby to get his drink, I pull on Sean's hoodie and we head to our usual spot for a bit of people watching.

We sit on the bench and watch the world go by. "Do you think Sean bought this too?"

"I dunno, maybe." I don't think Toby really cares where it came from as he shoves his half a sandwich in his mouth. "And what would he think about you sharing it with a sexy guy like me?"

"It's tough, whatever he thinks."

"Have you thought any more about what he said? Or even if you're gonna take up this offer on Tokyo?"

"I've been doing nothing but thinking. I just haven't got any answers yet." I sigh and take a bite of brownie. "Anyway I'm not sure the two go hand in hand."

"What do you mean?"

"Well if I choose Tokyo, that means I give up the chance with Sean. And if I choose Sean then he's not gonna want me to leave."

"Maybe he'd go with you?"

"I doubt it. He has his job, which he loves. And I don't think it would be fair to ask him to give it up." I sigh again. It would be lovely to have both, but that's hardly likely. "Right time's up. Best get back to work."

We dawdle back to the gallery and push through the doors. This afternoon is Toby's turn to be on reception and I have the job of cataloguing some new pieces that have come in. But when we get to reception there have been two more deliveries – one parcel and one letter, both addressed to me. I reach for the card, while toby looks over the parcel for any signs of the sender. I open the envelope and pull out a Valentine's card. Either this has been lost in the post for several months or there's some kind of mistake. On the front it says *With Love to my Girlfriend*. I open it to find the message inside reads.

> **To Hannah**
> **We missed our first Valentine's but hopefully we can spend many more together.**
> **Love Sean x**

Cute! I pass it to Toby for his inspection and he shrugs. I grab and rip open the parcel. It's some kind of clothing. They're cream with hearts all over them. I pass them to Toby, unsure of what they are and read the note attached to the front.

> **To Hannah**
> **For all our cosy nights in together.**
> **Love Sean x**

"Ah, I know what they are." Toby holds the clothes out in front of him. "His and hers matching pyjamas. Look, the pocket has your initials on – HS." He points to the detail. "And the other has his – SH. Wow! You've even got matching initials, that's freaky."

"God yes, I never even thought about that before. Do you think I should message him?"

"I think you should wait and see what else comes." Toby has a mischievous look on his face.

"Do you think there'll be more?"

"If you tell him now that it's working there definitely won't be any more." He giggles and claps his hands.

"Who says they're working?" I narrow my eyes at him.

"The gooey look on your face says it all."

"Shut up." I punch him in the arm.

The rest of the day goes by uneventfully.

· ♥ · ♥ · ♥ · ♥ · ♥ ·

Waking up with a jolt I look at my phone to see the time. It's 9am already and I'm late for work. I jump out of bed, throw my pyjamas on the bed and rummage around in my drawer for some clean knickers. Grabbing the nearest clothes from the chair and start to pull them on. I take out the toothpaste from my wash bag – there's no way I want to keep my toothbrush in the shared bathroom. Just think of what could happen. I shiver at the thought and put a tiny bit of paste my brush. Quickly cleaning my teeth, using the opened can of lemonade on my bedside table to swill my mouth and swallow the rest, I pull on my trainers and head out.

I make it down stairs and out of the door by 9.10. Running the few streets distance to the gallery. When I barge through the door, and am greeted by Toby with a smug smile on his face. "What time do you call this?"

"Why didn't you ring me?"

"To be honest, I only just realised." He pulls a sorry face. "But the reason I realised was, you have more parcels." He does an understated jazz hands to avoid bringing attention to us.

The first one is more of a thick envelope, so I open that one first and pull out a home furnishing catalogue. The note on the front says:

> **To Hannah**
> **Because couples build flat pack furniture together.**
> **Love Sean x**

What an idiot. Doesn't he realise that 90 percent of flatpack furniture building results in divorce? Okay I made that up. But it could be true. I open the next parcel which seems to be a lot squashier. I rip it open to find a toy bear holding a big red heart. The note attached says:

> **To Hannah**
> **I was gonna win you one, but you'd have to have been with me for it to count. I hope to do that sometime soon.**
> **Love Sean x**

"Let's see then." Toby can barely conceal his excitement. I pass the card over for him to read. "Aww. He's really laying it on thick. I wonder if you'll get lunch again?"

Lunch time comes around and there is another delivery from the deli, the same as yesterday. And again, Toby and I go and sit on a bench in the park and share it. The sun is shining and there's more people about than usual. We sit and eat in silence, both of us seem to have our heads full.

"Have you thought about what you are going to do about Tokyo?" He asks, breaking through my musings.

"I have, yes."

"Are you gonna share with me?"

"Well, I actually rang Julian, and he went through what it would entail. It's a really good opportunity for me. I said I'd let him know by the end of the week."

"And what about lover boy?" He nudges me with his shoulder.

"I don't know. He seems to be making an effort. But what will happen when I tell him that I'm leaving for six months?"

"Well, if he's really that into you he'll be okay with it."

"It's absolute torture for me being without him, especially when I know he's here. If I take that Tokyo job and get back with him, it will be a whole next level of torture. I've just got to work it out in my head first."

"So you want both?"

"Yes! I just can't see how."

"Are you gonna tell him?"

"Not until I have something solid in my head."

We pack up our rubbish and head back off in the direction of the gallery, talking about Toby's new plan to get Luigi to notice him. I laugh at all his weird plans and promise to be his wing woman when he goes out.

We get back to reception and there's another padded envelope with my name on it. It's labelled with same handwriting as the rest. I open it and pull out a key. Attached to it is a big enamel pink heart. The note attached says:

> **To Hannah**
> **This may not be the key to my heart, but it is the key to my flat. It's not the same there without you.**
> **Love Sean x**

Now he's gone next level. I pass the note over to Toby with raised eyebrows.

"Wow." Is all he can muster.

"Wow indeed. This throws another spanner in the works. Does he want me to move to Edinburgh with him?" My head spins.

"I though he lived in the same town as you?"

"He does temporarily, but he has a permanent place in Edinburgh."

"Does this not show he wants a permanent place with you?"

"Oh I don't know anymore." I'm so confused. I think the more these parcels keep coming, the more questions I have.

And so the storm within my brain is taken to another level. I so wish I could have it all, but it would mean a considerable amount of compromise, and is that really fair on either of us? I need a dark, quiet place to calm my head. Maybe I could hide in the gallery's dark rooms for a few hours?

Chapter Thirty-Four

Toby

I feel like all I do in this job is run errands for other people. First, it's coffee for the boss, then it's organising lunch for the meeting in the conference room, then tidying up after everyone. Today I have to nip out to the shop to get milk because the office manager forgot.

I'm walking down the street, past that lovely deli, when I see him walking towards me. He hasn't seen me because his head is in his phone. Just as he gets to me, I call out to him. "Sean?"

"Yes." He lifts his head with a smile, but when he realises it's me his face drops.

"I'm glad I bumped into you." I have a feeling he's going in to the deli to place our lunch order. I hope it'll be something nice.

"You are?" As if he doesn't know…

"About these parcels you keep sendi-"

"Look, if you're gonna tell me to stop and back off, that's not gonna happen. Ever."

I start to laugh. "Good."

"What's so funny?" His face is flushed, he seems to be getting really furious now.

"Can I just set something straight? Hannah is not my type. For a start she hasn't got a beard."

He looks confused. "What about the hotel room and the touchiness, and the lunch dates?"

"How do you know about the hotel?" Are there no secrets in the world anymore?

"Funny what you can find out from friends and social media." Ahh he's got spies out. Well good for him, shows he's upped his game.

"Calm down, I'm on your side. but there are things you need to know."

"Like what?" His eyebrows knit together.

"Hannah has been offered a job."

"That's brilliant news!" A genuine smile spreads across his face.

"In Tokyo." His face falls again. "She can't seem to get her head around being with you AND going to Tokyo. So if you're not prepared to support her with this job, can you just give it up so she doesn't waste what an immense opportunity this could be for her."

"Why wouldn't I support her?"

"Some men wouldn't and I don't know you enough to know if that's you."

"Why would she think it's an either/or choice?"

"Because you didn't choose her last time."

"That was different." He folds his arms across his chest, like I've pissed him off.

"She wants Tokyo, she wants you, but she doesn't want long distance." He ponders for a minute.

"Thanks for letting me know. Could we keep this conversation to ourselves for now?"

"Absolutely, she'd kill me if she found out." He smirks. "I need to get on." He nods and we both set off the way we were going. I turn and shout back to him, "Oh and just so you know, my favourite is hummus and roasted peppers on wholemeal."

"I'll bear that in mind," he says without slowing his pace. I can see why Hannah is taken with him.

Chapter Thirty-Five

Hannah

I was expecting to be told there were more parcels delivered this morning. But there was nothing. It makes me feel sad. Maybe he's lost interest or given up because I haven't been in contact. Maybe I should message him.

I'm covering reception today and it's been very quiet. I haven't even had Toby here to annoy because he's been in and out on errands every hour or so. The last one, he came back with a big smile on his face that makes me think he's bumped into Luigi in the street. He had a big spring in his step, something I wish I had, but the weight of all these decisions I have to make is getting a bit too much.

Toby walks into reception. "Is it lunch time yet?"

"It is."

"Have we had any deliveries today?"

"Nope." His face falls, it seems like he is just as invested in these little treats as I am. The main door opens and it's the deli girl. I light up.

"Two today. One tuna and mayo, no sweetcorn, the other hummus and roasted peppers. This time you won't have to share."

"How do you know we share?" I ask her.

"I don't, that's what's written on the ticket." She puts the bags on the reception desks and leaves.

"Oh cool, hummus is my favourite."

"So he knows we've been sharing?"

"Maybe he's seen us eating lunch. It's a popular place to walk through."

"Maybe." There's something a bit suspicious about this. How does he know?

Just as we gather our things together the postman comes through the doors. He doesn't have a parcel but he holds out two letters addressed to me. The first one is a postcard with a picture of two adjoining hands, with one half of a heart on each side of their outer palms. Holding hands completes the heart. I turn the card over and see the words he's written:

To Hannah
These are the matching tattoos I was thinking we could get.
Love Sean x

Matching tattoos! Has he gone totally insane? I pass it to Toby and pick up the other to rip the envelope open. Inside is a greetings card with two ducks on the front in a watercolour painting. One is flapping, the other is swimming next to it. Handwritten under each duck are our names. Tears prick my eyes. He remembers the ducks in the park. I have a photo similar to this. We discussed how they seemed like a married couple. He's got the names the wrong way round though, because he has me as the flappy one. Cheek. I open the card and look inside.

> **To Hannah**
> **These two reminded me of us.**
> **Love Sean x**

I have no words left. My stomach rumbles and Toby nudges me. I better get something to eat before I do anything else.

"Ready?"

"Ready."

We sit at our usual bench, which is funny because the place is really busy – I didn't think we'd get any seats. We eat in silence, the storm in my brain raging. Toby has usually asked me a million questions about what the gifts meaning are and how I was feeling about it all. But he remains quiet today, watching people go by as he eats his lunch.

"Maybe you should ring him," he says, out of nowhere.

"Hmm?"

"I'll go back to the gallery and cover reception whilst you stay here and give him a call."

It takes me a few minutes after Toby has left to pull myself together to ring him. I've stared at his contact picture a while before I press the call button. It only rings twice before I hear his voice. "Hey." I feel a warm glow wash over me.

"Hey." It's all I can manage.

"Are you okay?"

I pull myself together. "Yes. I got your gifts."

"And what did you think?"

"I think maybe we should meet up to talk."

"Can I take you out for dinner tonight?"

"That would be nice." I smile, because it would be more than nice.

"If you send me your address, I'll pick you up from there."

"No pick me up from the gallery." I can't have him seeing what a dump I'm living in.

"Okay. 7 o'clock?"

"Okay, see you then. I hang up so I don't get flustered. Just hearing his voice makes me all nervous and excited at the same time, so much so that I can't be sure what might come out of my mouth.

• ♥ • ♥ • ♥ • ♥ • ♥ •

I'm running late. And all because the people in the house are an absolute nightmare. I haven't been able to have a decent shower for nearly a week and because I'm meeting Sean, I am now desperate. But people have been hogging it.

I've just got out, water dripping down my back, to find several messages from Sean all asking where I am. I pick up my phone to message back.

Sean
> Hey, I'm heading to the gallery now
>
> I'm here, are you nearly ready
>
> Hannah where are you?

Me
> I'm really sorry, running late, I'm still at home

Sean
> Send me the address so I can come and get you

Me
> Fine
>
> *location pin drop*

Sean
> I'll be there in 5

And true to his word I hear him shouting up the stairs five minutes later. "Hannah, are you here?"

"I'm on my way down." I grab my bag and rush out of my room and down the stairs. The less time he is in this house and sees what a state it is, the better. "Let's go." I rush past him out of the door and I'm down the street by the time he catches up.

"The door was wide open. That place isn't very safe." He's looking back over his shoulder, a concerned look on his beautiful face.

"I know. But it's the only place I've got."

"I can't have you living there. There's absolutely no way."

I stop still in the street without warning and the man behind me bumps into me. He swears under his breath before moving past us. "Listen here, I've done things without you for three months. You can't just rock up and tell me what to do." It pisses me off that he thinks he has a say in how I've lived my life when he didn't want to be part of it.

He holds his hands out in surrender. "Okay sorry." We carry on walking. "I thought we could go to this little restaurant I've seen on the main road."

I put my hand up to stop him before he gets too carried away. "I'm sorry Sean. I just don't really do that whole candle lit dinner thing. There's a place round the corner with a load of street food. The food is amazing, and we can sit in the park and talk."

"Sounds good to me."

I expected him to protest. "Are you sure?"

"Yes, of course. I just want to be with you."

We walk round the edge of the park where there are seven or so vans selling street food of some description. Sean opts for noodles and I go for my favourite Greek Gyros. We collect our food and find somewhere to sit. The park is not mine and Toby's usual hang out but one a bit further away from the gallery. It's more a square in the middle of the bustling intersection of streets. It has grass, trees and a water feature with a winding path that branches out to each street it borders.

Finding a free bench we sit together and pick at our food. We haven't said much of any real meaning to each other so far. Just general chit chat, so I try to ease us in gently. "So you're here on business?"

He takes his time to answer and he looks me straight in the eye. "No Hannah, I'm here for you. I decided that while I was here, trying to win you back, I would look up some work colleagues and scope a few things out."

"Oh." I didn't expect that answer. I thought the visit was just convenient for him.

"You are not a second thought Hannah." He turns on the bench to face me. "You are my one and only thought."

"So why did it take you three months to come for me?"

"I didn't want to interfere and distract you from what you were doing. I knew it was important." Well that puts a whole different slant on things.

"The gifts were..."

"Thoughtful?" He looks so cute and hopeful.

"Some were weird."

"I thought cute."

"I am not getting matching tattoos."

He laughs "Okay we can draw the line there. If you hadn't called, I was gonna suggest we got a puppy together."

"Idiot!" I nudge him but can't keep the excited laughter I feel inside.

"I wanted to get your attention."

"I think you got it."

"And I wanted to prove that I'm all in, if you'll have me." He leans into me.

"I still need some time to think things through."

"I'll give you as much time as you need." He shifts in his seat again and looks me right in the eye. "But please, even if just for one night, don't go back to that house. I have rented an apartment. Stay with me, no expectations."

"We'll see." I eat more of my food to give me a bit more time to think. "What made you change your mind?"

"About what?" He picks at his noodles.

"About being in a relationship."

"You. Apparently, I'm a miserable fucker without you." He thinks for a moment. "But also someone pointed out that the barriers I had put up to stop me from getting hurt were now actually hurting me more." I definitely need to thank them, I feel a little flutter in my stomach, surely this is a good sign.

"How do you know I'm the one?"

"Because I don't feel whole without you."

"Very deep. What if I don't feel the same way about you?" His face falls and I feel a bit guilty for letting him think that I'm not totally and completely in love with him.

"I don't know, maybe I have to just live with a broken heart." How do you follow that? I look at his serious face, his eyes searching mine. He pulls a puppy dog eyes face to break the tension.

"I'm sure you'd find someone else to put up with you." I joke.

"Never."

I need to change the subject. "I'm sorry about my reaction the other night. I was a bit overwhelmed by you being there."

"I'm sorry too. I could have timed that better. I didn't want to overshadow your opening night. But those photos just threw me and I couldn't leave telling you how I felt for another minute."

"I want my photos to invoke a reaction, but what was it that affected you so much?"

"I don't know. The first one you took, I was feeling really lost. I didn't know my place in anything and I couldn't believe you could see that when no-one else could. The second was from when I found you."

"I'm finding it hard to believe that someone like you could fall for someone like me."

"Is that a joke?" He sounds irritated.

"No. It's not a joke. Have you seen you?" I indicate his body. "And have you seen me?" I spread my arms to make my point.

"I can't answer something I don't understand." His face void of expression.

I feel a drop of water on my leg, then my hand. I look up to the sky. The rain has come out of nowhere. Sean looks up too. "Shall we take this back to mine?"

"I'm sure it'll pass." I'm not sure being alone with him right now is a good idea. But just as I speak the heavens open and the torrential rain begins. Sean stands, grabs my hand and pulls me up off the bench. We start running through the park, trying to avoid the newly formed puddles. This could be tricky.

Chapter Thirty-Six

Sean

We reach the flat and stumble in through the door. We are soaked from head to toe, water dripping from our hair and off our noses. We look at the state of each other and laugh. Wrapping my arms around her and lean in to kiss her.

She's soft and I can taste her lip gloss. I can't escape the taste of her, I have missed it. Pressing firmer and run my tongue along her lips so she opens up to me. Hold the back of her neck as I angle myself to take her deeper, her mewing noises do something else to me. But she stops still.

She pushes me away and looks up into my eyes. "Can we please not put sex into the mix. If we start down that road right now, I'll say yes to anything and that's not fair to either of us."

"Okay. Sorry."

"There's no need to be sorry, I just don't want to blur the lines right now, before I can sort my thoughts out."

"That's fair. But we do need to get out of these clothes." We both start toeing off our soggy shoes and I pull off my t-shirt.

She looks at me as if she may just change her mind about the sex part. "I'll go get you something to wear." I head into the bedroom and search through the draws for something she can put on. Then I change into a new t-shirt and some joggers.

I meet her back in the hall. She has started to shiver. "The bathroom is down there." I point. "Here's a t-shirt and some shorts while your clothes dry out."

She takes them and heads to the bathroom.

It amazes me that this woman can look so beautiful in just about anything. Here she is, coming out of the bathroom, drying her hair with a towel, wearing an oversized t-shirt so long that she doesn't need the shorts, but she looks amazing. I'll need to think about something else, or she'll notice the affect she has on me. "Feel better?"

"Yes. I'm not sure how long it will take to dry those clothes because they're soaked." She holds out the sodden pile.

"Well, you can stay here tonight. I'll sleep on the sofa."

"That's not really fair, it's your apartment."

I shrug and point to the sofa. "How about we watch some TV. I have some snacks here, and a few cans of lemonade." She nods her approval and we settle in.

I angle myself so I can watch her without being obvious. She looks so beautiful.

We choose a film to watch and snuggled up on the sofa but she fell asleep almost as soon as it began. I didn't want to disturb her. I watch her eyes flutter like she's mid dream. I really don't know what I'll do if she doesn't choose me. I hope she's felt the chemistry we have between us – I certainly have. I move her legs from my lap and stand up. I scoop her up into my arms and walk her over to the bedroom. I kick the door open softly, walk over to the bed and place her down gently. The deja vu hits me in the chest as I remember the first time I did this. When she had me all of a fluster.

This woman is absolutely perfect. I think about getting into bed beside her, but right now I'm not sure I could sleep, so I pull the covers over her and go back into the living room to find something else to watch.

· ♥ · ♥ · ♥ · ♥ · ♥ ·

I wake with a start. The room is dark but there's something heavy on top of me. A kiss lands on my cheek and I smile. She came out looking for me. I move over slightly to let her lay down and her head fits perfectly under my chin as I wrap my arms around her. This just feels right and my heavy eyes close as I drift back off to sleep.

Chapter Thirty-Seven

Hannah

I woke up on the sofa curled into Sean. I didn't want an awkward morning chat, but I did need a shower. So I showered and dressed in the bathroom and sneaked out of the apartment. I didn't even leave a note, but I'll message him later.

The time we spent together yesterday proved how much I love being with him. He's easy to get on with and I can safely say he is still as hot as hell. Now to figure out how we can be with each other and still live the life we want to.

I reach the gallery earlier than normal and get started on sorting all my things for leaving in a few days' time. I've loved being here. I've learnt so much from the other photographers and also from the gallery manager. It has even made me think I might want to have my own gallery one day. And it's a definite that I'll pick an up-and-coming photographer to intern for me – give them the chance I have had.

Toby walks into the office and does a double take. "What are you doing in here so early?"

"I came straight from Sean's"

"So did you have a night of passion?" He gives a cheeky grin, his eyes hopeful.

"No. We had a night of talking and then fell asleep."

"So you've made a decision then?"

"Not quite."

"What's it gonna take?" he says in frustration.

"What do you mean?"

"What's it gonna take for you to make a decision? Can't you just speak to him and tell him what's on your mind?"

"It's not as easy as that. I need to get everything straight in my head so he can't throw me off balance."

"Hannah. You've got two days."

"I know, I know." I wave him off because he's beginning to annoy me. I have my head in HR sign off forms and I need to concentrate.

A few hours go by without me even noticing, when my train of thought is interrupted by the phone ringing on my desk.

"Yes." I answer.

"Hey Hannah, There's someone in reception for you." Lottie is covering the desk this morning.

"Right, I'll be down in a minute."

I wonder if it's him. I realise I completely forgot to message him after I left the apartment. I check my phone. It's been on silent all morning, and there's a missed call from him but nothing else. I make my way downstairs and into reception. He's standing there as gorgeous as ever, hands in pockets, looking out of the window. He sees me and gives me a small smile.

"I'm so sorry, I was meant to message you and I just got overtaken by work."

"You didn't wake me to say bye."

"You were fast asleep. It looked like you could do with the rest."

"Right. Anyway." He straightens up and takes his hands out of his pockets. "I thought I'd hand deliver my final gift." Final? Does this mean he's giving up? Have I spent too much time procrastinating?

He puts his hand into the inside pocket of his jacket, pulls out an envelope and hands it to me. I take it and look at him, searching his face for any clues. There are none. I turn the envelope over, open it up and pull out a folded piece of paper. Inside are two tickets to go up the Tokyo Skytree tower. I look up at him and then back down to the tickets. How does he know about Tokyo? I check the tickets again. The date is for three weeks' time. "What is this?"

"It's for one of our first dates as a couple." I can't quite get my head around what this means.

"Tokyo?"

"I wanted you to know that if you choose to be with me, I'll go with you, anywhere you want, always."

"You'll come with me?"

"If you'll have me."

I can't believe this. "What about your job?"

"Oh. Didn't I say? I've got a new job." He searches his pocket again, finds a little business card and hands it to me.

Sean Hutchinson
Chief Camera Bag Carrier

I look up at him again, tears in my eyes. "Seriously?"

"Seriously! If the position is vacant."

"It is. Are you sure?" is he really choosing me?

"I've never been more sure about anything in my life. I love you Hannah and I don't want to spend another moment away from you. So what do you say?"

"To what exactly?"

"Hannah Spencer, will you be my girlfriend and take me on all your adventures."

"Yes. I think I will."

He bends down and kisses me on the lips, then turns to Lottie. "Tell the boss Hannah is taking the rest of the day off to plan for Tokyo." He puts his arm around me and turns me towards the door to lead me out. "We have some serious making up to do Miss Spencer."

I stop, remembering I need my things from my office, but Toby is immediately beside me holding out my bag. "Did you know about this?" He just shrugs as Sean pulls me out of the gallery, a huge smile spreading across his face.

Chapter Thirty-Eight

Who knew there'd be so much to sort out. We spent the first few days of being a couple in bed making up for lost time. But also chatting about things we wanted to do and see. Then came the practicalities. This is when I am grateful that Sean and Ben work in property management and know the logistics around house moves. I just wouldn't know where to start.

We've made our way back up north, after a tearful goodbye with Toby. I'm not sure why he was so emotional, we're gonna see him again in a month when he joins me at the new gallery. I rang my new boss, and pitched the idea of an extra set of hands and he agreed.

Things are pretty straight forward for Sean. Ben is looking after the Edinburgh flat and Dionne gets the house to herself. I'm not sure whether she's pleased or not, but I think she may miss him more than she's letting on. His things will either be taken with us or kept in storage, but to be fair he doesn't have much in the way of personal possessions.

My little place, on the other hand, will need to be sorted and packed up. I've decided to rent out while we're away. I don't want to sell it, but I also don't know if we'll ever come back and live in it either. And that is where I currently am. Sat on the floor of my living room looking through boxes of nik-naks, boxes of old bills and photos. It's gonna be a big job.

"What about these?" Sean walks in from the kitchen, for what seems like the hundredth time, waving something random in the air He's been making me choose whether to keep things or send them to charity. It's a not very amusing game that usually ends in my saying *whatever* a lot.

I hear the front door open and we both look at each other. "Expecting anyone?" I shake my head as my mother emerges from the hall.

"You're back then?" Her face looks all smug, like she's caught me out.

"Clearly." I say curtly. I haven't heard from her since I left for London, so I have no idea why she's here now.

"Come back to reality to start looking for a real job have you? Need bailing out?" My step father steps through the doorway and scoffs at her comment.

"No I'm packing up the house and moving away." A look of panic crosses my mother's face.

"Wwhat do you mean?"

"Exactly that. Oh and I'll need your key back." I say matter of factly.

"You can't sell the house, we bought you this place."

"I can't believe I have to say this again. I bought the house. You gifted me the deposit." I sigh at having to go through this again. "But if you are so strapped for cash, I can give you the deposit back. I made an absolute mint from the sale at my photography exhibition. Although it isn't a real job."

She's lost for words, the look on her face is a picture, so I may as well get another shot in. "You'll be happy to know that I have finally found myself a suitor. However, we will be having a completely open relationship and traveling round the world, staying in communes, sharing our souls and bodies, in exchange for food and shelter."

Sean is leaning on the door frame with a smirk on his face, watching the whole thing unfold. I've filled him in on the relationship I have with my parents, so he knows the score and doesn't even flinch.

My mother's face turns a funny shade of puce, she practically throws her keys on the coffee table and storms out of the house, followed by my step father, who shakes his head saying things about going too far. The front door slams and I can't help but burst out laughing. "I actually feel a little bit sorry for her now. I thought she might just pass out." Sean says.

"What goes around comes around." It felt good to give it back to her.

"Do you want me to send them some money to cover the house deposit, cos they'll forever bring that up."

"I already have, when the money from the exhibition came through. They just haven't realised." I shrug. It was the right thing to do, because it would always be brought up and thrown back in my face.

"Anyway, we'll need to keep an eye on the time. We are meeting for drinks in the Dog in an hour."

· ♥ · ♥ · ♥ · ♥ · ♥ ·

Sean pulls open the door to the pub and we walk in hand in hand, but something seems off. The noise for one, or lack of it. I stop dead still and take in the scene for a moment.

"Surprise." I properly jump out of my skin as the whole pub erupts in cheers. I look towards Sean and his face is just as shocked, as our friends come rushing over.

"What's all this." I eventually manage.

Dionne comes to the front of the crowd. "Well we couldn't have you leave with out a proper send off."

And as I take in the group, I see the faces of all our friends, smiling back at us.

"Did you know about this?" I turn to Sean.

"Nope."

"Do you think they're sorry to see us go or are having a party because we're leaving?" Sean laughs and pulls me in for a hug.

"That's what friends are for." He replies with a grin.

Epilogue

Sean

18 months later

I'm looking down at my shoes in the cold, draughty church. Nerves are getting the better of me. The anticipation of seeing her has my stomach in knots. Jonathan stands beside me. He squeezes my shoulder. I'm so grateful for our friendship. He's really pulled me through.

The music starts up and I shake my hands out, trying to get my head and body in gear. I look up the aisle, past all the people dressed in their best clothes. The light pours in as the door at the back opens and my heart races, waiting for the first glimpse of her.

I hear the footsteps start and see her floating down the aisle, the light from behind her highlights her blonde hair, which is pulled off her face. She's like an angel and she's mine. As she gets closer, I see her face, her beautiful lips turn upwards as she smiles at me, her face lighting up. And all the anxiety washes from my body, because she's here and she's mine. The love of my life.

She reaches the alter and, with a smile, turning to the back of the church. She lifts the camera to her eye and aims its towards the back of the church. This woman is my everything and I can't take my eyes off her. A tap on my shoulder brings me back to reality.

I look across the aisle and see Ben with a wriggling Ava, his little girl that runs rings round him, fairy wings and all. His face changes when he sees Emma coming towards him, arm in arm with her son Noah. Then I see my best friend Megan, looking incredible, making her way to the front of the church, flanked by a grown up looking Jacob.

Jonathan steps out into the aisle to greet Lizzie. Head to toe in lace, Lizzie is the most beautiful bride. Something I never thought I would say. But the two of them are made for each other, although its only taken them nearly two decades to realise it. But their faces say it all. The love they have for each other shines through. And I am taking the credit for today.

· ♥ · ♥ · ♥ · ♥ · ♥ ·

Hannah

So much has happened in 18 months. We spent six months in Tokyo, then onto Sweden and we've flown back from California this week to attend Lizzie and Jonathan's wedding. The speeches have all been done, Sean made everyone laugh with his tales about the two of them. All the food has been eaten, champagne – and fizzy grape juice – have been drunk, and everyone is sitting chatting, waiting for the evening to begin.

I can't believe how long we have been a couple. It seems like two minutes, but also a lifetime. I can't imagine my days without this man. He's funny, sexy and moody when he's hungry. And we are always together. After me being so independent, we spend every last minute together, and I wouldn't change it for the world.

We see Megan come back in from the garden. Here eyes are red but she's beaming with a beautiful smile. She comes up to Sean, kisses him on the cheek and whispers in his ear. She puts her finger to her lips in a shush motion and takes Myles' hand before she continues through the room. "What was that about?"

"Megan and Myles just got engaged. But it's top secret."

"Ah." I'm so glad for them. Megan is just as amazing as Sean said. We've become very close, and have been known to gang up on Sean. It's like having the sister I always wanted.

"Would you want a big wedding like this?" I turn to Sean, his face serious.

"What a question! God, no. All I would want is me and you on a beach, a celebrant and no one else for miles around." I was never into the big puffy dress, even as a little girl. I think it mainly because it was what my mother always wanted. I was always the rebel.

"Sounds perfect. Let's do it." I laugh at him and he turns towards me, taking my hands in his. "I'm serious. Let's do it when we get back to Cali." I kiss him on the lips and I know he's completely serious.

California will be our home for the near future. I'm setting up my first gallery there and I'm happier than ever. I do miss my friends and the Dog and Swan, but we have virtual catch ups and the girls are loving that they can come out to the States for their holidays. Lizzie and Jonathan are even having their honeymoon following route 66 and ending up at ours.

Life is perfect.

The END

Afterword

Thanks for reading my book, I hope you enjoyed it. It would be just awesome if you could put a review over on Amazon and Goodreads. Reviews are like little tips that keep us authors motivated to write more stories.

If you would like to follow updates on my work, find me on **Instagram** and **Facebook @carriemcgovernauthor** or **www.carriemcgovern.com** and join my Facebook group for chats about books and life in general at www.facebook.com/groups/carriesbooksandbanter.

I love getting all your messages about my books and their characters, so come and tell me what you think.

The Hello Series

This series of books focus on a strong friendship group. The books are individual stories with interconnected characters.

Hello Happiness
Emma's story
Hello Mr Beckett
Megan's story
Hello Handsome
Hannah's story
The Other Mr Beckett
Coming late 2024

Acknowledgements

There are loads of people to thank who have supported this journey. Thanks to my friends and family who have supported me and put up with my constant talk about *The Books*. Thanks to Emma and Marian my Beta Readers, Helen for being a very patient and supportive editor, Lauren for being so patient with changes to my artwork.

I want to thank my author mentors, TL Swan and her *Cygnets* authors, without you guys for support, my journey would never have begun, your ongoing help is much appreciated. The continuing support and cheerleading from lasses of **The Northern Lass Lounge,** especially my *Mean Girls* group chat, you have kept me sane and motivated, thank you. A special thanks to Mara Robinson from *Alchemi Art,* who helped with my photography refresher, I appreciate you answering my millions of questions.

But the biggest thanks goes to those of you who have read my books, reviewed them and sent me some lovely messages of encouragement.

About the Author

Carrie McGovern

Carrie is a contemporary romance author based in the UK. She writes relatable fiction with strong female characters. Her books have a strong emphasis on friendship and female empowerment.

Carrie has been writing since the age of sixteen and has a BA(Hons) in Communication Studies, specializing in Journalism. It is only recently, through the love of reading, that she has taken up writing again.

She is married with two boys and a cat.

As well as reading she enjoys binge watching crime dramas and growing random plants.

Printed in Great Britain
by Amazon